Trap Queen

Trap Queen

Christine N. Davis

www.urbo

Urban Books, LLC
300 Farmingdale Road, N.Y.-Route 109
Farmingdale, NY 11735

ISBN 13: 978-1-64556-365-5
ISBN 10: 1-64556-365-0

First Trade Paperback Printing September 2022
Printed in the United States of America

10 9 8 7 6 5 4 3 2 1

This is a work of fiction. Any references or similarities to actual events, real people, living or dead, or to real locales are intended to give the novel a sense of reality. Any similarity in other names, characters, places, and incidents is entirely coincidental.

Distributed by Kensington Publishing Corp.
Submit Orders to:
Customer Service
400 Hahn Road
Westminster, MD 21157-4627
Phone: 1-800-733-3000
Fax: 1-800-659-2436

Chapter 1

Lihanny (Le-ha-knee) aka Li (Lee) Wright

June 18, 2014

"Bitch, didn't I tell you I was going to bust you in your fucking face if you missed another appointment? Huh? Didn't I?" Patty, aka Patrice, yelled in my face.

I wanted to roll my eyes so bad, but I didn't feel like fighting with her ass tonight. "I told you to push it back because I had to walk across the stage this morning."

Thankfully, by the grace of God, I was able to graduate high school. Despite all the shit I went through with my mama, I promised myself that, no matter what, I was going to walk across the stage come June 18, 2014. And that was exactly what the fuck I did. I didn't give a damn about these stupid-ass appointments.

"I don't give a fuck, Lihanny. I don't fucking play about my money. I told you not to play with me about my money."

"One fucking appointment isn't going to hurt your ass," I muttered.

Patty grabbed me by my hair and wrapped it around her hand, pulling me to her. "What the fuck you say, bitch? Huh? Say that shit louder for the people in the back."

I tightened my lips, trying my hardest not to scream out because of how hard she was pulling my hair. After a second she let me go. "That's what I thought. Now get yourself together. You have another one in thirty minutes." Turning on her heels, she walked out of my room and slammed my door behind her.

My hands immediately went to my hair. I needed to make sure my shit wasn't bleeding. Once I felt around and saw that it wasn't, I sighed and walked to my mirror in my room. I was proud of myself for sticking through it and graduating. I couldn't lie. I didn't think I was going to make it, but seeing myself in my cap and gown was a realization for me that I could do anything.

Coming out of my thoughts, I took off my gown and hung it up in my closet. After stripping out of everything else as well, I grabbed my towel and hopped into the shower. I was ready to get this dumb-ass appointment over with so I could go to work. For the confused minds as to what kind of appointment it is, I'll be glad to tell you.

Ever since my father was gunned down in a drug deal gone bad, my mama had been selling my body for money. I was 15 when she called me downstairs to "play" with one of her friends. The sick-ass nigga paid almost $5,000 to have sex with me because I was a virgin. My mother was down bad after my father was killed and the banks froze his accounts and repossessed everything we owned. We went from living in a mini mansion in Ghent Square to staying in the Timbers townhouses. It wasn't bad, but it wasn't anything that I was used to either. Even though Patty had all the money she needed to live comfortably, she continued to sell me out to the highest bidders. I was 18 now, and as soon as I got what I needed, I was moving the fuck out and away from her ass forever.

After I got out of the shower, I walked back into my room and put lotion on my body. I couldn't lie. For me to be so young, I had a really nice body thanks to my mama. In some cases it was good, and in others it was bad. I looked at myself in the mirror, admiring my beauty. Many people said that I favored Lulu Simmons, the model, with my milk-chocolate skin tone and long hair that stopped in the middle of my back. My eyes were a deep hazel, and I had big, full lips. My breasts were the size of cantaloupes, my stomach was flat, and my butt was phat as hell.

I went into my drawers and grabbed a pair of light blue jean shorts. It was going to be ninety-seven degrees today, and I refused to wear jeans. I tossed the shorts and my gray crop tank top onto my bed. I grabbed a pair of panties and the matching bra and put them on. Looking at the time on my dresser, I saw that I needed to be leaving in five minutes, so I quickly put my clothes on and went into my closet to pull out my gray and white Jordans. After I put my hair in a cute ponytail, put a few coats of lip gloss on, and grabbed my phone, I was out the door.

When I walked outside, my eyes squinted immediately because of the sun glaring in my face. I rolled my eyes at the sight of my mama sitting on our poor excuse of a porch and smoking a cigarette with her ugly-ass boyfriend, Karl.

She looked up at me and turned her nose up. "Hurry the fuck up and get there, Lihanny. I told you, you had thirty minutes," she fussed.

"You didn't give me a damn address yet," I replied.

"Bitch, who the fuck you talking to?"

I refrained from saying anything.

"I'll text you the address. Now bye."

I looked over at her before shaking my head and walking off the porch. When the message with the address came through, I opened the Uber app and called for one.

It didn't take long before they got here and drove me to my hell.

Two Days Later
Saturday at 2:30 p.m.

I turned around and checked to make sure that my black thong bikini bathing suit was looking right. It was showing off my cheetah tattoo, which went from the top of my shoulder down my back and to mid-thigh. My bikini showed off my double belly piercing that I had. I did my hair in some cute wand curls, and I had all of my gold body jewelry on. The sound of my phone ringing made me quickly throw my cover-up on and grab my phone. I knew that it was my best friend, Alondra, telling me to come outside. We were going to the biggest beach party of the year down on the oceanfront.

Grabbing my phone and overnight bag, I slipped my feet into my Gucci slides and left my room. Alondra was waiting for me in her car when I walked outside. Quickly, I walked over and got into the car.

"Damn, bitch, where did you get that bathing suit from?" Alondra asked as she pulled out of the parking spot.

I buckled my seat belt. "Some website called Romwe," I answered, plugging my phone in. Even though it was at 80 percent, I needed it to be fully charged for the night because it was going to be epic.

"I'm going to have to look up there."

"Are you going to get Cassie?" I asked her, referring to my other best friend.

Alondra, Cassie, and I had known each other for a good five years. We met in middle school when I transferred to Norview from Blair. We all had the same homeroom, and we clicked instantly because we were all pretty as hell, not to sound cocky though.

"She said she was riding with Nigel, so she'll meet us there," she replied.

Nigel was Cassie's boyfriend of three years. He was a good dude, I'd give him that, but personally, I didn't think he was for her. Mainly because Nigel was a bitch while Cassie was the exact opposite. Her ass popped off on any- and everybody, not giving a fuck. But sometimes it backfired on her because she got in nigga's faces, too, and her nigga was a punk. You couldn't tell her shit about him though.

"Did your cousin get the room for us? I am not trying to go back home tonight," I said just as my phone vibrated. I picked up my yellow iPhone 5c and rolled my eyes at the sight of Patty texting me.

The Devil: Bitch, didn't I tell you that you have two appointments tonight?

Instead of responding, I blocked her number for the night. I was getting really sick of her money-hungry ass. I needed this weekend to do me without having to fuck some sloppy little-dick-ass nigga. I was just going to deal with her wrath tomorrow.

"Yeah, she got it. You have the money?" She looked over at me for a second before turning back to the road as she got on the interstate.

I went into my bag and pulled out the $50 before passing it to her. She, Cassie, and I were splitting the money for a room for the night. We were going to stay at SpringHill Suites, so when we were kicked off the beach, the party would resume in our room. I had gotten some weed from our weed man yesterday so we could smoke something before we walked on the beach.

After I gave her the money, I pulled the bag of weed out and rolled it up. "You got a lighter?" I asked after realizing that Patty took mine with her annoying ass.

"Yeah, it's in the armrest."

I opened it up and grabbed the lighter before lighting the blunt and taking a long pull from it. A bitch really needed this. I plugged my phone up to the aux, and we jammed out the whole way to the beach. This shit was about to be epic.

It took us a good fifteen minutes to get to the beach, and when I say the shit was packed, it was packed. I was glad that we were getting hotel parking because if not, we weren't going to have anywhere to park. Alondra called up her cousin to get our room keys and parking ticket. We went up to the room to put our stuff away, then headed down to the beach. As soon as we stepped on the boardwalk, a huge smile spread across my face. There wasn't an empty spot on this beach, and I'm not even exaggerating.

"Bitch, look at all of these sexy-ass niggas," Alondra squealed, biting her lip at the group of chocolate niggas who walked past.

I giggled, "It should be a sin to look that good." We laughed and high-fived before walking onto the sand.

"Heeeey, bitches!" The sound of Cassie's voice caused us to turn around.

"Hey, ho." I walked a few feet to hug her and nod at Nigel.

I couldn't lie and say that Nigel wasn't fine because he was. But you needed to be more than fine to get a pass.

"Y'all look good. If I were gay, I would have both of y'all on lock," Cassie said, playfully smacking Alondra's butt.

"Bitch, you gay," I laughed.

She shrugged her shoulders and bit her lip at me, and I just shook my head. Cassie always played like that, but I was starting to think that she was really like that.

"Let's go get some drinks," Alondra suggested.

We walked through the sand with our shoes in our hands and headed over to where the DJ and the drinks were. We had to hold hands so we didn't lose each other. It was so crazy out there. As we were walking through the crowd, some nigga grabbed my ass, causing me to turn around quick as hell. I didn't play that shit even though I allowed niggas to do that and more for money.

"Excuse you, nigga," I fussed, eyeing him up and down.

He was fine as hell. Like pretty boy kind of fine. His light skin was glowing under the sun, and his big brown eyes looked lighter than they really were. He had a low cut and a few tattoos here and there. His lips were pink and soft, not too big for his face but just enough to bite on. He had to be about six feet as he stood next to my five-four frame. He wasn't wearing a shirt, so I could see his muscles and what looked to be almost a six-pack coming in.

"You're excused, beautiful." He licked his lips at me, and I turned my lips up.

Sucking my teeth, I turned on my heels and started back to the drinks.

"Damn, baby girl, where you going?" he called after me, but I ignored him and continued.

"Girl, you are tripping. He was fine," Alondra yelled over the music.

I shook my head as I opened the cooler and pulled out a fruity alcoholic drink. "Rude as fuck, too."

After I took a few sips of my drink, I damn near ran over to where everybody was dancing when my song, "Handsome and Wealthy" by Migos, came on. This was my shit, and Quavo was my man. I bent over with my drink still in my hand and started popping my ass and swaying to the beat. Alondra and Cassie weren't far away, doing the same thing. We were having so much fun. Fun that I hadn't had in a long time.

By nightfall, I was a little more than tipsy. The police were starting to kick people off the beach, so we decided to head to the Hookah Lounge for a little bit.

"I'll be back. I need to go to the bathroom," I told them before getting up and heading to the back.

I went into the girls' bathroom and into one of the stalls. As I was peeing, I heard a huge bang as the door of the bathroom came open. I quickly finished up so that I could get the hell out of there.

"Check the stalls," I heard a dude say, so I quickly stood on the toilet, almost falling in. I almost peed on myself, even though I just finished using the bathroom, when another dude came and looked under the stalls.

I held my breath when he came to the one I was in. He was trying to open the stall, but because I was in it, it was locked, so he just looked under it again. I let out a quiet sigh of relief when he moved to the next one before saying, "They're empty."

"So explain to me why you don't have my fucking money," the first voice said.

"M . . . man, listen. I told him I needed a little more time," a different voice answered and almost sounded as if he was crying.

I couldn't honestly tell you how many people were in here with me, but I was too scared shitless to care.

"You don't get fucking time for owing ten Gs, muthafucka. You get a bullet in your head."

Pow!

I gasped but covered my mouth because I didn't want them to hear me, but it was too late.

"Nigga, I thought you said there wasn't anybody in here," the first nigga said before I heard footsteps.

"There isn't."

They got to the one I was in and banged on it before he bent down to look under. But when he looked, he stuck his whole head under it and saw me. It was the same dude who touched my ass on the beach.

"Get out here," he said, but I just stood there. "I don't want to have to kill you."

Sighing, I got down and hesitantly unlocked the door. When it swung open, he grabbed my arm and pulled me all the way out. I wanted to yell at the sight of the dude lying on the floor with a hole in the middle of his head. The blood was going everywhere, spreading on the floor. I backed up a little as it moved closer to us.

"You clever little bitch. You want me to kill her?" he said, pulling out his gun from behind him.

"Titus, chill," ass-grabber told him before turning back to me. "You didn't see anything, right?"

I nodded my head frantically. "This is none of my business."

"A'ight, give me your number."

I quickly rambled off my number to him. "Can I go now?"

Before he could even finish nodding, I was bolting out the door. Everybody was chilling and acting like they didn't even hear the gunshot. It was loud, so how couldn't they hear it? But then again, the music was blasting. I quickly walked over to the table that Alondra, Cassie, and Nigel were at.

"Wait, where are you going?" Cassie asked.

"Uh, my stomach is cramping. I'm going to the room." I gathered all my stuff and left.

Without looking back, I hurried across the street and started walking back to the hotel. The feeling of my phone vibrating in my pocket scared the shit out of me. I took a deep breath to try to relax myself. I felt like if a pen dropped from miles away, I would jump out of my damn skin.

757-556-6659: Bitch, you think you could block me and I wouldn't get to you? Bring your ass home now!

I shook my head because I knew that it was Patty texting me. I looked at my notifications and saw that she had called me five times from that number. I knew it had to have been Karl's phone. I blocked that number, too. I was going to have to deal with her when I got home. Too much had happened tonight.

What a fucking night . . .

A Week Later

I was walking down Chesapeake Boulevard and listening to my music. I had just come from one of those damn appointments out at the Oaks. It was going on two o'clock in the morning, and I had to be to work at Food Lion at seven. My body and my feet were hurting from having to walk all over damn Norfolk. It was crazy how Patty had me doing all of this shit, but she didn't have the decency to at least drop me off and pick me up from the places where I had to go. That bitch had two cars. Hell, I could even drive myself, but she wasn't going for that either. I was just waiting until the day I hit my $10,000 goal. I was going to get my car and move out of Patty's house. Hell, out of Norfolk as well. Since I had graduated, there was no purpose for me here. I loved my city, but there were way too many bad memories for me. I was even transferring my job to wherever I moved in case Patty decided to come looking for me.

Bobbing my head to DeJ Loaf's "Try Me," I looked both ways before I crossed the street. I knew for a fact that I made sure no cars were coming, so I was confused as fuck when this BMW almost smacked my ass.

"What the fuck!" I yelled, smacking my hand on the hood.

The music in this shit was blasting and the windows were tinted, so I couldn't see who was inside. The door swung open, and none other than ass-grabber stepped out. Annoyance and fear immediately spread across my face. I was annoyed because this nigga was rude as fuck, and I was already tired. And I just wanted to go home. I was afraid because I knew what he was capable of, and I wasn't trying to be the next bitch found dead.

"Damn, if it isn't my future wife. What's your sexy ass doing out here this late with that tight-ass skirt on?" He smiled wide, showing his perfect white teeth.

All I could see were his lips moving because I had my earbuds in still, so I took them out and paused my music. I looked over at him with a stank expression on my face. "What?

"Ay, fix your face, baby girl. I ain't do shit to you. Now come get in the car and I'll take you home."

By that time, there was a car behind him, blowing the horn like crazy. But he didn't give a fuck, because he was still parked there. I shook my head. "No, thanks. I'm almost there."

"I didn't ask you that, sweetheart. I simply told you to get in the car." His tone was stern, which made me roll my eyes but get my ass in his fucking car.

My body melted as soon as it touched the leather seats. The inside of this car was beyond beautiful. Patty had one, too, but my ass couldn't even touch the bumper on that bitch. Ugh, I couldn't stand her ass. Ass-grabber climbed in the car after me before speeding off, making an illegal-ass U-turn right before the entrance of my neighborhood. I quickly strapped my seat belt across my body before looking at this nigga like he was crazy.

"Where the fuck are you going? My house is over there." I pointed behind us.

"We gotta make a quick stop first," he said, making a left onto Chesapeake Boulevard.

"Look, I don't want any problems. All I want to do is get home because I have to work in"—I hit the lock button on my phone—"five and a half hours, and I am exhausted."

"I got you, shorty. Just sit tight."

Oh, I was sitting tight all right. Stiff as a muthafucka because I was scared as fuck. I was clutching my imaginary pearls something serious. This nigga could easily take me somewhere isolated and chop me up for witnessing that murder at Hookah's. Now I was regretting not running when I had the chance. I should have just taken the fuck off. Hell, I used to run track in my middle school days, so I was pretty fast. He would have most likely caught up to me, but at least I would have tried.

The ride was quiet except for the loud-ass music he had playing. He would occasionally look over at me, then back to the road, but I kept my eyes straight ahead. I knew my way around Norfolk like the back of my hand, so if he was trying to kidnap me, I could jump out right now and find my way home with no problem.

"What happened to your face, baby girl?" he asked, looking over at me briefly.

Last week when I came home, as soon as I walked in the door, Patty went ham on me. By no means was I a punk, and I could go round for round with the best of them. But at the end of the day, Patty was my mama. And although she was a horrible mother, I couldn't disrespect her by beating her ass. I just couldn't.

"I was in an accident."

"What kind of accident?" he inquired.

"Car accident," I lied.

"Oh, yeah?" he said like he didn't believe me.

I just nodded, not up for conversation. All I wanted to do was go home. I had no interest in wherever he was taking me. None. But all that changed when we drove into a dark-ass alley. I sat up in my seat and looked over at him before looking to where he stopped. Placing the car in park, he looked over at me.

"You know I should have killed you at Hookah's last weekend, right?" he said in a calm tone.

I swallowed hard as fuck before nodding. He gave me a grin that had me looking at him sideways.

"But I didn't because I saw something in you. I could tell by the look in your eyes that you've been through a lot, but you're a hustler. And I like that about you. I know you're confused as to why I brought you here. It's not to kill you," he said.

I released a breath that I didn't even know I was holding. "So why did you bring me here?"

He took the keys out of the ignition. "Come on and I'll show you."

Climbing out of the car, he started toward a door that I didn't notice before. Probably because I was scared out of my mind. I got out, making sure to have my phone on me in case I needed to call the police on this nigga. I knew he said he wasn't going to kill me, but I wasn't taking chances. Hell, I didn't even know this man's name. But I reluctantly followed him.

He opened the door and allowed me to go first when I reached him. My nose scrunched up at the smell of something that smelled like piss, shit, and feet. I covered my nose and looked back at him so he could lead the way. He walked ahead of me, and we went down a long hallway before he opened the door to a room. I peeped my head around him to see some dude tied up in a chair, causing me to gasp. His head was down so you couldn't see his face. Dude grabbed a bucket of water that was on the floor and threw it on him. The man jumped up immediately, and I saw his face. It was the dude Titus from Hookah's. I was confused about how he got him here because I was just with him.

"You see this muthafucka betrayed me," ass-grabber said.

"Malaki, what the f . . . fuck, man?" Titus looked up at him before looking over at me, and his face turned into a frown.

"Yeah, that was what I was thinking too. Because you knew I was going to make her my bitch, but you fucked her anyway. And to make shit worse, you paid for it," Malaki said, causing my eyes to widen.

How the fuck did he know that?

"Look, I didn't mean to do the shit, man. Jus—" Titus pleaded.

Malaki's laughter stopped him in his sentence. "You didn't mean to do the shit, huh?"

Titus shook his head frantically.

Malaki just nodded before playing with his little beard. "Okay, cool. Well, to make shit even, I'm not going to mean to let my bitch kill you."

If you'd have thought that my eyes couldn't get any bigger than what they were right now, you'd have thought wrong. Because when Malaki pulled the gun from behind him and held it out to me, my eyes popped out of my head, literally.

"Uh, no. I can't." I shook my head.

"You can and you will. Either that or I kill you right along with his bitch ass," he spat.

I just wanted to disappear right now. I was just seconds away from crying my eyes out. My ass just couldn't win for losing. My eyes went to Titus, then the gun, and Malaki, then back to the gun. You would have thought there was an earthquake by the way my hands were shaking as I reached out for it. Malaki stood back and watched as I pointed the gun at Titus and closed my eyes. I was trying to drown out his screams and cries, but it was hard. My heart was beating a mile a minute. I turned my head to the side and pulled the trigger, but nothing happened, so I opened my eyes to see Malaki laughing his ass off.

"My fault, baby. I thought you knew the safety was on." He walked over and took the gun from me to take the safety off and cock it back before giving it back to me. "All right, try again."

I took a deep breath before closing my eyes again. I put my finger on the trigger and pulled it again.

Pow!

"Damn, baby, you almost had him. You gotta open your eyes or you'll keep missing. I don't have any more bullets," Malaki said.

I slowly opened my eyes and looked over at Titus. I mouthed, "I'm sorry," before pulling the trigger.

Chapter 2

Lihanny Wright

December 31, 2016 at 11:59 p.m.
Five, four, three, two, one.

"Happy New Year!"

I blew my horn before turning to my right to give my man a big-ass kiss. My smile faded to a frown when I saw him in another bitch's face, whispering in her ear and shit. I was baffled as fuck because I didn't even remember seeing him leave my side. We'd been attached at the hip for this whole fucking party, so how the fuck did his sneaky ass get over there? Fed up, I turned to walk over there when I felt somebody grab my arm.

"Li, don't go over there," Cassie said with a pleading face.

I kindly took my arm away from her before continuing my mission. When I got over there, I stood right next to Malaki.

Honk! "Why the fuck do you keep testing me, Malaki?" I spoke, scaring the shit out of both of them. I was in both of their ears, but I didn't give a fuck. They were in my house disrespecting me? Yeah, okay.

Malaki looked over at me with a frustrated expression on his face. "Why you tripping? I'm just talk—"

Honk!

"I don't give a fuck," I said, cutting him off. "You should be on stage tonguing me down because that's what couples"—I turned my horn on the girl before turning back to Malaki—"do, nigga. Not over here yapping in this horse-looking bitch's face."

"Who you calling a horse?" The girl bucked, taking a step toward me.

By now, the party had stopped, and everybody's attention was on us. I put the horn in her face. Honk! "You, bitch."

"Get that horn out of my face," she said.

I laughed at her. "Or what?"

"Ay, chill, man. What the fuck? It's New Year's."

The sound of Malaki's phone ringing cut us short. He pulled it out of his pocket and walked away. I watched him the whole way because I was about to beat this bitch's ass. But when I turned to her, the bitch was gone. I turned in a full circle looking for her ass. She really had done a Casper on me.

"That bitch peeled." Alondra came up behind me, laughing her ass off.

I shook my head before joining her. "Yeah, that's her best bet. I was about to beat her ass."

"Li!" Malaki called my name from behind me.

I rolled my eyes hard as hell before turning around to face him. This man was so fine, but he was toxic as hell. Lord knows he was. When he forced me to kill Titus two years ago, my life changed forever. After he took me home, I thought he was going to leave me alone, but boy was I wrong. The very next day, he picked me up from work and took me to a trap house. This nigga taught me how to cook up dope. I was doing that for a week before he moved me to the block and taught me how to sell it. Then after that I was the runner, and then I was picking up and counting money, and then I was looking over shipments. Now here I was. I was that bitch, and anybody could agree with that.

"What do you want, Malaki?"

"Ay, watch your fucking tone, Lihanny. Don't play with me," he said, getting in my face.

"Yeah, whatever. What do you want?"

"I need you to go to the pier and see what the fuck those niggas talking about. Kent said something about the boat being caught on fire or some shit."

My eyes popped out of my head. If that was true, that was fucking kilos gone. "Malaki, we both need to go."

I was confused as to why he only wanted me to go handle it. Hell, he was really the one who needed to be dealing with this shit, because our connect didn't play at all. If he knew that this shit had caught fire, he was going to think some funny shit was going on and have us killed. I was enjoying my life and damn sure not ready to die tonight.

"Just do what the fuck I told you to do. Hit me up with details later." This nigga walked away from me without saying anything else.

I so badly wanted to take my shoe off and knock him in his big-ass head, but I had more important shit to deal with. Since I became like Malaki's prodigy, this nigga had been lazy as fuck with everything. Every time somebody called about something, he sent me to do the shit, unless it had to do with the connect because he refused to speak with anybody but Malaki. It was frustrating as fuck because even though this position was basically handed to me, I took it seriously, and I worked my ass off to make sure nothing fell apart. It was like he didn't give a fuck if the shit would crumble and fall today, and that didn't sit well with me at all. I loved Malaki, but I loved what I did more. If he didn't get it together, and soon, I was going to have to do what I needed to do. Simple as that.

"I have to go. Enjoy the rest of the party, and call me later," I told Alondra and Cassie.

Alondra poked her lip out like she was pouting. "Bitch, this is your birthday party. Malaki's ugly ass needs to be the one to handle business." She rolled her eyes.

Yes, it was my twentieth birthday, but that never mattered when it came down to business. I nodded and walked away so that I could get my jacket. It was forty degrees tonight, so I was wearing a burgundy velvet strapless leotard with a low dip to my belly button, a pair of black jeans, and burgundy thigh-high, heeled boots. My hair was straight and flowing down my back. When I got to the door, I grabbed my fur jacket from the rack and quickly put it on along with my black leather gloves. Opening the door, I stepped out and the cold smacked me in my face almost immediately.

I quickly walked to my 2015 candy red Jeep Wrangler and jumped in. After starting the car, I turned the heat on, then wasted no time pulling away. It was risky bringing in a shipment on New Year's because there were going to be cops everywhere, but they were going to be so busy trying to pull over drunk drivers that they weren't going to be worried about the shit I had going on.

It didn't take me long to get to the harbor that was in Norfolk on the base. I parked my truck and hopped out. My heart dropped at the sight of my boat burnt out. That was millions of dollars' worth of merchandise in that boat. It was crushing my soul just looking at it. I walked over to Dezmond, one of my closest workers, to see what the fuck happened. He must have heard my heels clicking because he turned around and shook his head.

"Where the fuck is Malaki?" he said.

I sighed and shook my head. "He sent me . . . again. Just tell me what happened, Dezmond."

He threw his hands in the air and shrugged his shoulders. "The shit was coming in like this. The muthafuckas who was driving the boat wasn't even on the fucking boat. I can't make sense of this shit Li, honestly."

I looked around before walking over to the boat. Carefully, I climbed on it and looked around to see if there was anything that could explain the fire. I removed my glove, bent down, and lifted up the tarp. I looked at Dezmond. "Thank God that this isn't all of it."

Dezmond leaned in. "What? That's not it?"

"This isn't all of it." I placed the tarp back and stood up. "That's about one-third of it. Did Malaki not tell you about the change of the shipment?"

When Dezmond shook his head, I rolled my eyes. This nigga had one job and couldn't even relay a message.

Two months ago, Malaki was drunk off his ass and got pulled over with the weight in the car. Why it was there I didn't know, but it almost cost us a lot of money. It might sound sickening, but he let him go because he used to be somebody Patty set me up with in those days. I saved all our asses. But because he wasn't on his shit, everything could have crumbled. So I made sure that our shipment came in threes: one by ship or boat, one by train, and another by truck. This was half a mil that we were going to have to explain to our connect, but that part was on Malaki.

"Find out who did this, and call me as soon as you figure this shit out. Not a minute later, Dezmond. I mean it," I warned him, and he smiled and nodded.

"You know I got you, and Happy Birthday," he called after me.

"Thank you." I placed my glove back on, then pulled my phone out to call to check out the other shipments. I waited until they answered.

"We're all clear," he simply said.

Without another word, I hung up and dialed the other number. Once I got confirmation that he was also on his way to the warehouse, I headed straight there. I needed to make sure myself that the rest of it was safe. Malaki was going to have to set up a meeting with our connect to explain what happened when we did figure it out. Hell, for all we knew it could have been his plan. We were going to find out for sure though.

It was going on four o'clock in the morning when I got home. I was tired as hell and knew I needed to get up later to make sure everything was being transported right. My feet were killing me, so it took no time for me to pull my boots off.

I looked around the house and rolled my eyes. Malaki let the housekeepers go home without cleaning up. I was beyond over him. Lord knows I was. This man was going to give me gray hairs. There was no way that I was going to be able to go to sleep knowing that my house looked like this, so I got to work.

It took me a good three hours to clean the entire house. I had an hour and thirty minutes before it was time for me to head out, so I headed up the stairs to hop in the shower. I climbed the last stair and walked to the left, to my bedroom. All of the blood in my body started to boil as I watched Malaki sleep in my bed with another bitch. She stirred, and I realized that it was the same bitch I caught him talking to during the party.

Without another word, I jumped on the bed and started beating her ass. I didn't give a fuck if she was asleep. She started screaming, obviously confused as hell. I dragged her out of the bed by her hair as I rained blows on her. I was pulling her out of the door when Malaki jumped out of his sleep. He looked to the side of the bed—

my side of the bed, where the ho was sleeping—before he looked over at me with wide eyes. Malaki jumped out of bed, dick swinging and everything, trying to get to us.

"Baby, what are you doing, yo? Stop!" he yelled, trying to pry my hands away from her.

"Get the fuck back!" I yelled before I dragged her to the stairs and let her go.

I didn't even watch as she tumbled down because I could hear it, but I was more concerned about beating Malaki's ass next. "Muthafucka, you got me fucked up! You in my muthafucking house and in my bed laid up with some bitch!" I hauled back and punched the shit out of his ass right in his face, causing him to stumble a little bit. I didn't miss a beat running up and throwing punches left and right. I was fucking him up.

He eventually grabbed a hold of my hands and punched the shit out of me. I fell back on the floor, looking at this nigga like he lost his mind. I had been by his side since he forced me to be two years ago. I had done everything he asked me to without question, and all I got in return was him treating me like gum on the bottom of his fucked-up shoes. I was over it, and he had to go.

"You got me fucked up, bitch." He stood up and over me. Bending down, he grabbed my throat roughly, damn near cutting off my air. "Don't forget, before me, you were nothing but a run-through ho with nothing. I made you." He held on tighter. "And I will break you if you ever put your fucking hands on me." Malaki squeezed a bit tighter before releasing me.

I inhaled so much air before coughing a couple of times. Tears fell from my eyes, not because I was crying, but because I was coughing so goddamn hard. I was pissed but fuck him! My eyes trailed over to Malaki, who was putting on his sweatpants like he didn't just violate the fuck out of me.

Standing, I calmly walked to the closet to pick my outfit for the day. As much as I wanted to blow this muthafucka's head off, I had other shit to do. More important shit. I had to think rationally about it. If I killed him right now, where he stood, shit would spiral out of control. So I needed to wait and lay shit out, but he was going to get his, believe that.

Once I picked out my outfit, I went into the bathroom and locked the door. Looking into the mirror, I placed my hand on the bruise that was starting to form on my neck. Turning away, I turned the shower on and waited a minute before getting in.

My energy for fighting over this man was gone. I was physically and emotionally tired of his bullshit. He was going to regret putting his hands on me. I could bet my life on that.

Once I showered and brushed my teeth, I walked out of the bathroom to put my clothes on. Malaki was still sitting on the bed, scrolling through his phone. His eyes moved across my body as I got dressed. That was the furthest anything was going to go, because if he came over here trying to feel up on me, I was going to knock him out.

Once I was dressed in a purple off-the-shoulder sweater, a pair of dark blue jeans, and my purple VSL pointy heels, I grabbed my watch and necklace that had my name on it before putting them on as well. I placed my hair in a bun so that my diamond earrings showed before I walked down the stairs. My eyes landed on the ho who was just lying on the last stair. She was most likely dead with a broken neck.

Pulling my phone out, I dialed the cleanup crew's number and instructed them to put the bitch back in bed where Malaki was. When they said they were on their way, I walked out of the house. *That muthafucka had better watch his back.*

Chapter 3

Lihanny Wright

Later That Day

I walked around the warehouse observing everything that was going on. With only having two-thirds of the shipment, we were going to have to ration it. Prices were going to have to go up, or demand was going to have to get smaller. I had to think about what the customers were going to deal with. Whether it was paying more or getting less, it was going to be all on me how this turned out because Malaki didn't give two fucks.

I sighed, shaking my head. He was really useless at this point. He couldn't even just show up to show his face when I asked him to. Just thinking about him calling me earlier made me laugh. I told my cleanup crew to put the bitch back in bed with Malaki since his ass went back to sleep after I left like nothing happened. He called me, snapping, but I just hung up on him, not wanting to hear anything that his dusty ass had to say to me. He didn't even have the decency to wish me a happy birthday. *Bitch ass.*

But on a more important note, I stopped walking and turned to Dezmond, who was right by my side like always. "Up the price. They'll pay whatever to get their fix," I muttered to him.

He just nodded. "What about Malaki? He texted me not too long ago asking what was going on."

I rolled my eyes. "Tell him everything is good. The boat fire wasn't our boat. He doesn't give two shits anyway."

Dezmond just nodded before pulling out his phone and stepping to the side while I continued to walk around to make sure shit was going right. As soon as it was done being cooked and bagged up, it was going to hit the streets. I just prayed the outcome was going to be the same.

I stayed until I felt like everything was going how it was supposed to. I was meeting Alondra and Cassie for lunch, and then we were going to go to the mall to do some shopping. I was willing to do anything for me to not have to go back home where I knew Malaki was.

"Dezmond, I'm out. Call me if anything happens. I mean anything." I glared at him. Dezmond was known for trying to handle everything himself before he called me. But shit was crazy right now, so I needed to be informed about anything.

He chuckled, already knowing what I was thinking. "I got you. Get out of here." He nudged me.

I stared at him for a second. Dezmond was really cute, reminding me of Quincy Combs with his light skin and thick-ass eyebrows. His teeth were beautiful, and his eyes were brown. Dezmond's lips were nice and pink, very kissable. He kept his hair in one of those man buns like Quincy, too. Dezmond stood at about six two and had a very muscular build. But he wasn't really my type. Plus, I thought he had a crush on Alondra.

"I'm not playing with you, Dezmond." I pointed my white claws at him before turning on my heels and walking out of the warehouse.

Climbing into my Jeep, I looked down to see Patty calling me. I rolled my eyes knowing that she was calling me for money. Hell, that was what she always called me for since I left her two years ago.

“Yes, Patty,” I answered, pulling away from the warehouse.

“Well, hello to you too, *daughter*. Happy Birthday.” She coughed.

“Yeah, thanks,” I said dryly. “What do you need, Patty?”

“I wanted to see if you could come over for a little while. I need a favor,” she said.

I rolled my eyes. “I will send someone over with some money.”

No matter how much shit she put me through, she was my mama. After I left, Patty went down bad. Karl stole all her money and jetted. The nigga left her a grand, and that shit didn’t last long. It wasn’t that long before she was calling me and begging for money. I wasn’t tripping though. She was my mama, and it was the right thing to do.

“Thank you.” The phone got quiet before she spoke again. “Lihanny, I’m so—”

I shook my head as if she could see me. “No, Patty, don’t do that. Look, I have to go. Somebody should be by there soon with the money.” I hung up before anything else could be said.

For the last few months, all Patty had been doing was apologizing for being such a horrible mother. Every time she called asking for money, she was trying to say that she was sorry. I just didn’t want to hear it. I felt like all those times when she was sending me out to make her money she could have stopped and done better, but she didn’t. She was only doing it now because she needed me. I’d told her time and time again if I was ever to get away from her, I was moving on and not looking back. But that all changed when Malaki came into my life.

It didn't take me long to get to the Cheesecake Factory in Virginia Beach. When I walked in, I looked around until I saw Alondra and Cassie, then made my way toward them. They stood to hug me when they saw me coming in their direction. I eyed the gift bags that were on the table as we took our seats.

"Happy Birthday!" they sang together, causing me to laugh because neither one of those bitches could sing.

"Thanks, y'all, but please don't ever do that again." I giggled, shaking my head.

Cassie laughed and playfully rolled her eyes. "Bitch, don't do us. You know we can sing."

Alondra nodded, agreeing with her. "She just hating."

I smiled. "Yeah, whatever." Looking up at the waitress who came over, I smiled at her. "Can I have a glass of red wine please?"

She took their orders before walking away. Lonny looked at me. "So what are the plans for tonight?"

I sighed, "Bitch, I'm going to sleep. I haven't been to sleep yet."

Cassie looked at me, confused. "What time did you get home after you left the party?"

"I got in at four, but I had to clean up the house. That alone took three hours. After that, I had no time to sleep, especially because Malaki had that bitch lying in my bed."

Both of their mouths went slightly agape just as the waitress came back with our drinks. I took a sip of mine, and as soon as she walked out of earshot, they started bombarding me with questions.

"Who was it? Did you beat her ass? What did Malaki say? Why didn't you call us?"

I waved my hands, signaling for them to stop. "Okay, first, I wasn't thinking about calling y'all. I jumped on the bed and started beating that bitch's ass. It was the same girl who was in his face at the party." I took a quick sip of my drink. "I threw that bitch down the stairs."

They looked at each other, then turned their attention on me before bursting into a fit of laughter. "Bitch, I know you didn't," Alondra said.

I looked at her sideways. "You damn fucking right I did. Both of them had me fucked up."

Cassie threw her head back in laughter, but then she stopped and looked at me with her eyebrows raised. "Wait, your stairs are steep as hell, Lihanny." She looked around before leaning in, and I sat back in my seat, getting comfortable because I already knew what she was about to ask. "Did you kill her? Is she a dead bitch?"

Crossing my right leg over the other, I picked up my drink and sipped it before shrugging my shoulders. "She might be."

"Oh, shit, bitch," Alondra said, taking a huge gulp of her drink.

I waved my hand in the air, stopping the conversation about that ho. What happened, happened. I wasn't one to dwell on the past, just shit on niggas and bitches in the future. They always said karma was a bitch. Plus, it was my birthday, and I wanted to have fun.

"Enough about that." I sat up and flagged our waitress down. "Since I'm going home after this, I need to drink. A lot."

I ordered us a bottle and then some food because I hadn't eaten all day. If I was trying to get drunk off my ass, then I needed to eat something first.

As we ate and drank as much as we could, we talked about everything. I wanted to say something about the fact that Malaki hit me, but then again it wasn't their business. I was going to handle that on my own.

Chapter 4

Hendrix Brown

One Week Later

"Muthafucka, why the fuck am I just now finding out that a third of my work caught on fire?" I looked to my right as I blew the smoke from my blunt in his face.

"What you mean? Nothing was set on fire. That was a misunderstanding," he said.

I chuckled and elbowed the shit out of this nigga in his face. "You thought I wouldn't find the fuck out, my nigga? Huh? How do I know you didn't set this whole shit up? You trying to get over on me or something?"

Malaki held his nose as he shook his head. "Nah, man. I sent my bitch to check shit out, and she told me that the shit was a misunderstanding, that they had the wrong boat."

"You sent your *bitch* to do your muthafuckin' work?" I snarled. That was the reason why I didn't like this nigga.

"I mean, yeah. She knows what she's doing. I taught her everything I know, and I learned it from your pops."

Gritting my teeth, I ran my tongue across my teeth. "It's your job to make sure shit is going as planned, and if not, to report back to me. I don't give a fuck who taught her what. This shit is on *your* hands. The only reason why I still fuck with you is because my pop begged me to keep your bitch ass on. Other than that, I would drop you like a bad muthafuckin' habit. I want all my fucking money come February, and if not, you and your *bitch* will be done for. Get the fuck out of my truck, nigga."

The door opened, and my driver yanked his ass out before closing the door. I watched as Malaki used his shirt to wipe his bloody nose and pulled out his phone. Shaking my head at his pathetic ass, I took a pull from my blunt. "Let's go."

Without another word, he pulled off, merging into traffic. I hated that I had to take a trip to Virginia because muthafuckas continued to test me. Malaki was one of the niggas who used to work with my pops before he stepped down. I had every intention of canceling all those muthafuckas and recruiting new people, but my pop damn near begged me to keep Malaki on. All was good until his ass started slacking. He never wanted to do shit anymore and was always sending his girl to do the dirty work. It'd been like that for a good year now, and I was seconds away from putting a bullet in his fucking head. I wasn't feeling the fact that his bitch was even around my shit in the first fucking place. I believed women were only good for two things: fucking and cooking. Not running around trying to have bigger balls than the next nigga. I didn't know the bitch, nor had I ever seen her, but I had heard about her. I had eyes and ears everywhere, and my people informed me that she had been running shit. I ain't have nothing against her, but with bitches came feelings. And I damn sure wasn't about to lose all my shit over some bullshit-ass Bonnie and Clyde relationship. Fuck that. I was going to be watching this muthafucka like a hawk. He had one last strike, and if he didn't come up with my money, it was lights out for that muthafucka.

"Where to, boss?" Jerry asked.

I looked down at my watch and saw that it was time for my meeting. "Take me to the Marriott downtown."

As he redirected his route, my phone vibrated, and I looked down to see that it was my girl calling. Shaking my head, I picked up the phone.

"Yes, Nylah."

"Baby, where are you? I'm hungry," she whined.

"I told you I had to fly out to Virginia to handle some business."

"Oh, yeah. I wish you had brought me with you."

I shook my head. "Nylah, you're nine months pregnant. You're not allowed to fly."

I looked at my watch again. "But I'm bored here without you, Hendrix."

"Go shopping for the baby or something, Nylah. Look, I have to go. I'll call you later." I hung up before she could say anything else.

Nylah and I had been messing around for three years. We met when I moved to Miami. She was in the club with one of her friends when I saw her. I was high and drunk as fuck when I hooked up with her, but she was cool as fuck about it, so we clicked. We were together for a couple of months when I found out she was fucking one of my workers on the low. She made an excuse like she didn't know that we were exclusive yet because I was fucking with other women, which wasn't true. I said fuck her after that shady shit, but I was still fucking her. The only reason why I was claiming her was because she was carrying my child. At first, I thought she was only saying that shit to get me back, but I took her to the hospital that morning and they confirmed that she was pregnant. I knew it was mine because I made sure she shut all that shit down when I started fucking her again. We were cool right now, but I was only doing the shit for my kid who could come at any minute.

We pulled up to the hotel, and I got out of the car and buttoned up my suit jacket. "Stay here. I'll be back," I told Jerry, and he nodded before getting back in the truck.

I usually would make him wait outside, but it was cold as fuck, so I was letting it slide. This weather was nothing like Miami. It was cold as fuck in Virginia. When I walked in, I went straight to the executive boardroom on the top floor. Just as I expected, my men were waiting for me. I nodded at the four who were standing outside before opening the door to go in.

"Mr. Garrett. Mr. Walker," I spoke as I walked in, heading to my seat.

"Mr. Brown, thank you for meeting with us on such short notice," Garrett said, standing up to shake my hand.

I held my fist out instead. I didn't shake muthafuckas' hands. Never had. I didn't know what type of shit they were carrying. Unbuttoning my suit jacket, I took a seat in one of the chairs and intertwined my hands, placing them on the table. I looked between the two of them. "What can I help you gentlemen with?"

Walker looked at Garrett before turning his attention to me. "Well, for the past few months, our oil company has been crashing because we both had to file for bankruptcy," he explained.

I nodded before leaning back in my chair. I pulled my mints box out of my suit jacket and opened it. Taking the blunt out, I grabbed the lighter and lit it. After taking a pull and letting it out, I shrugged my shoulders at them both. "So what do you need from me?"

"A loan. A big one," Garrett simply said with Walker just nodding his head.

"Just get to the fucking point. I don't have all day," I said, blowing out some smoke. After this blunt, I knew I was going to be hungry as fuck, so I was going to go to my mama's crib and get some of her food that I knew she was cooking. As soon as she found out that I was coming into town, she told me to come over for dinner. Hell, a nigga was almost ready to skip this shit and go straight there.

"A million," he all but yelled.

"Okay, but I hope y'all understand that with me giving money comes interest. A lot of it with the amount that you're asking."

They both nodded, and I sat up because this was where shit needed to be clear as fuck for them. "Y'all came to me because y'all need money, and a lot of it. I'm sure y'all knew what y'all were getting yourselves into when you made that call, correct?" They both nodded their heads. "A'ight, so this is how this shit works. I give you my money, and you return it with half a million more. Y'all have exactly six months to pay this shit back, and if not . . ." I shook my head. "If not, then it'll be bad. I have all of the addresses to any living family member y'all have. If y'all can't deliver and y'all try to hide from me, then they will be who I visit for my money. Is that understood?" I said.

They looked at each other before nodding. "Yes, we understand."

"My people will see you soon." With that I stood and walked out.

Buttoning my jacket, I headed to the elevators. A nigga was anxious as fuck to get to my mama's house. I was hungry as fuck and in desperate need of a home-cooked meal. Nylah cooked for me from time to time, but since her ass was damn near ready to pop, I had been eating out all the fucking time now. I was a grown-ass man with a big-ass appetite, and I needed to eat.

Stepping off the elevator, I ran smack into some female, causing her to fall onto the floor.

"Shit," she hissed, pulling her hair from her face and reaching for her phone.

"Damn, I'm sorry. I didn't even see your little ass coming." I bent down to help her up, and she snatched away fast as hell.

"Then maybe you should look where you're going next time," she said, moving past me and pressing the button for the elevator that had long gone back up.

I just smirked at her, not wanting to disrespect shorty even though she was rude as fuck. I took a second to look at her because she was sexy as fuck. That wasn't hard to see, but her attitude was fucked up, and I just met her ass. Well, ran into her. "You got it."

She gave me a fake smile before walking into the elevator. I waited until it closed before continuing to walk to the front. Once I was outside, Jerry got out of the car and opened the door for me. Nodding to him, I jumped in, and we immediately headed in the direction of my mom's crib.

"Ma! Where you at?" I called out as I walked into her house. It was feeling good as hell in here being that she had the heat on.

"In the kitchen," she replied, and I started making my way to her.

I heard little footsteps coming down the stairs, and a huge smile spread across my face. I already knew that it was my baby girl coming to look for me, but I continued to walk into the kitchen. When my eyes landed on my mama, I walked over and kissed her cheek before looking over her shoulder at whatever was smelling so good in those pots.

"Daddy!" Hydiah yelled, and she wrapped her arms around my legs to hug me.

I stepped away from my mama to pick my baby girl up. "What's up, baby girl? Did you miss me?"

She nodded fast as hell before wrapping her little arms around me. I kissed her cheek a couple of times, then took a seat on one of the kitchen chairs and placed her in my lap.

"Ma, where Pop at?"

She looked over her shoulder at me for a second before turning her attention back to her food. "Probably in the living room watching the game."

I looked down at my daughter, who was playing with my beard. "How you been?"

She giggled, showing all her teeth. "Good."

"Good, huh?" I tickled her stomach. "You ready for your sister to come?"

"Yes. Am I going to be able to come see her when she's born?"

I nodded. "You and Grandma are going to fly down to meet her as soon as she is here. Is that cool with you?"

Hydiah smiled at me. "Yes."

I kissed her head before placing her down and standing. "I'm about to go in here with Pop."

"Okay, baby," my mama responded.

I walked out of the kitchen and headed toward the back of the house where the living room was. Just as my mama said, Pop was sitting on the couch with a beer in his right hand and the TV remote in his left. I walked around the couch so I was in his line of sight.

"What's good, Pop? How you been?" I dapped him up and took a seat in the recliner that was slightly across from the chair he was sitting in.

"I'm good, young'un. Where the fuck you been at?" He looked over at me briefly before turning back to the TV.

"You know I live in Miami, Pop," I said, taking my suit jacket off and placing it on the back of the chair.

"Yeah, so?" he said. "Your rich ass can afford to come down and see your old man at least twice a month. It's been what? Three months?" He shook his head.

"Damn, let me find out your old ass missed me," I joked, looking at him sideways with a grin on my face.

He scrunched up his nose. "Hell no. No shit like that. My ass just be bored as fuck here when your mama is at work and baby girl is in school."

I turned my lip up in confusion. "Work? When the fuck did Ma start working? I thought she retired."

Pop looked at me and shook his head. "See, if your ass called or came down more often, you'd know that she went back to teaching, but she's a professor now."

My eyes bucked out of my head as I looked at my dad. "You let her go be a professor at a college?"

He shrugged. "Why not?"

I shook my head. "For one, Ma is getting too old to work, and two, some young nigga might try to steal your wife."

Pop let out a hearty laugh before turning up his beer. When he swallowed, he looked back at me. "Like I said, if you had called, you'd know that I had a conversation with each and every one of those muthafuckas in all of her classes, including the females because your mama is the type to make them bitches go gay."

I burst out laughing. This nigga was a fool. "Yo, get outta here, Pop. You didn't go threaten those kids."

"You damn right I did. I couldn't stop her from going back because you know your mama. She loves teaching, and nobody is going to stop her from doing that shit. Not even me."

I nodded, understanding. My mama was stubborn as fuck. And spoiled, so whatever she said went. No questions asked.

"So I had to make sure those muthafuckas knew to respect her but don't get too close, or I will break their faces." He smirked, causing me to shake my head but smile.

I didn't even blame him. My mama was beautiful and didn't look like she was 40. At all. She was deep chocolate with brown eyes and short hair she always kept done. She stood at about five six with a thick body. She put me in the mind frame of Angela Bassett with a thick body. Niggas always threw themselves at her, but most already knew who she belonged to.

"So what you doing here, young'un?" Pop turned the TV down and turned his beer up as he waited for me to answer.

I sighed and shook my head. "Your boy is fucking up."

He raised an eyebrow. "Who? Malaki?"

I nodded. "Shit is being burned, and ain't nobody saying shit. Then he got his bitch running around town doing all this work for him."

Pop chuckled as if I said something amusing. "You haven't met her?"

Frowning, I shook my head. "No. Why would I want to meet her? It's not her that I'm doing business with."

All he did was finish off his beer and slowly nod. "You should find the time to meet her, sonny. I'm telling you. I've met her, and she isn't anything to play with."

I waved him off. "Nah. I don't do any business with females unless it's about her giving me some pussy. I just wanted to let you know that Malaki might not be around long if he continues that bullshit he's on. I already have somebody in place to take over for his ass."

"Listen to the wise man, Hendrix. If you cancel Malaki, talk to Li. Don't try to change nothing in Norfolk, or it will be some shit."

My father only called me Hendrix when he was serious about something, but I wasn't trying to hear that. I was sticking by what I had always stood by. Bitches were only good for cooking and fucking. But I just nodded my head.

"I hear you, Pop."

Chapter 5

Lihanny Wright

Later That Night Around 9:15 p.m.

I walked into the hotel room and kicked off my heels. Looking at my wrist, I saw that I had fifteen minutes before it was time for me to get home and handle what I needed to handle. I placed my purse on the couch after I plopped down next to it. I was sleepy as fuck and was so ready to get into bed and lie down. Unzipping my purse, I pulled out my phone to see if I had a message.

Unknown: We're on the way to your house.

Me: Is he drunk?

Unknown: Yeah, he's knocked out in the passenger seat.

Me: Okay, stick to the plan.

Unknown: Will do.

Locking my phone, I let my head fall back on the chair. After this, shit was going to get hectic real fucking fast, but I was more than prepared for it. When my watch read 9:30, I got off the couch and grabbed my purse, then walked to the door to put my shoes back on. I headed to the elevators and waited for them to open. My phone rang with a message.

Unknown: We're all set.

Me: OMW. Get rid of the phone.

I deleted the messages, then texted a friend of mine from Sprint to remove them from my records as well. When I got to the main lobby of the Marriott, I looked to my left at the front desk and nodded at the girl who was there. She returned it before going to the back. Tightening my jacket around me, I walked outside and got in the car.

It took me about fifteen minutes to get to my house, which was perfect. I parked my truck around the corner, then walked the rest of the way to my house. When I got inside, I went straight to where the security cameras were and took the tape out, slipping it into my purse. I opened the hidden compartment I had in my countertop and pulled out the Desert Eagle that was in there. Grabbing the silencer, I twisted it on. Taking a deep breath, I walked to the stairs in my house and ascended them one by one, making sure to be as quiet as possible.

I looked in the doorway of my room and watched as Malaki fucked my best friend. I had been waiting for this moment for a long-ass time, and it was finally happening. It was crazy how shit worked. I told that muthafucka he was going to regret putting his hands on me and disrespecting me like I wasn't that bitch.

"Wow, Malaki," I spoke, making my presence known.

He stopped mid-stroke and jumped up. My eyes landed on Cassie, who looked just as surprised to see me. Malaki's eyes darted to Cassie before looking back over at me and the gun I had in my hand.

"Baby, wait. It's not what it looks like," he said, holding his hands out with his palms facing me.

I crossed my arms across my chest. "Oh, it's not, huh? Then explain it to me, Malaki. What exactly could be going on that includes your dick in my best friend's pussy?" I looked at Cassie. "And you, bitch. I knew you wanted to fuck my nigga all along, but I didn't think your ass would have actually grown the balls to do the shit. I mean, damn, Cass, you're supposed to be my bitch," I said, actually sounding hurt.

Cassie looked at Malaki, then over to me before she burst out laughing, causing me to laugh right with her. "Bitch, you need to be an actress. You really sounded like you were about to cry." Cassie climbed out of bed to get dressed.

"I told your ass to watch my fucking skills. I think I'ma go to college for that shit."

Pulling my eyes away from Cassie, I looked at Malaki, who was looking confused as shit. I gave him a warm smile. "Oh, shit, my bad. You seem a little confused."

I gave him a second to take it all in before he looked at me with hate in his eyes. "Bitch, you set me up."

Smiling, I shrugged my shoulders. "I told you, you were going to regret putting your hands on me, Malaki."

He let out a sarcastic laugh. "So you gon' kill me? Bitch, I made you! The faster you realize that shit, the faster we can get past it. Like, what the fuck, Lihanny?"

I rolled my eyes. "I can admit that you did help turn me into the person I am today, but *I* perfected me. *I* worked hard to get to where I am, so don't even try that."

"So what? You kill me and take over everything?" he said with a raised eyebrow.

Shrugging my shoulder, I replied, "Maybe, but either way it doesn't matter. You don't give a fuck what happens. I'm the best thing that's ever happened to you business-wise, because without me, the streets wouldn't be what they are today. So you're welcome," I said before putting a bullet in his head.

Out of the corner of my eye, I could see Cassie putting her shoes back on. That was the cue for this to be over with. I turned on my heels and left with her right behind me. She was going back to her man, and I was going to the hotel where I never left.

***

I woke up the next morning to my phone vibrating like crazy. Already knowing what it was about, I left my phone sitting on the hotel bed, then got up to go handle my hygiene. Once I was finished, I walked back over to my phone in my robe and decided to answer the phone for Dezmond.

"Hello?" I answered, sounding like I was asleep.

"Li, yo. I cannot believe your ass is still asleep. You need to get up, shorty. Malaki was killed last night."

"What? What are you talking about, Dez?" I said, looking at my nails. *I need a fill in.*

"Man, one of his homeboys found him dead at your house last night. The police is surrounding the shit. You need to get over there."

"Oh, my God. I'm on my way." I made sure to sound like I was crying before I hung up the phone.

I took my time getting dressed and checking out of the hotel. As I drove back to my house out in Lakewood, my phone continued to ring, and I had the right mind to cut the shit off because it was starting to get on my nerves. I thought it was crazy how worried everybody seemed to be about Malaki being dead. Nobody fucked with him.

It didn't take long before I was pulling up across the street from my house. I couldn't get to the driveway because the police cars were blocking it. I turned the car off and quickly jumped out, running to the front where the officers were scattered all over my yard and coming in and out of the house.

"Ma'am, you can't go in there." An officer placed his hand up to stop me from going any farther.

"What do you mean I can't go in there? That's my house," I said with tears rolling down my face.

"Ma'am, I'm sorry, but you can't."

I looked at my front door to see the coroner coming out with a black body bag. I knew right then that this was my chance to act a fucking fool, so I did. "Nooooo! My baby!" I cried, trying to get out of his embrace. "Malaki, I'm so sorry. I should have never left you." I dropped down to my knees and cried my eyes out. I swear to God I deserved an Emmy award for this shit.

"Ma'am, please come with me," another man walked up in a suit and said while trying to help me off the ground. I knew him immediately as one of the head detectives from the Norfolk Police station on Virginia Beach Boulevard. Detective Roy was his name. I did my research on him before I planned this whole thing.

Standing up, I followed him to an all-black truck. He opened the back door for me and closed it before going to get in the front seat. When he closed the door, he immediately looked back at me and said, "You're doing a good job acting this out."

Smiling, I wiped my face and shrugged my shoulders before sitting back and crossing my arms. "I try."

"So my boss is on his way here. This case is going to be bigger than we thought because our narcotics department has been looking into him."

That part made me sit up because, as far as I knew, Malaki wasn't on anybody's radar. I made sure to keep his name out of anything that had to deal with the police because that meant my name wasn't too far behind, and that was some shit I didn't need. That was why I went to Detective Roy. I was paying a lot of damn money to keep our name off their radar.

"Okay, what exactly does that mean?"

"I mean, it can mean two things. One, they'll leave it alone because he's dead, or two, they'll dig deeper to find his killer because they'll believe it's drug related."

"And when were you going to tell me this shit, Roy?" I shook my head. "Fuck!" I sat back and went into deep thought. "How much will it cost to keep my name out of any of this?"

He let out a big breath before shrugging his shoulders. "I don't know. I might not be able to."

I looked at him like he lost his mind. "I pay you way too fucking much for those words to even slip through your lips."

Nodding, he responded, "I'm going to do whatever it takes, but I just want to warn you, I am going to have to take you to the police station to question you."

"I know. Don't worry. I have that part covered."

"In the meantime, try to stay low. Focus only on planning his funeral, because they will be watching your moves. My boss is coming, so cry," was all he said.

Chapter 6

Hendrix Brown

One Week Later

I sat in the back of the church watching as everybody stood to pay their respects to Malaki. I couldn't even lie. I was surprised as fuck that this nigga was dead, but then again, I was low-key pissed somebody got to him before I could. I mean, I was glad that I didn't have to do the heavy work. But now that it was done, it was time to put somebody in place. Just because the nigga was dead didn't mean the money had to die too.

"There she is." My pop pointed to a female who stood and walked to the casket at the front of the church.

I sat up a little bit, trying to get a good look at her face, but the veil she had on was covering her face. Her body was looking right though, and she was short as fuck. I wasn't believing that this was the shorty who had been taking over for Malaki. Her little ass didn't look like she could burst a grape. As she stood over his casket, looking down at him, she bent down and got closer. Since I was in the back, I couldn't make out what she was doing.

"I think she killed him," he said, and I looked over at him, shaking my head.

"Nah, I doubt it."

"Don't doubt her. She might be little in size, but she's nothing to play with. Her pops is Karter Wright. Besides me, he was the biggest drug lord out here. That shit is in her blood."

I was impressed by that little fact. Karter and my pop were enemies before he passed, and most people thought it was Pops who killed him, but it wasn't. Dude was hot shit back then. Hotheaded as fuck from what my pop told me. He tried to be partners with him on multiple occasions, but Karter wasn't having it. He wanted to do everything on his own. He didn't believe in having a partner. Only one nigga could be king to him. I felt like that was his downfall. But then again, whether or not you had a partner, niggas would be gunning for you.

After the service was over, everybody left the church since there wasn't going to be a burial. Pop and I stayed back because he wanted to talk to Li one-on-one. I wasn't feeling it though because she didn't know who I was, and I was trying to keep it that way. I knew my pop was going to want to introduce me to her, and that wasn't something I wanted. I preferred to keep my identity anonymous until I felt otherwise. Besides, I wasn't going to be working with shorty anyway. She had better find something else to do with her free time.

Rising to his feet, my pop headed to the front where Li was sitting by herself watching his casket. When he reached her, he touched her shoulder, and she looked up at him and stood. She immediately embraced him in a hug. After they broke apart, they stood and talked for a while, and I was surprised when my dad walked back in my direction minutes later. She watched him and looked over at me before turning back around and taking her seat. I stood when my pop got back in my personal space so that we could leave.

I saw the smile written all over my pop's face, and I frowned in confusion, wondering why he was smiling. "What's funny?"

"She definitely did it," he said, walking ahead of me.

I stood still for a minute before looking back at Li, who was also looking at me. We stared at each other for a second before I continued to follow my father out of the church.

5:32 a.m.

Five hours later, I was standing back in my room in Miami, looking Nylah over. Her pregnant frame was draped over a long-ass pillow. She had her hair tied up with a few strands falling around her face. All she had on were panties, and my dick instantly bricked up at the sight of it. Kicking my shoes off, I pulled my shirt over my head and pulled my jeans off. Once I was only in my boxers, I climbed into bed behind her. She squirmed a little when I kissed her cheek.

"I was trying to stay up," she muttered softly with her eyes still closed.

My hand found its way to her stomach, and my baby girl immediately started kicking. "It's cool, baby. Go back to sleep."

It was quiet for a good five minutes before Nylah jumped out of her sleep, causing me to do the same. I watched as she grabbed her stomach, crunched over.

"Baby, what's wrong?"

Nylah looked at me with her mouth ajar. "I think my water just broke."

I felt between her legs, and sure enough, it was leaking everywhere. I jumped out of the bed and slipped some sweats on, while Nylah slowly threw her feet over the side of the bed so that she could put some clothes on.

"Baby, it hurts," she cried out.

"I'm coming, Ny. Just don't move." After I slipped my slides and a shirt on, I walked over to her side and helped her put on one of my shirts and a pair of pants. She put her feet in her slippers, and I bent down to help her stand up.

"Grab the bag," she muttered.

"I got it, baby. Come on."

We walked out of the room and down the stairs. I grabbed my keys off the rack as she headed to the garage. When she got into the car, I climbed in right behind her before pulling out and heading to the hospital. We were pulling up in no time, and the doctors were already outside waiting for her. As soon as she was on the stretcher, they rushed her to the back. I pulled out my phone to call my mama.

"Boy, why the hell are you calling me at five thirty in the morning?" she spoke.

"Ma, Nylah is in labor. I'm getting suited up right now to go in there with her." I held the phone between my ear and my shoulder as I pulled the blue pants over the sweats I was wearing.

"Oh, goodness, okay. Byran. Byran, get up. Nylah's in labor. No, I'm not joking. Hendrix is on the phone. Nigga, get your ass up," she said before coming back to the phone. "We're going to be there as soon as possible. I'm going to pray for a safe delivery. Good luck, and I love you guys."

"I love you too, Ma."

When she hung up, I slipped my phone into my pocket, then finished putting on the scrubs they'd given me. Once I was dressed, I walked back out of the bathroom, and the doctor was waiting to show me to Nylah's room.

At 6:46 a.m. Haylee Nia Brown was born. She looked just like Hydiah when she was a baby, with a head full of hair and bright hazel eyes. My baby girl was beautiful, and she had me wrapped around her little finger already. I was so in love with her, and I already knew that I was going to have to get my AK ready for these niggas who thought they were going to try to get with her. Smiling down at her, I leaned over to kiss Nylah on her lips.

"Thank you," I whispered in her ear before kissing her again.

We admired her for a little while longer until the doctors had to take her to clean her up. I was chilling while they cleaned Nylah up and prepared to move her to another room. She fell asleep as soon as Haylee left the room. The sound of my phone ringing caused me to quickly pull it out so I could silence it before it woke Nylah up. I looked down to see that it was my homeboy Vince.

"What's good?" I answered, leaning back in the chair.

"Ay, man. I know you just left Virginia, but we need you to come back."

I shook my head. "For what?"

"I mean, well . . ."

"My nigga, spit the shit out," I barked, then looked over to my right to make sure I didn't wake Nylah up. Once I was sure I didn't, I stood and walked out of the room.

"Well, I did what you told me to and placed Serge in charge of the Norfolk part, but that nigga is dead now."

I frowned. "Fuck you mean he's dead? How the fuck did that happen, and where the fuck was everybody when the shit happened?"

"I don't know. All I know is that everybody I sent to take care of the traps out in Norfolk is missing. Don't know how the shit happened."

"So how the fuck you know they're missing?"

"One of the corner workers who worked with Malaki saw the shit go down."

"Do you know who?" I asked, kind of already knowing.

"Nah, I don't. I guess since Malaki is gone, niggas think they can step up and try their luck."

Running my hand down my face, I sighed, "A'ight, yo. I'll be there by tonight." Without saying another word, I hung up the phone.

This was not the right time for this shit. Nylah was going to flip the fuck out when I told her I had to go back to Virginia. She was going to think it was some bullshit I was on. I was just going to wait until my mama got here so she wouldn't flip on me too much. I was pissed that I had to leave my baby girl not even a few hours after her birth. A nigga wasn't expecting this shit to happen. Everything always ran smoothly because niggas knew not to fuck with me. It wasn't hard for me to put fear in these niggas' hearts. All it took was a look. I didn't have to say shit. I thought it was really crazy how, as soon as I left, all this shit happened, but I was going to get to the bottom of this shit.

My parents got here a few hours later with Hydiah, who was excited as hell to see her baby sister. My heart smiled a million times as I watched her fawn over Haylee. I looked over at my father, trying to get his attention, and when I did, I gave him a look, and he nodded.

I turned to Nylah, who was playing with Hydiah and Haylee. "Baby?" I called her, and she took a minute before giving me her attention. "I gotta go handle some business back in Virginia."

Her pretty-ass face immediately turned into a frown. "You just got back not even twelve hours ago, Hendrix. I just had our daughter."

"I know, baby, but it's important."

Looking away from me, she shook her head. “Do you,” was all she said.

I was going to have a lot of making up to do when I got back. Standing, I walked to her bed and bent down to kiss her lips, but she turned, so I kissed her cheek instead. I understood she was pissed, but I didn’t have time for her shit. So I didn’t even acknowledge her as I kissed my baby girl and Hydiah.

“Daddy, where you going?” Hydiah said, trying to jump off the bed and come over to me.

“I have to go handle some business. I need you to stay here to help Nylah with Haylee, okay? You finally get to be a big sister.”

She smiled wide, showing all her teeth. “Okay. Don’t be long.” She pointed her little finger at me before going back to the bed with Nylah.

“I love y’all. I’ll call when I land,” I said before leaving the room with my dad following me.

Once we were out of the room and into the hallway, my pop looked over at me. “What’s going on?”

“Somebody kidnapped the muthafuckas I put in to take over shit for Malaki,” I said.

Pops smirked like that shit was amusing. While he thought the shit was funny, I was fuming on the inside. “You should know who it is. I told you she wasn’t going to be with no niggas trying to take what she fought so hard to keep up.”

“I don’t give a fuck about none of that. I said I wasn’t fucking with her like that. She’s not offering to suck my dick or make me some steak, so I’m not trying to hear it.”

“Go down there and talk to her about that.”

“Nah, ain’t no talking about to be done.”

Chapter 7

Lihanny Wright

The Next Day at Noon

I was going through Malaki's phones trying to get in touch with whoever the connect was. I called every number in them, using the code word I always heard him say before they started talking about the shipment. So far, nothing was happening. I was getting frustrated as fuck because it was almost time for us to get another shipment in, but if I couldn't get in touch with his ass, then we were going to be shit out of luck. That was definitely something I didn't need right now.

Since Malaki died, niggas on the west side were thinking they were going to come to our side to start some shit and reign supreme. I needed to prove to them muthafuckas that I could handle this whole shit without Malaki being here. Yeah, I handled everything when he was alive, and niggas respected me because of Malaki, but now that he was gone, I was going to have to work twice as hard to try to prove myself. They thought that Malaki was the bug in my ear telling me what to do and how to do all the shit. Nobody knew that I was really doing all this shit on my own for as long as I could remember. I didn't have a problem with proving myself because I knew this shit like the back of my hand. I was more than capable of handling everything. It was just my turn to show it.

"Dammit," I yelled in frustration, throwing one of the phones against the wall. None of the numbers in there were it. Most of the numbers I called were bitches, which infuriated me more. If I could, I would have brought his ass back to life, then killed him again for disrespecting me. *Bitch-ass nigga.*

Knock! Knock!

I looked up at the door. "Come in," I yelled.

Seconds later, Dez was walking in. "What's good wit'chu? Any luck?" he asked, closing the door behind him.

Rolling my eyes, I shook my head. "No. Neither one of those phones led me to the person I need to talk to."

Dez came and took a seat in one of the chairs in front of me. "I mean, the nigga has to come get his money. He's going to pop up now or later for his bread. Just tell the nigga what it is then."

I looked off to think about that. "Dez, I swear I don't know what I would do without you," I said.

That shit definitely made sense, and I couldn't wait until the day I would come face-to-face with this man. I knew it was going to be hard to try to convince him to let me be the one to take over for Malaki, but I was going to do my best. If he wasn't feeling me, then I was going to find somebody else. Nothing or nobody was going to stop my money. He could kiss my ass and go cry about it to somebody who gave a fuck.

"Let's just hope this nigga not on no funny shit," I said, standing. "What's good with the niggas we got held up in the basement?"

"They not saying shit," he said, standing as well.

"Let's just pray they agree to work for me. I'd hate to have to kill anyone."

Dez chuckled, "Look at your li'l gangsta ass trying to be in power and shit. I see you."

I looked back at him and laughed, "Nigga, shut up."

We walked out of my office and down the two flights of stairs that led to the basement of the warehouse. Flicking the lights on, I looked around at at least fifty niggas who were tied up and sitting on the floor. I didn't know what the fuck dude was thinking trying to push some niggas in my spot. I didn't give a fuck who he was. This was my shit, and nobody was going to knock me out of my place.

Walking around, I looked at each and every one of them. Some of them were still unconscious from when we brought them here, and the others were awake with tape on their mouths. I stopped in my tracks and crossed my arms across my chest, just looking around.

"If they don't want to trade, we burn all these muthafuckas up. I don't have time for this shit," I muttered to Dez before turning my attention to our guests. "Let's wake everybody else up before we start."

I grabbed a bucket of water that was lined up on the wall, then walked to the first person who I saw was unconscious. I splashed the water over him, and he jerked out of his sleep immediately, gasping for air.

"Wakey, wakey." I smiled down at him.

He looked up with the biggest mug on his face. "Bitch—"

Before he could even finish his sentence, I slapped the piss out of him. I didn't give a fuck. He wasn't about to disrespect me. "Watch how you talk to me before I say fuck being nice and just burn your ass alive."

He chuckled as if I just said something amusing. "You must not know who the fuck I work for. When he finds out about this bullshit you pulled, trust and believe you won't be burning nobody else alive . . . bitch," he said.

Saying fuck this nigga and setting him on fire, I pulled my gun off my side and lit him the fuck up until he resembled Swiss cheese. "Let this be a lesson for all of you muthafuckas. I don't give a fuck who your boss is. You work for me now. And if you don't like it, to hell you go."

***

Later That Night Around 1:30 a.m.

I unlocked the door of my apartment and walked inside before locking it behind me. After setting the alarm and putting my gun in the vase by my door, I kicked off my heels, then headed straight to my room to get in the shower. I'd just gotten in from a long day of burning niggas until I ran out of gasoline and lighter fluid. I was tired and needed to sleep before I had to get back up in the morning and get back to work.

I walked right into the bathroom, not bothering to turn on any lights or get my clothes. I was definitely in the mood to sleep naked. My body was drained from a long day of work. Turning on the shower, I allowed it to get hot as I undressed, then brushed my teeth. Once I was done, I checked to make sure it was hot but not too hot, then stepped inside. My body immediately relaxed at the touch of this steaming hot water. I just stood underneath it for a good five minutes before I grabbed my washcloth to wash up.

Fifteen minutes later, and after washing my hair, I was walking out of my bathroom with towels wrapped around my body and my hair. I walked back into my room and took the towel off my hair to put it in a bun. I flicked the switch for my fan, then snatched my towel off my body and climbed into bed. Once I plugged my phone in, my body melted into my mattress, and it took no time for me to fall asleep.

Feeling like something was off, I woke up to see a dark figure sitting in the corner of my room in the chair. I thought I was seeing shit, but I didn't hesitate to pull out another gun from under my pillow and aim it in the direction of the person. I half expected for him to be gone by the time I looked back in that direction, but he wasn't. And he didn't even flinch as I aimed my gun.

"I heard you been looking for me," the deep, raspy voice sounded throughout my bedroom.

"How the fuck did you get in my house, and who are you?" I questioned.

"Don't worry about all that. You been looking for me, and you been causing a lot of problems for me."

As soon as he said that, I knew who he was. Placing my gun down, I climbed out of my bed, not caring that I was naked, and walked to the safe that was on my wall. After putting the code in, I grabbed the bag that was in there and threw it to his feet. My hands went to my waist as I watched him. I still couldn't see his face.

"What is this?"

"That is the money that I owe you. I need more product," I simply said.

He laughed like I had just told the funniest joke in the world, which caused me to frown. "What's so damn funny?"

"You're funny, sweetheart. You're standing in front of me as a *woman,* butt-ass naked, asking for some work. How do you expect me to take you seriously?"

"It shouldn't matter that I'm a woman or that I'm standing in front of you in my birthday suit. You can look in that bag and see that I'm nothing to play with. I handle what I need to. Even after a third of our shipment caught on fire, you still got exactly what was owed to you with no problem. I'm the one behind that."

"I don't give a fuck." He sat up, placing his elbows on his knees. I could now only see his nose and the outline of his lips due to the little lamp that was in my room. "You could get me a million dollars in a week, and that still won't change the fact that I don't work with your kind."

I scoffed, "My kind? You sound childish as fuck. Obviously, your ass has some serious issues, because money is money. No matter if I'm blue, green, purple, woman, or trans, you don't turn down money. I'm trying to help your pockets."

"I'm not hurting for shit. I don't work with emotional-ass women who will be quick to call the Feds on muthafuckas when shit don't go their way. I mean, you just killed your own nigga, and now you're trying to take over his shit. I don't got time for the bullshit. And you can stand your fine ass there and preach about how you don't mix feelings in your business. I'ma save you the trouble. I'm good on you, and the next time I hear some shit about you trying to fuck with territory that belongs to me, the next visit won't be so nice. I'd hate to have to body a fine-ass bitch like yourself. Now if you not trying to fuck or cook me a hot meal, stay the fuck off the streets and stop looking for shit."

"Ha! You think you scare me, nigga? You don't. Just like you said, I killed my own nigga for what *I* worked for. Just imagine what I would do to somebody I don't even know. I don't give a fuck what you claim to be yours. I built that shit, and I am the one who's been holding that shit down on all ten toes. So you can miss me with that bullshit. I don't give a fuck if you don't want to work with me. Somebody will. Trust and believe I will make mine, and ain't nobody, and I mean nobody, is going to stop me, not even your pussy ass. You may leave through the front door."

I was beyond pissed. Hell, that wasn't even the word that described how hot I was right now. This nigga had me fucked up insulting me. Like, who the fuck did he think he was? God? He wasn't going to stop shit that I was building. If I had to, I would cook up my own shit for all I cared. My pockets would stay fucking fat. Fuck him.

"I ain't even going to lie. You turning me the fuck on with this gangsta-ass attitude you got going on. But don't let this front you put up be the reason why you're buried beside your nigga, sweetheart." Standing, he picked up the bag and headed to my bedroom door.

When the light hit his face, I was surprised to see that it was Big B's son. I remembered seeing him at the hotel that night and at Malaki's funeral. I didn't know how he knew about Malaki. Maybe he was just fishing for something and I gave myself up because I was talking big shit. I didn't care though. His fine ass didn't seem like the type to run to the police. I watched as he left my room and headed toward the front door.

"Just like your guns work, mine do too. Don't underestimate me and find yourself six feet deep," I yelled after him.

He didn't say anything as I heard my apartment door open and close. I leaned over to the wall and set the alarm before sitting on my bed. I knew he was serious about not wanting to work with me. I was already prepared for the shit to happen like that, since from the beginning he only wanted to work with Malaki. Malaki used to tell me all the time that he used to get in his ass for letting me handle certain shit, but everybody knew that Malaki didn't give a fuck and nobody told him what he could and couldn't do. That was one of the things that I loved about him before he turned into a complete asshole and met one of the bullets in my gun.

I reached behind me and pulled out my phone. After dialing Dez's number, I waited for him to pick up. When he did, I didn't even give him a chance to talk before I was speaking.

"Plan B," was all I said before hanging up the phone. He knew what that meant, and he knew that it meant we were possibly going to go to war with this nigga. It was time to prepare and still make money in the streets. This nigga had woken up the beast that I was trying my best not to let out.

***

The Next Day

“So look, this is what’s about to happen. I’m running this shit now, and a lot of shit is going to go down,” I said, looking into the eyes of every soldier in attendance.

From the back of the room, I could hear snickers. I squinted to see that it was a couple of Malaki’s friends. They were loyal to him and always had been. They never liked me since the day Malaki introduced me. All of his friends blamed me for killing Titus even though I was doing it against my will.

“Y’all niggas got something to say back there?”

They looked up at me, smiling like shit was funny, before one of them known as Cade spoke up. “Yeah. Fuck we look like working under you? What? You think just because you were handling shit with Malaki, you become top dog now that he is gone?” he chuckled. “Fuck that.”

Everybody else started nodding and shit, agreeing with him. I looked back at Dez, who was just shaking his head. One thing that I wasn’t about to do was explain myself to these dumb muthafuckas. Either they wanted to get money or they didn’t. Either way, the shit didn’t make any damn difference to me. So I walked to the door with Dez right behind me. When I got outside, and he was right there, I closed the door to the warehouse and secured the bolts on them with the key I had.

“What are you doing? Locking them in there?” Dez looked at me, confused.

Ignoring him, I looked around until I saw the stacks of steel drum containers filled with gasoline. I looked up at the window, then back at Dez. I was too short and not strong enough.

“Put this in there,” I told him, pointing to the steel drum and then the window as I twisted the cap to open it.

"Girl, you're crazy as hell." He shook his head before doing what I asked.

As soon as the shit hit the ground of the warehouse, they started going crazy. I grabbed the blunt from behind his ear before lighting it and throwing it through the window. Dez looked at me like I was crazy as we walked away from the warehouse. Those niggas were trapped in there. If they didn't want to follow my lead, then they were going to die. It was as simple as that. I didn't have time for all the extra shit. It was nothing for me to find a group of niggas who wanted to make some money. So that was what I was going to do.

We left and parted ways because I had to go see Patty. She called me, saying that it was an emergency. Even though I knew better, I was still going to go see her. It'd been a minute.

Before I went there, I stopped at Feather 'n' Fin on Tidewater Drive to get some food. I had been fienin' for their chicken and macaroni, and I was happy that I found time to finally get some. I sat back in my car and waited for my food to be finished. The sound of Rihanna's "Needed Me" blared through my speakers just as my phone started ringing. I looked down to see that it was from an unknown number. Against my better judgment, I answered.

"Hello?"

"You're making shit hot." His voice sounded through the phone, and I caught myself unintentionally biting my lip.

Clearing my throat, I responded, "How do you seem to continue to have connections to me and I still don't know your name?"

"That doesn't matter. I told you to stay off the streets, yet you're on the news for arson and the murder of almost fifty people. You too reckless, and it's going to backfire."

"This has nothing to do with you."

"This shit has everything to do with me. They are my streets, and you're fucking it up because you're in your feelings, right?" That must have been a rhetorical question, because he continued before I could say anything else. "Stay the fuck away or you will regret it, sweetheart. I'm usually not into killing women, but I'll have no problem making an exception for you. This is your last warning," he said before hanging up.

I placed the phone in the cup holder. Feeling like I was being watched, I stuck my hand out the window and stuck up my middle finger. The faster he realized that he didn't scare me, the better. He was just being annoying now. I guessed I was just going to have to show him what I was about, just like he was trying to do. I never had backed down from a fight and wasn't about to start now.

It wasn't long after that that I was pulling up to Patty's house. She was still living in the same house from when I moved out. I was guessing that it was because she couldn't afford anything else. Getting out of the car, I got my food and closed the door, hitting the locks. There were niggas sitting on the green box who nodded and others who spoke as I made my way to the front door. I pulled my key out and opened the door. My nose immediately scrunched up at the smell. For as long as I could remember, Patty had always been a clean person. She didn't play that dirty shit, so I was confused as to why the house smelled like must and balls.

"Patrice!" I called out, walking farther into the house. I was pissed because I wasn't going to be able to eat my food now. I was about to throw up just from the smell of it. When she didn't say anything, I placed my food and drink on the table before starting to walk around the house. She wasn't in the kitchen or the bathroom, so I walked up the stairs to her room. My heart dropped at the sight of her lying in the middle of the floor in my old room. She looked unconscious. I ran to her side, and I started shaking her to wake her up.

"Patty! Patty, get up." I checked her pulse, and it was really faint, so I quickly pulled out my phone and called the ambulance.

Not even fifteen minutes later, they were putting her on a stretcher and rushing her out of the house. I ran out of the house behind them after locking the door and then followed them in my car. I said a prayer for my mama. I prayed that God would help her. I knew Patty wasn't the most holy person in the world, but she was still my mother. And I wouldn't feel the same if she died. I wouldn't be the same.

Chapter 8

Lihanny Wright

A Few Hours Later

I was sitting at Velocity Urgent Care with Patty. I was waiting for her to wake up so the doctors could tell me what was wrong with her. It seemed as though Patty was keeping a lot of stuff from me about her health. Even though we didn't talk much or get along, I was still her daughter.

I looked down at the sound of my phone ringing. My eyes darted to Patty before I got up and left her room, then answered.

"What?" I hissed as soon as I pressed the green button.

"You need to come down to the station for questioning," Detective Roy whispered through the phone.

"I can't right now. I'm busy."

"Well, you need to get unbusy. Either that or they'll arrest you. I told them that there was no need for that, and I could give you a call and have you down here," he said.

Rolling my eyes, I sighed. "I don't have much time to give y'all for this bullshit. My mama is in the hospital," I said and looked at my mother's doctor, who was walking past. I signaled for him to meet me in her room, and he nodded before going inside. I waited for Roy's response.

"It won't take long. Just a few questions," he said.

I didn't even respond. Instead, I just hung up the phone. Running my fingers through my hair, I took a deep breath before turning on my heels and going back into my mother's room. Her doctor was checking her vitals.

"I have to go make a quick run. Would it be possible for you to tell me anything about my mother?" I asked, picking up my jacket and keys.

After walking to the clipboard, he flipped through the papers before looking back up at me. "Your mother has stage four brain cancer."

"Wait, what? That's not possible. I send her to the doctor every month to make sure she's free of anything, and she's always told me that she was good."

"Do you ever see the results for yourself?"

"Yeah, sometimes. I even make her doctor call me," I assured him. I would know if my mama had cancer. Even though we weren't close, I made sure she took care of herself.

"What's her doctor's name?" he questioned, going through the papers.

"Dr. Ros . . . Rosland . . . Rosando . . ." I snapped my fingers, remembering the name. "Dr. Rosando."

"I will have to look into that because it says here that your mother hasn't been in for a check-up since sometime around Easter last year," he informed me.

My eyes went over to Patty. How the hell was that possible? I made sure that she was good. I always made sure she was good. "Okay, so when can she start chemotherapy? I don't care how much it costs. Just get it done."

He sighed, "I'm afraid that chemo won't help. It's too late—"

"That's not what I asked. Get her started on chemo as soon as she wakes up. If my mama dies, you better start counting your fucking days." Without saying anything else, I walked out of her hospital room and headed to the police station.

"Where were you the night your boyfriend was robbed and killed?" Detective Roy asked.

"At the Marriott on the waterside. He and I got into an argument because I caught him cheating again, so I went to a hotel for the night," I responded.

"And when did you check into that hotel?" he asked, looking through some papers that I assumed were the records from the hotel.

"I checked in around four in the afternoon. I'm sure you can see if I'm lying by the tapes from the hotel."

"Do you know anybody who would have wanted revenge on Malaki?"

I shrugged my shoulders. "I don't know. Malaki had a lot of enemies because he didn't know how to keep his mouth shut and talked shit to a lot of people."

"We have reason to believe that Malaki had dealings with drugs. Before he was killed, there was a file being built against him. Now—"

Before he could finish what he was saying, there was a tap on the glass mirror. Detective Roy looked up at it before looking back over at me then leaving the room.

I was guessing that his ass was saying too much. They were at a dead end now with the case on Malaki now that he was dead. That was exactly how I needed it to be. After today I was going to have to switch up some shit though in case they came sniffing around. I had Roy as my inside man, but I didn't trust that muthafucka one bit. At any second now, he could turn on me and have me in jail for the rest of my life. Which was why I had plans B and C if anything were to go wrong.

A few moments later the door opened, and in walked another guy. "Miss Wright, you are free to go," he said.

As much as I wanted to question it, I got up and walked out. I was going to hit Roy up about it later. Right now, my focus needed to be on finding a new connect. The mystery muthafucka thought he was going to stop something. He wasn't going to fuck with me because I had a vagina between my legs, and it was annoying as fuck. But it was time for me to put some shit in motion.

I called up Dez and waited for him to answer as I headed to my Jeep.

"What's good wit'chu?"

"Get dressed. We're going out."

I didn't say anything else. I had gotten word that the son of Jose Ortiz was in town for his birthday party. We'd crossed paths on more than one occasion, and he always had this little crush on me. Tonight I was going to use that to my advantage. I headed straight home so I could shower and get dressed. I was hoping this was going to turn out in my favor.

I walked into Origami with Cassie to my right and Alondra to my left. Dez and Nigel were walking in behind us. I swore that nigga was a fucking leech on Cassie, but if she liked it, I loved it. I wasn't about to judge my friend for the choices she made with her nigga. Clearly, she didn't mind it.

We walked up to the VIP I reserved that was right across from where Juan was having his party. I could see him clear as day, popping bottles, surrounded by almost every female in the building. I looked toward the DJ, and he looked back up at me before turning the music down a little bit.

"I see the Queen of Norfolk is in the house. Li, baby, what's up? We 'bout to turn this shit up!" Everybody cheered and got hyped when he played "Jumpman" by Drake and Future.

Out of the corner of my eye, I could see Juan getting up from the chair he was sitting on. I knew he was on his way over here. I looked over at Alondra as she turned her drink up, smirking. Pouring myself a glass, I sat back in the chair and crossed my legs as he walked up to me.

"Damn, girl, how you come in here and steal the show at my party? Where they do that at?" He grinned, looking fine as hell.

Juan was a full-blown Cuban through and through. He kind of put me in the mind frame of the nigga who played in *Coach Carter,* Timo Cruz, but a slenderer version of him. He rocked a low cut that was tapered on the sides. Dressed down in a plain black Gucci shirt, the matching pants, and all-black Giuseppe Zanotti sneakers, he was looking like a snack for real. But I could never mess with Juan like that. He wasn't my type, I'd have said. He had no problem with living in his dad's shadow and accepting his dad's money as his. You never heard "work" or "hustle" in the same sentence with Juan's name in it. Ever. That shit was a complete turnoff, and it was something I couldn't deal with. Yeah, Malaki was a dog-ass nigga and a piece of shit, but he was a hustler before he got lazy. Niggas only fucked with Juan because of who his father was. Including me.

I smiled up at him. "Not on purpose. I just kind of have that effect. Happy Birthday though."

"Why don't you come celebrate with me?" he offered.

I shook my head before nodding toward his section. "I'm not into big crowds."

"Shit, just say the word, and I'll kick all those mutha-fuckas out. Or at least come dance with me. Come on, baby. It's a nigga's birthday." He held his hand out to me.

I looked over at Cassie, as she moved her body to the music while sitting on Nigel's lap, before I shrugged my shoulders at Juan. "I guess I can do that." Setting my glass on the table in front of us, I stood and pulled my skirt down a little bit before grabbing his hand. I was wearing an olive green skirt with the bandeau top to match. On my feet were a pair of nude glass heels. My hair was in curls, pinned to the side and showing off parts of my tattoo.

He led me down to the middle of the dance floor. "Down In the DM" sounded through the club, and I started moving my ass on him. He held my waist, trying to catch my rhythm. I looked up and could see Lonny, Cassie, and Dez laughing at my ass. I stuck my middle finger up. This shit was not funny. I could feel that he was having a hard time keeping up with me. This shit was embarrassing as fuck for the both of us. I stopped dancing and turned around to face him.

Leaning toward his ear, I licked it a little before whispering, "I know a better way to say Happy Birthday." Turning on my heels, I grabbed his hand and led him to the bathrooms.

I slightly looked up at Dez, and he already knew what to do next. When we got to the women's bathroom, I locked the door before pushing him into the wall. I kissed him as he groped my ass. I was too much for him. My head fell back as he attacked my neck with his soft lips. His tongue moved its way down to my breast. Pulling my shirt down, he took my right nipple into his mouth. This was my cue.

"Wait, baby. I need a favor." I bit my bottom lip and moaned a little at his warm mouth on my nipples. As much as I didn't want to admit it, this shit felt good. "Juan . . ."

"Yes, Li."

"I need a meeting with your father." I pulled his head up and kissed his lips roughly before kissing his jawline. He was breathing hard as hell. "Do you hear me?"

I made my way down before squatting so I was right in front of his jeans. I rubbed my hand on the bulge in his pants. My eyes found his face, and I knew I had him when I saw him looking at me with low eyes while biting his lip. I unbuckled his pants. "I said, do you hear me, Juan?"

He nodded. "Yes, baby. I hear you," he muttered.

"Will you set up a meeting for us?" I said, looping my fingers in his boxers.

"Yeah, baby, I got you," he said.

Taking that, I started to pull down his boxers. Just before he sprang out, gunshots sounded through the club. I hopped up and moved toward the door while Juan struggled to pull his pants up. After opening the door, I speed walked toward the emergency exit. When I got out there, I hopped in the black truck that was waiting for me. As soon as the door closed, the driver sped off.

I passed Juan's phone to Dez. "Get this to Zeke so he can crack the code on it," I said, pulling my phone out of my handbag.

"No need. There isn't one."

My eyes went to the phone, which showed the home screen. A huge smile spread across my face. *What a dumbass.*

Chapter 9

Lihanny Wright

Two Weeks Later, Thursday Night

"Patty, I'll be right back. You gon' be good?" I peeped my head in her room.

She was sitting on the bed, staring up at the TV. She looked over at me briefly before slowly nodding. "Yeah, go ahead." She coughed.

"I'll send somebody up to look after you. Take your medicine," I said before heading to the door of the hotel.

Here I was in Cuba heading to meet up with Jose. I was praying this shit went as planned, because if not, I was fucked. I was all out of options at this point. I needed this more than anything in the world. This shit had to work out. It had to.

I got into the truck that Jose sent for me, and we were off. I made sure I had my gun on me in case shit went wrong. I was going to be outnumbered, but I wasn't going to go out without a fight. That was for damn sure.

As I sat in my seat, I thought about what my life might have been like if my father were never killed, or if Patty had never seen me as her meal ticket. Life before my father dying was one only a girl could dream of. I had everything a preteen could dream up. But most importantly, I had two parents who loved and cherished me. I felt like as soon as the police came to pick my mom up to identify my father, all of that shit went out the window. Patty hated me; I was convinced. She'd always beat me if I breathed wrong, and she blamed me for my father being killed. It was horrible.

I always thought that if Patty had gotten on her shit and worked to take care of us, I wouldn't have been in the streets as heavy as I was. Had she been the mother I needed, I'd have probably been in my junior year of college to be a lawyer or some shit. But instead this was where I was. I wasn't complaining, because I was the shit, but this wasn't where I thought I'd ever be. But I couldn't complain, because shit could have been worse. I was able to say I worked my ass off for everything I got, and that was something to be proud of.

We rode up to two gates, and the driver stopped so the security could check the truck. They opened the back door and made me get out. When they patted me down, they took my gun before opening the gate. I climbed back into the truck, and the driver drove me to the house. He got out and opened the door for me. Thanking him, I turned and walked up the stairs that led to the front door. I looked around at all the men posted up surrounding the estate with big-ass guns. This shit was something straight out of a movie for real.

It was hot as fuck out here, and I was instantly regretting wearing a pantsuit. But I was looking cute, so I didn't care. As soon as I hit the last step, the door opened, and a big Cuban nigga greeted me. He moved to the side so that I could walk fully into the house.

"Damn, Juan wasn't lying. You are fine as shit," one of the other men said after the door was closed. He was young, just a little older than me I would say. He was cute, too, but nah. I didn't come here for that.

Some young broad wearing a maid's outfit came out to get me. "Mr. Ortiz will see you now."

I followed her down this long-ass hallway where there was only one set of doors. Big red doors to be exact. When we finally reached them, she knocked twice before turning and leaving me standing there. I turned back to the doors just as they opened. Walking in, my entire body got hot at the sight of Malaki's old connect sitting in the chair in front of Ortiz's desk. He turned to look at me with a smug grin on his sexy-ass face. I was pissed. His being here meant nothing good at all. Ortiz was turned around near a table filled with liquor, so he hadn't seen me yet.

"Well, are you going to come in?" he said, smiling like something was fucking funny.

I was livid, and I wasn't hiding it either. "What the hell are you doing here?"

Ortiz turned around with a smile on his face. "Oh, great, you know Hendrix already? So no need for introductions. Please, come have a seat," he said before walking back over to his chair to sit down.

Slowly, I walked all the way into the room, and they closed the doors behind me. "I'm good standing."

"That wasn't me asking," Ortiz said, glaring at me.

I shrugged my shoulders, not feeling this whole shit. I didn't even know why I was still standing right here. This shit wasn't going to turn out how I expected. "Well, I'm telling you that I'm good here."

Hendrix threw his head back with a little chuckle before looking at me. "Damn, shorty, why so tense?"

Ignoring him, I looked over at Ortiz. "So what exactly did he tell you about me?"

Ortiz took a sip of his drink. "Nothing much. Just that you're very disobedient."

I looked at Hendrix. "Disobedient, huh? Why, because I'm about my shit and I don't care about nothing else but my money?"

He shrugged his shoulders but didn't say anything. Ortiz looked up at me. "I'm so sorry, love. You seem like somebody who's about her business, but I can't help you."

"Why, because he says so?" I pointed at Hendrix, who was nonchalant as hell. That annoyed the shit out of me.

Ortiz shrugged his shoulders and leaned back in his chair before crossing his hands. "Y'all have shit going on, and I respect this man enough to not get in the middle of it."

"You don't respect my father enough to at least give me a chance?" It was a low blow, but I was out of options at this point.

"Damn, shorty, that's cold." Hendrix shook his head.

"You're not your father," was all he said before he looked over at one of the guards.

Dude opened the door, and I took that as my cue to leave. My eyes darted over to Hendrix, who held his glass up at me before turning back around. On the inside I was fuming. But I walked out of the room with my head held high. When I made it to the front door, the dude from earlier smacked my ass, and I turned around and sliced his stomach with the blade that I had under my tongue.

"You bitch!" he yelled out, holding his side.

"Keep your hands to yourself, bitch," I spat just as everybody drew their guns on me. I continued to walk out the door.

"Li!"

The sound of Hendrix calling my name made me roll my eyes.

I hopped into the truck and locked the doors. I didn't know where the driver was who brought me here, but he needed to bring his ass because I was ready to go. Stupid muthafuckas had me fucked up. They both were going to regret this, that was for damn sure. I pulled out my phone to call Dez to let him know about this bullshit, but the tapping on my window stopped me.

My eyes rolled so hard that I thought they were about to get stuck. Hendrix was standing there looking so damn good it pissed me off. "Fuck away from me!"

"They not going to take you home, shorty. You might as well come get in my car so that I can."

"Fuck you! I'll call an Uber," I said, going to the app on my phone. This nigga was crazy if he thought I was getting in the car with him.

"There aren't any Ubers in Cuba, shorty," he said, laughing.

"I'll walk then, shit." Unlocking the door, I jumped out of the car, making him jump back to refrain from getting hit. I started walking down the long-ass driveway. It was too hot for this bullshit, seriously. Cuba had to have some cabs or something.

As I walked, I pulled my phone out to Google the number for a cab company. The sound of an engine caused me to look behind me to see Hendrix driving slowly beside me in a pretty-ass sky blue Ferrari.

He rolled the window down. "Girl, get your ass in this car. By the time you get to the gate, your feet going to be hurting like a muthafucka."

I shrugged my shoulders. "I'll just take my shoes off."

Speeding up, he drove in front of me, stopping me in my tracks. I just shook my head because I never understood why people did that, like the person couldn't just go around. *Idiot.*

Hendrix hopped out of the car. "Why the fuck you being difficult? All I'm trying to do is give you a ride."

I placed my hand on my hip and shifted all my weight to my left foot. "And all I'm trying to do is make money, but you keep fucking that up, acting like a pussy bitch," I spat.

He clenched his teeth before grabbing me by my face and squeezing my jaw hard as hell. "Listen to me and listen good. You should be counting your fucking blessings and thanking me for not sending a bullet through your damn head. You're disrespectful as fuck, and I've killed niggas for less. Fucking recognize who the fuck I am before you be in a grave next to your boyfriend."

"See, that's the best thing about me. I don't give a fuck who you are or who you've killed. I'm not a nigga. I'm that bitch. You bleed the same way I do, so you fucking recognize, and get your fucking hands off me." I pushed him off me, then pushed past him to get in the car.

I was turned on so damn much I had to walk away so he wouldn't see the wet spot that was forming through my pants. This nigga was so dangerous it was sexy as hell. But I couldn't look past the fact that right now he was the enemy. He was stopping me and my crew from eating, and I just couldn't look past that. He fucked up for not putting that bullet in my head like he planned to, because now I was about to be his worst fucking nightmare.

Chapter 10

Lihanny Wright

April 13, 2017 at 2:30 a.m.

Ducking down on the roof, I quickly walked until I was at the edge. Bending down, I dropped my bag, then quickly unzipped it to pull out my baby: a M40A5 sniper rifle. It belonged to my father before he passed away. I found it in his storage when I cleaned it out last year. I had it cleaned and painted red, which was my father's favorite color. After that, I paid Alondra's cousin, who was a sharpshooter, to teach me how to shoot it. The shit was hard, but now that I'd gotten the hang of it, I was loving it. Hell, I never missed.

Once I put the gun together, I lay down on my stomach and looked through the scope to see how many people were outside. "I count three," I said through the mic that was attached to my shirt.

"Whenever you ready," was all Dez said.

I looked through the scope, making sure to piece my measurements together. Lightly I placed my finger on the trigger. "Dez?"

"Yo?"

"Count to three," I told him.

"One." Pew! "Two!" Pew! "Three." Pew!

I caught the last one who was just about to run in the door. I looked up from the gun and smiled. “Go in.”

Sitting on my butt with my arms wrapped around my knees, I watched as my crew ran up into the main house in Chesapeake that belonged to none other than Hendrix. Since he wanted to continue to make sure I didn’t get any work from anybody, I was just going to take his. I had a nigga on the inside who told me that this was where they kept their work. I made sure to do this on this particular day because a shipment just came in. I smiled. This nigga should have just listened to me, sucked it up, and accepted that I was that bitch in the streets so we could all make some money. He was losing it.

“Dez, y’all good?”

“Hell yeah, we good. This shit is beautiful,” he said, and I could hear the smirk all in his voice.

“Bag that shit up and let’s go then. We got work to do,” I said as I placed my rifle back in the bag and headed to the door. I looked back at the house as they started coming out and smiled. “His ass should have just worked with me.”

Later That Day

“Bitch, you need to give this shit a rest. You look fucking horrible,” Alondra said when I walked into her house.

“Damn, bitch, you rude as fuck.” I yawned and rolled my eyes at her.

“Shit, I’m just telling you what’s real. You looked stressed the fuck out,” she said, passing me a bottle of water.

“Nope, not stressed at all.” I twisted the cap off before taking a sip.

Alondra came and sat on the chair next to me with her feet tucked under her. Taking my shoes off, I lay back, placing my feet on her lap. My arm moved over my eyes.

"Lihanny," Alondra called out to me.

"Yes, Alondra. I told you that I am fine," I said. I was sick of people asking me if I was okay. Like, damn, didn't I look okay?

"Li, it's been almost two months. You can't—"

"Oh, my God, Alondra, please. I said I'm fine. Okay? Let it go."

"I can't let it go, Lihanny. You lost your mother almost two months ago, and you haven't said a word or shown any emotion behind it." As she talked, I sat up and swung my legs off her. She continued to talk while I placed my shoes back on my feet. "You are running the streets like it's going to make you forget everything. You can't, Li. It's not healthy."

"No, what's not healthy is you continuing to press an issue that doesn't have shit to do with you. She was my mother, Lonny, not yours." I walked to her door and opened it before slamming it shut behind me.

I was so over people trying to preach to me about how I should be dealing with the fact that my mom died. I wished they would just leave it alone. After climbing into my Jeep, I sat there thinking about when I found my mom face down on the floor.

"I thought you were bringing me home and then you were leaving," I said, rolling my eyes. I was annoyed that this nigga was following me. He was supposed to drop me off and then take his ass on, but here he was right behind me as the elevator finally came down. We walked onto it, and I pressed the floor that I was staying on.

"I'm being a gentleman and making sure you're good," he said.

"Do you call stopping my money being a gentleman as well?" I snapped, closing my eyes. I absolutely hated elevators.

"How many times do I have to tell you that it isn't your money, baby? All that shit belongs to me. Why you want to be in the streets so bad anyway? Didn't you used to work at the Food Lion before you started fucking with Malaki's lame ass?"

I opened my eyes and turned to look at him. "How do you know that?"

"I'm Hendrix, sweetheart. I know everything there is to know about all my enemies." He smirked.

I looked him up and down before walking off the elevator. "So you take me as a threat?"

His face got serious as his eyebrows dipped. "Hell no. But you're a problem because you don't listen to shit I say. And I consider all of my problems my enemies."

I rolled my eyes. "That's dumb as hell. You clearly have issues."

"I've been told that once or twice."

I shook my head and continued to my room. When we reached the door, I turned to look at him. "I'm fine, and you can go."

His eyes looked down to my feet and back up as he licked his lips before biting the bottom one. "Yes, you are. Now open the door."

My face scrunched up at him. "Hell no. I don't know what the hell you got going on. But you're right about one thing, we are enemies, which means this is where this shit ends. Hell, you shouldn't have even come this far."

"Girl, shut the hell up and open the fucking door. You are so fucking difficult for no reason."

Ignoring him, I placed my key card in the slot, gaining access. I opened the door and stopped in my tracks at the sight of Patty lying on the floor facedown. A coffee cup was broken around her. I quickly ran over and turned her over so that I could see her face. I could tell she was gone just by looking at her. While Hendrix called for an ambulance, I just sat there.

I didn't know how exactly I was supposed to feel. I hadn't had to deal with any serious death since my daddy died almost seven years ago. But it was different with him because we had an actual relationship. He was my best friend when I was 13 and the only person who understood me. He loved me unconditionally, and that was something that I hadn't had since he'd gone. I never felt that love from Patty. Ever. Since my dad passed, she had never even uttered the words "I love you" to me. All she saw when she looked at me was money, and people expected me to cry over somebody like that? They expected me to break down and go into this sunken place over somebody who, for all I knew, didn't give two fucks about me? No, I wasn't going to do it. I didn't have it in me to give her the satisfaction of shedding tears for her. The only thing I could give her was to hope she was happy now that she was reunited with my dad.

The sound of my phone ringing snapped me out of my thoughts. Sighing, I picked it up to see that it was Roy calling me. Rolling my eyes, I pressed the green talk button before putting it to my ear.

"What?"

"They're looking for his killer," he whispered.

I sat up in my seat. "What? I can't hear you."

"I said they are looking for the person who murdered Malaki. They think it will lead them to the person who's supplying everybody."

Looking off to the side, I said, "Fuck! How the fuck did this shit happen? You were supposed to make sure this shit didn't fucking happen. What do I fucking pay you for?"

"This one is out of my hands."

"It shouldn't be out of your fucking hands. You're the number one detective there, which means you should be able to persuade them to leave well enough alone. Like, damn, do I have to do all the work?"

I sat back in my seat frustrated. This was something that I didn't need right now. "I'll take care of it. You just keep me updated."

"I can do that."

Rolling my eyes, I hung up the phone. Sighing, I leaned back in my seat and rested against the headrest. I felt bad for the way I talked to Alondra because she was only worried about me. As if she sensed me thinking about her, my passenger door opened, and she slid in.

I looked over at her. "I'm sorry," I muttered.

"Girl, you don't even have to do all of that. I know you are just in your feelings because you're having mixed emotions. I'm just here to tell you that it is okay to miss her even though she was a fucked-up mom. She still is your mom at the end of the day," she said.

I nodded and closed my eyes. "I know. I just . . . I don't know, Lonny. Is it bad that I don't miss her though? Like, I feel so much at peace now that she's gone. When she was here, anytime I was around her I felt like she had some type of hold on me. But all that weight lifted off my shoulders when I saw her on the floor face down in Cuba. Does that make me a monster?"

It sounded so harsh to say out loud because I was basically saying that I was happy that my mother was dead. She couldn't control me anymore. Yes, I moved out two years ago, but that didn't change anything. My body still felt like it belonged to her, and I hated it.

"No, it doesn't, Li. You went through a lot of shit at the hands of your mother at such a young age. No child should ever go through that, Lihanny, so you have every right to feel the way you feel. Everybody who is anybody knows how bad of a parent Patty was to you. She's gone now though, Li, and you can finally move on with your life the right way."

I wiped my face as tears slowly fell. I wasn't crying over my mother. I was crying because I was finally free. She held me down for so long, and I never expressed that until now.

"Come on, Li, let's go chill and watch movies. I'll call Cassie, and she can bring some food," Alondra encouraged me.

I sniffled. "Feather 'n' Fin?" I said, looking up at her.

The face she gave me before rolling her eyes and laughing made me laugh too. That was why she was my bitch. "Your ass is going to get fat if you keep eating that shit like you do. Bring your ass on." She shook her head and opened the door.

"Bitch, my ass already phat! But you knew that already," I replied, turning the car off and climbing out with her.

"Ew, don't nobody want to hear that, gay ass." She switched up to her front door, and I followed.

"Girl, whatever. Stop acting like you never wanted any of this," I joked, closing the door behind me after I walked in.

She turned her nose up and plopped down on the couch, picking up her house phone. I burst out laughing because I hated that ugly-ass shit. It was one of those rotary phones, but hers was pink. Alondra loved that phone though. "Bitch, use your cell phone." I sat on the love seat next to her, kicking my shoes off.

"Girl, shut the hell up and leave my phone alone." She picked up a pillow and smacked me with it. "You don't be saying shit when your childish ass want to prank call people up here."

I started laughing. “Because niggas don’t pick up for private numbers no more. That 1920s shit was the only option.”

Alondra rolled her eyes before calling Cassie. Just to fuck with her, I said, “Bitch, put it on speaker.” She shot me a look, and I burst into laughter. I had to chill seriously.

Chapter 11

Hendrix Brown

7:00 p.m.

"Daddy, can we watch *The Little Mermaid* now?" Hydiah asked as she sat on the floor playing with her dolls.

I scooted to the edge of the couch. "Not yet, baby. Daddy's game goes off in ten minutes, and then we can watch *Mermaid,* okay?" I briefly looked down at her before turning back to the game. The Dolphins were down by two touchdowns, and if they didn't win this shit, I was going to lose twenty Gs. A nigga hated losing.

"Okay, Daddy. Uncle Hussein, you want to play Barbies with me?" Hydiah asked my brother when he walked through the door.

He looked up at me before looking down at Hydiah. "Yeah, Uncle got you." He smiled, and I shook my head before laughing.

"She gets your ass every time."

Hussein shook his head before taking a seat on the floor with Hydiah. "I can't tell her no. This my dawg."

"Yeah, Daddy. Uncle Hussein is my best friend," Hydiah said matter-of-factly, passing him one of her dolls.

"Is that right? I thought I was your best friend, Hy," I said, looking confused.

Hussein played like he was hurt. "Dang, Hydiah, you switching up on me?"

She shook her head fast as hell, causing her beads to go all over her head. "No. I never told my daddy he was my best friend." Looking over at me, she frowned. "Daddy, when did I tell you you were my best friend? Never," she answered herself, causing me and Hussein to burst into laughter.

"You right, baby girl. My apologies," I said.

"See, Uncle?" She crossed her arms.

"My dawg." He held his hand out to dap her up before grabbing one of her dolls.

I shook my head and chuckled because they were a mess. My brother Hussein just got home from being in Kuwait for three years. He went into the military as soon as he graduated high school, and I was proud of my li'l nigga. I didn't want him in these streets because it was nothing nice. Shit, I was in the highest power, and I barely made it here. My ass had been shot a couple of times, stabbed, and picked up by the boys. But I made it out. I didn't want that for him, which was why I was all for him going into the military.

"How's baby girl doing?" he asked, looking up at me.

"Shit, she good. Nylah is pissed the fuck off with me because I haven't been back home yet." I ran my hand down my head before looking up at the TV just as the Dolphins scored. I jumped up. "Let's fucking go!"

"So you can sit here and scream at the game, but you can't answer my phone calls or texts?" The sound of Nylah's voice stopped me mid-cheer.

I looked to my left to see her standing in front of the elevator with my daughter's car seat in one hand and her bags in the other. I walked over to them and took the car seat and the bag that was on her shoulder. "Yo, what the fuck you doin' here? How did you even get here?"

"A fucking plane, how else, nigga?" She bucked, causing me to turn around and look at her like she was fucking crazy, because clearly she was.

"Ay yo, who the fuck you talking to?" My voice boomed throughout the penthouse I was staying in.

She rolled her eyes but said nothing.

I set Haylee's car seat on the floor next to Hussein. "Watch her for me really quick," I told him before putting the bag down and walking over to Nylah.

I grabbed her by her hand and pulled her to where my room was located. When we got in there, I closed the door behind us before pushing her slightly. "Who the fuck you think you talking to, Nylah? Huh?"

"Nobody," she muttered.

"That's what the fuck I thought. Now, what the fuck are you doing here? Who told your ass to get on a fucking plane with my daughter and come here?"

Nylah turned her nose up at me. "Nigga, she's *our* daughter. Not just yours. I came here since you didn't want to bring your ass back home where the hell you belong."

I ran my hand down my face and sighed. "I fucking told you I was handling business, Nylah."

"For three fucking months though? You've only seen our daughter once since she was born, Hendrix. One fucking time. What type of shit is that?" She shook her head and plopped down on the bed.

"You know I would rather be there with her in Miami, Nylah. There's a lot of shit going on out here, and I need to fucking handle it myself. You never complained about that shit before, so what's the fucking problem now yo?"

"The problem is that we just had a damn baby, Hendrix. For three fucking months, I've been taking care of her by myself! By myself, nigga. I'm fucking tired. My body hurts all while you down in Virginia slinging dick and 'handling business.'"

"Did you just listen to anything that just came out of my fucking mouth? That's your fucking problem now. You always so fucking quick to assume shit. I just told your ass that I'm handling business, and you jump right to me fucking bitches. Shit, if I had the time to do the shit, maybe I would."

Nylah jumped up and slapped my face. "Fuck you! Don't you ever in your fucking life disrespect me like that again." She tried to raise her hand to slap me again, but I caught it and turned her around so that she was against the door.

"Don't fucking ever raise your hand to hit me again, or I will fuck you up." I gritted my teeth, looking in her eyes.

My mood softened seeing her tears forming. A nigga started feeling bad for saying the shit I said, but she pissed me off. I was tired of being accused of cheating on her ass. For one, we weren't even together like that. And two, if I wanted to go out and fuck some bitches, I could and would with no problem. But I had too much fucking respect for her, as the mother of my child, to do some shit like that.

"Yo, stop crying. I ain't mean that shit." I used my thumb to wipe her tears away.

Seeing her pout with her lip poked out made my dick hard. It'd been a minute since I'd had some pussy, and now that her six weeks were up, it was over with. I bent down and kissed her soft lips. She hesitated for a second, but after no longer being able to fight it, she relaxed and kissed me back. I eased my tongue into her mouth before bending down and scooping her up. Walking over to the bed without breaking our kiss, I placed her on her feet facing me. I bit my lip as I looked down at her. Nylah was sexy as hell. Grabbing the hem of her shirt, I pulled it over her head and licked my lips at the sight of her titties sitting up. A nigga couldn't help himself, so I grabbed her, pulling her close before wrapping my mouth around her nipple.

"Aww." Her head slowly went back as my tongue flicked across her nipple. "Mmmm, baby."

I ignored her and moved to the other side to repeat the same thing. My dick was standing up by now, and I was about to say fuck the foreplay. But Nylah pulled my head away from her nipple and squatted down so that she was face-to-face with my dick. Looking up at me, she smiled before pulling my sweats down, and my mans jumped up, standing at attention. Nylah grabbed it in her hands before wrapping her pretty-ass mouth around it. My eyes drooped, and I bit my lip as I watched her. She continued to let her mouth slide up and down on my dick as she twisted her hand around my shaft.

"Make it nasty for daddy, baby," I muttered to her, closing my eyes. I thought my eyes were playing tricks on me when I opened my eyes and saw Li down there instead of Nylah. That shit made me even harder.

"Move your hands," I whispered to her before grabbing the back of her head and slowly starting to thrust into her mouth. "Damn, girl." It wasn't long before I was busting in her mouth. That shit felt so fucking good, and now I couldn't wait until I slid up in her fine ass.

After she swallowed it, I helped her up and bent her over. Her ass was looking right in the pink tights she was wearing. I couldn't help but to smack her ass before I pulled them down. "What'd I tell you about not wearing panties, Nylah?"

"Sorry, daddy." She looked back at me, biting her lip. I held my dick in my hand as I massaged her ass before pushing her waist down.

"Stay just like this." I ran my dick up and down her slit before pushing myself inside. She hissed and tried scooting away. "Stop moving, Nylah."

"I can't help it. It's been so long," she whined.

I pushed myself in, and as soon as she started pulling away, it was over with.

We got out of the shower, and as I was getting my clothes out to get dressed, my work phone started ringing. Nylah looked at me and shook her head before walking back into the bathroom. I picked it up, holding it between my ear and shoulder.

"What's good?"

"Hendrix, we were hit. Bad. Some niggas ran up in our main shit and took everything except the money. I can't get in touch with Willie either. That nigga not answering his phone or nothing. I don't know yo. I was trying to talk to that nigga before I called you up because I already know," Joie said, sighing.

"I'm on my way." I hung up the phone and tossed my towel off before grabbing my boxers and throwing them on. After that, I grabbed a pair of sweats and a white tee. I slipped some sneakers on before grabbing my wallet and keys, and I left.

"Where you going, bro?" Hussein asked, getting up from the floor.

"Gotta go take care of some business. You going to Ma's house?" I asked, pressing the button for the elevator.

"Nah, I'm going with you," he said, stepping onto the elevator with me.

"No, you not. I don't need you in no shit, nor do I want to hear Ma's mouth. So no, you not. Go home," I told him.

He sucked his teeth and shook his head. "Bro, I'm not a damn teenager anymore. I can handle it."

I shrugged my shoulders. "I don't give a damn what you can handle. I said no." The elevator hit the first floor, and I stepped off with Hussein behind me. I turned to him. "Take your ass home, Hussein. I'm not playing with your ass. I'm about to call Pop right now," I told him before turning back around and heading out the door.

I walked outside and climbed into my truck. I wasted no time speeding out of my parking spot and heading to the house on Thirty-sixth and Debree. It was the safe house in case some shit like this happened with our main house on Colonial Avenue.

This was some bullshit that I did not fucking need right now. I already had a clue about who was behind this shit. Fuck a clue. I knew exactly who was behind this shit. I didn't understand this girl. I had given her many passes, and she still managed to say fuck me and continue to piss me off. I was done being nice to her. She was going to fucking feel me if she was behind this shit, which I knew she was.

It didn't take me long to get there. When I did, I looked around at the niggas who were just standing around, drawing attention to the house. I placed my truck in park and hopped out, not caring to turn my car off.

"Why the fuck y'all just standing around this shit? Get in the fucking house," I barked as I watched them damn near push each other over to get into the house.

When they were all in, I walked in behind them and closed the door. "Somebody want to tell me what the fuck happened?" I asked, walking into the living room where everybody was at.

They said nothing as their heads fell down. Not one of these muthafuckas could look me in my face. Not one, and that pissed me off. Frustrated, I flipped the table over. "Start fucking talking!"

"Look, we were in the house counting shit up and bagging up the work. We had Douche, Kimp, and Set outside watching shit. They came in and took everybody out who was in the front room. Everybody else was in the back. We heard the shots, but shit, I thought these niggas were playing *Call of Duty* or some shit. So we didn't think nothing of it. But they busted inside of the back room, hemmed us up, and took everything." Everybody else nodded in agreement.

"Okay, so y'all didn't see any faces or nothing? A fucking tattoo or hear a voice you recognized?"

"Nah, they had masks on," another nigga said.

"Wait, I recognized one of the niggas. He used to roll with Malaki before he passed and his bitch took over. What's the nigga's name?" He snapped his fingers before pointing at me. "Dez. He be with Malaki's bitch now."

"Damn, why she gotta be all that?" one of the other dudes said.

"She a bitch, but a fine one."

"All y'all, shut the fuck up!" I yelled. They were all starting to piss me off. "None of y'all muthafuckas go anywhere until I figure this shit out. Y'all lucky that I don't shoot all y'all. Fuck do I pay y'all for, huh? Y'all got fucking guns and don't use them. All y'all were handpicked to protect that house, and all y'all fucking failed. Fucking idiots. Don't move." My eyes went to Joie. "Where the fuck is he?"

He shrugged his shoulders. "I don't know. I done called this nigga fifteen times. He blocked my number."

That right there was what let me know that his ass more than likely had something to do with this shit, which was blowing my mind. "Y'all don't go anywhere," I warned them before turning to leave.

I pulled out my phone and dialed Jerry. "Go find that nigga Willie. Call me back when you do," I told him before hanging up and climbing into my truck.

Chapter 12

Lihanny Wright

I sat up in my bed watching *Vampire Diaries* and eating my chicken and shrimp Alfredo. I was going to stay the night at Lonny's house with her and Cassie, but I felt like being home. I hadn't been able to be alone at all because everybody was always crowding me. Even when I was here, Cassie or Lonny would sneak into my house in the middle of the night and sleep on the couch. I appreciated them, but I needed my space.

The sound of my front door opening made me roll my eyes. "Didn't I tell y'all not to come over? Y'all bitches don't listen," I called out, putting my pasta down and climbing out of the bed.

All I was in was my bra and panties, but they'd seen me in less, so I wasn't tripping. When I didn't hear either one of them say anything, I grabbed my gun that was sitting on my dresser and walked toward my bedroom door. When I opened it, I almost peed on myself seeing Hendrix standing there with a hood over his head and his hands in his pockets. I grabbed my chest.

"You scared the shit out of me," I said, turning around to get back in my bed. I placed my gun in front of me and got comfortable.

"Why you keep taking my patience as a game?" he asked, walking in and coming to sit in the chair that was in my room.

"What could you possibly be talking about?" I said, putting a piece of shrimp in my mouth.

"Don't play me like I'm fucking stupid, ma. You're the only person with enough guts to do what you did tonight. I don't like to be played, sweetheart."

I shrugged my shoulders. "I don't know what you're talking about." I was in mid-bite when he yoked me up by my throat.

I could smell the mint on his breath as he spoke, "You think I'm fucking playing with you? I'm not. I have been giving you way too many chances."

"That was on you, not me," I slowly let out, licking my lips. He was so fine with his brow furrowed.

He squeezed a little tighter before letting me go. I turned around and bent over to catch my breath. Once I was good, I turned back around to face him. "You tripping like you're not going to benefit from this shit in the end. All I want to do is make money, and since you want to continue to block that, I have to find a way around it. I can't allow you to take food out of my crew's mouth. I won't do it. I have been proving myself to them for them to trust me, and it's happening. I'm the queen of the trap, and if you can't get with that, then we will continue to bump heads. The only way that's going to stop is if you agree to work with me or kill me." I rubbed my neck as I looked up at him.

He looked at me. "You are dead ass willing to risk your life for a title?"

"Not just a title, but for what I built and worked my ass off for," I said, taking my seat back on the bed.

He walked to me, towering over me as he looked down. "Why can't you just listen?"

"Because my daddy didn't. He went a long time doing what the fuck he wanted and gained a lot of respect also. I am my father's child. So if you're going to kill me, do it. If not, you can leave and allow me to get back to the peace that I haven't had in a long time," I said, looking up at him.

I studied his face as he did the same to me. We were just alike as we started to read each other. I couldn't tell what he was thinking, but I knew that it was going to be some shit. I could see it all over his face that he was trying his hardest to not take it to the point of killing me, but since I was hardheaded and didn't care, he didn't have any other choice. Hendrix knew that he couldn't tame me no matter what he did. His only move would be to put me down. I wasn't even going to try to fight him either. If it was meant to happen, then I was just going to let it happen.

I lost all my thoughts when his lips crashed into mine. It caught me off guard at first, but I relaxed in his mouth and started to kiss him back. This shit was so powerful, nothing that I had ever experienced before. He pushed me down without breaking the kiss as he lay on top of me. Neither one of us said anything as he pulled his sweatshirt and undershirt over his head. My panties instantly got wet at the sight of his tatted chest.

"You turn me on so fucking much it's dangerous," he whispered against my lips as he undid my bra and threw it.

His soft lips went to my erect nipples. His teeth attacked my bottom lips, and my head flew back. This shit felt so good it didn't make any sense. My right hand found its way to the back of his head while the other went for his sweats. I pulled at his pants until he pulled back to pull them down. I sat up on my elbows as I watched him remove the rest of what he had on. I swear he could hear me swallow when he pulled down his pants. That shit was beautiful, I swear to God. There was nothing like that that I had seen in my life, and I had seen a lot. Without hesitation, he grabbed my legs and pulled me down to him. I lifted my butt up so that he could take my panties off. Usually, when I was naked in front of a man, my hands would immediately cover myself because I was so ashamed and embarrassed. But as he looked down at me with his bottom lip tucked inside of his mouth, I didn't feel the need to feel ashamed. I felt beautiful, perfect even. He made me feel comfortable.

"You are so fucking sexy," he muttered as his eyes roamed my body.

I smirked. "You still want to kill me?"

"Shit, I'm about to murder this shit right now," he joked, and I burst into laughter at his corniness.

"I can't believe you just said that," I said, covering my mouth and trying to hide my smile.

He didn't say anything else as his lips met mine again, and his head found my entrance. It had been a minute since I had sex. I wasn't even fucking with Malaki like that when he was alive because I knew that nigga was on some funny shit. I didn't trust his dirty-dick ass. Hendrix lifted my leg and slowly pushed himself into me. My hands found his back as my nails started to claw into his skin.

"You okay?" he asked while still pushing himself inside.

I nodded. "It's been a while," I gasped loud as hell when this nigga pushed the rest of himself inside of me.

"Relax, baby," he whispered in my ear, and my entire body was covered in chills.

His fine ass was really doing something to me. Something that I couldn't control, nor did I want to. Hendrix started moving in and out of me at a slow pace. I could feel myself opening to adjust to his size, which was monstrous. After a while, the pain subsided, and it started to feel amazing. I lifted up my other leg so that he could go deeper.

"Aww, oh, my God," I moaned out.

"Damn, you wet as hell, ma," he muttered, biting his lip.

I smirked on the inside as I closed my eyes and threw my head back. I felt his lips on mine, and when I opened my eyes, he was looking right at me.

"Don't take your eyes off of me," he said before sitting up on his knees and grabbing a hold of my legs. "You hear me?"

I slowly nodded, biting down on my lip. I watched as he spread my legs apart and started going in. "Oh, shit, waaait," I whined, feeling him going deeper and deeper with every stroke. This nigga was trying to rearrange my insides.

"Nah, baby, you going to take all this shit. You want to be fucking hardheaded." He pushed himself in deeper.

In one swift move, I was on my stomach with my ass up in the air. I swear to God, I lost all my breath when he pushed himself back inside of me.

"Fuck, girl," he exclaimed, leaning down so that both of his hands were at the side of my face.

"Yesss, fuck!" This shit was feeling so good that it made me want to slap my mama. Yes, dead and all. God rest her soul.

He started to pick up his movement, and chills ran down my entire body. I didn't know what was happening. As much as I wanted him to move, I didn't want him to stop.

"Shit, this feels so good," I moaned out.

Hendrix bent down and kissed my lips before licking my earlobe. "I want you to cum all over me, a'ight?" he said, and I just nodded.

He pulled out slowly before slamming back into me, grabbing a hold of my waist and picking up his pace.

"Oh, my God, yesss. Don't stop!"

One stroke later and I was cumming all over the place. “Shiit.”

Hendrix delivered a few more strokes before he was right behind me, releasing everything inside of me.

“Fuuuuck!” He stayed in his position for a while before he kissed my shoulder and slowly pulled out.

I laid my ass right down. I was exhausted and ready to go to sleep now. He moved the food and gun that were on my bed before walking to the bathroom that was in my room. That was all I remember before I dozed off.

I didn’t know what time it was, but when I opened my eyes, I was in a dark room tied to a chair. My first thought was to panic, but when I remembered who was with me last, I had to laugh. This nigga came to my house, fucked me, then kidnapped me. That was some smooth shit. I had to give it to him.

“Hendrix! Your ass is real fucking slick!” I laughed, shaking my head. “You got me though,” I said, having no problem with giving him his props. He got my ass good.

I got no response for a few minutes, but a door opened in front of me, and in he walked, looking good as hell in a suit. I thought he was going to be by himself, but when I saw a few more bodies come in, a smirk came upon my face. Hendrix walked over to something, and lights started coming on. I was able to look down to see that I was only in my bra and panties. It was the same thing I was in before he pulled them off me.

“Well, hello to you too,” I said. “And all of you, whoever y’all may be.”

Hendrix walked over to me, unbuttoning his jacket. He bent down and smiled a little. “This is the person who has been causing us so much trouble these last couple of months.” He stood up before turning around to face them. “Y’all know my rules. I don’t kill women or children, but she"—he pointed at me—"she is making it hard for me to stand by that."

"So why don't you just kill her?" a voice sounded out.

"Yeah, why is she even alive right now?" somebody else asked, causing me to roll my eyes. All of them were bitches. I could see it from where I was sitting.

"That's a good-ass question, Greece. You too, Poe. Why not just kill the bitch? Why is she still alive?" He turned to look at me. "Why can't I just kill you?"

"Because my pussy is way too good to go to waste," I responded, looking up at him.

"That shit may be true, but pussy is pussy. I'm sure I can walk outside and find another you with no problem," he responded.

"Tuh!" I laughed. "You will never find another Lihanny, boo. I'm the realest bitch you've ever met and will ever meet. I got more balls than all of these niggas, including you, put together."

"Shit, that may be true also, but no. Ay, West, why is she still alive?" he asked one of the dudes who was standing there.

"Shit, I don't know."

"I'm alive because y'all are too pussy to kill me. Y'all have had many chances. I walk around this shit untouched. All of y'all know who I am and how to find me." I looked up at Hendrix. "Where the fuck did you find these niggas at? A bunch of bitches."

"Ay, who the fuck are you calling a bitch, shorty?" Poe asked, stepping up.

"You, nigga. I'm still sitting here, pretty as fuck. I'm more than positive all of y'all have guns, and nobody has done shit yet."

"Ay, Hendrix, can I just shoot this ho?" he snarled, mean mugging the shit out of me.

My smile never left my mouth because he wasn't about shit. He was just embarrassed and thought he had something to prove. I could see in his face that he had never killed anybody before. And he damn sure wasn't about to start now.

"See, that's your fucking problem now. You asking too many fucking questions. Had that shit been me, the bitch would have been gone," Hendrix said.

"Damn, you sure do switch up quick. Just a few hours ago I was 'baby,' and now all I'm hearing is 'bitch this' and 'bitch that.'" I shook my head, pretending to be hurt. While I was doing that, I got a glimpse of the gun that was on his waist.

Every single one of them could try their luck in killing me, but I wasn't going to go down without a fight. That was for damn sure.

"Shit, you ain't got to tell me twice." Before this nigga could even reach for his gun, I was on my feet and turning around so that I could grab the gun on his waist.

I turned around and released every bullet that was in that gun. I was letting off shots one by one, taking out every single one of them. They were all laid on the ground. I pointed the gun in Hendrix's direction and shot his ass right in his arm.

"Bitch, you fucking shot me," he said, coming in my direction.

"You fucked me then kidnapped me, so I think we're even now," I said, backing away from him.

"Nah, baby, that's not what you call even. Now, you're going to drive me to my parents' house so my pop can stitch me up," he said, grabbing a knife.

"What? You're going to stab me next?" I said as I watched him put it in his pocket.

"Nah, I need you to drive me home."

I took off running. There was no way in hell I was driving this nigga anywhere. Like, he fucking kidnapped me, then expected me to help him out? Hell no. I didn't care that I was only in my bra and panties. I peeled.

When I got outside the house, I looked around to see if I could recognize anything that was around me. I looked to my left and saw a 7-Eleven, Taco Bell, and McDonald's, and I immediately knew I was on Five Points. I walked to the 7-Eleven and went to the first car I saw. It was an old black lady. When she saw me, she clicked the locks to unlock the door, and I got in.

With wide eyes she looked at me. "Oh, my goodness, are you all right?"

"Yes, ma'am. Can I borrow your phone please?" I said, looking around.

"Yes, of course. Do you need to call the police?" she asked, pulling her phone out of her purse.

"No, ma'am. I just need to call my friend to come pick me up," I said, taking the phone from her.

I dialed Cassie's number because I knew that Lonny was most likely at work right now. When she answered, I wasted no time telling her where I was. There was no way that I was going to tell her about what happened with this lady watching me. Once she assured me that she was on her way, I gave her the phone back. It wasn't long before Cassie was pulling up.

"Thank you," I said to the lady.

"Whatever you're into, sweetheart, it's not worth it. Get out while you can," she said, giving me a small smile.

I just nodded before getting out of the car and jumping into Cassie's car. She looked over at me before pulling out of the parking lot.

"Bitch, where the fuck are your clothes?" she asked.

"Girl, long-ass story. I'm cold as hell. You don't have something for me to put on?" I said, looking in her back seat.

"My overnight bag is in my trunk, but you know you can't fit in that shit. Your butt is too big."

"Girl, I don't give a damn. I just need anything to put on. That nigga dropped some bomb-ass dick on me, then kidnapped my ass," I said, climbing in the back so I could open the trunk.

"Who, bitch?"

"Hendrix's fine ass," I said, using her spare key to unlock the hidden door that was connected to the trunk.

"Bitch, Hendrix who fucking owns the whole VA?"

I rolled my eyes, pulling out the bag. "Yeah, I guess. He came to my house last night to try to check me for some shit I did, but shit went left, and we ended up having sex. Bitch, why did I wake up and I was tied up in a chair in some empty-ass house? He was trying to prove a point to some niggas but ended up getting shot. Before he could get to me, I ran," I said, pulling up the tights.

"That's some shit I've never heard of. Y'all gon' fuck around and be fucking with each other for real."

I turned my nose up as I pulled the shirt over my head. "Girl, no, this nigga done fucked up. He should have killed me a long time ago. I know where that nigga's parents live."

"Girl, you better not play with that nigga's parents. I've heard stories about him, and he's nobody you want to piss off."

I sucked my teeth. "I've burned his people alive, stolen his product, and shot him. I'm sure the last one alone would piss anybody off, and I'm still standing."

"That's because you're fine as hell with a fat ass."

"No, it's because he isn't as tough as people make him out to be."

"I'm telling you, you're going to regret it."

Chapter 13

Hendrix Brown

Later That Night

"I done gave shorty one too many chances. I ain't fucking with it no more," I said, clenching my jaw. My father was stitching my arm up, and this shit was hurting like hell. I had to drive to their house leaking blood because that bitch bailed out on me.

"Sonny, I told you to just work with her. I'm sure it would make both of our lives much easier. Your mama is damn near ready to beat your ass for dripping blood all over her floor."

I shook my head and chuckled, "I would have gone to the hospital, but I wasn't in the mood to be answering all those questions that they were going to be asking me."

"Damn, bro, I thought you were big and bad. You let a bitch shoot you?" Hussein walked into the room.

"She didn't do the shit on purpose. She was taking out everybody else, and I just so happen to get hit."

"Nah, big bro, you need to do something about it. You're Hendrix Brown, my nigga. You can't let somebody disrespect you in more ways than one and allow them to get away with it. Now everybody else is going to think they can try you."

"You can't put your two cents in this because you don't know Lihanny. She is a certified nut. Just think of her as the female Hendrix," my dad said.

"Shit, you're in a situation now, aren't you?" Hussein said, shaking his head.

"Nah, she's not. She's hardheaded as fuck and has never had the right guidance in her life. Shorty ain't got nothing to live for, so she does whatever the fuck she wants."

"Yeah, sounds like you," Hussein said, pulling a bag of Skittles out of his pocket.

"Hendrix!" my mama called out before she appeared. She was holding the house phone in her hand. "Nylah is on the phone. She says you're not answering yours, and Hydiah has been crying for you since you left," she said, walking up and handing me the phone.

I took it from her and pressed it to my ear. "What's wrong with her, ma?" I asked Nylah. I could hear Hydiah calling out for me.

"I don't know, but I don't know what to do," Nylah whined.

"I'm on my way. Give her the phone."

It was quiet, and then a few seconds later my baby's sweet voice came through the phone. "Daddy, where are you?"

"Daddy's on his way, baby girl. Why you doing all that crying?" I asked, pulling a jacket over my arm.

"I don't like being here without you." She sniffled.

I didn't like how she said that, so I jumped up. "Okay, baby, Daddy's on his way, okay? I'll be there real soon. I gotta go, Hydiah, okay?"

"Okay, hurry," she said before hanging up.

I gave my mama her phone back. "Pop, call me later."

"Let me go with you." Hussein stood up from the chair he was sitting in.

"I hope you staying, because I'm not bringing your ass back."

"Yeah, I'm staying. I left my clothes over there," he said before coming to stand next to me.

We said good night to our parents before heading out. Instead of him following me with his car, he jumped into mine, and I sped out, heading to my apartment.

"Why haven't you killed her yet, bro?" Hussein asked, breaking the silence that was in the car.

I sighed and shook my head before running my hands through my waves. "I honestly can't even tell you, bro. I just get this feeling like I'm not supposed to." I shook my head, knowing that I was sounding like a straight bitch.

"You are feeling her, aren't you?" he said, eyeing me.

"Nah, nothing like that. I . . . shit, I can't explain the shit even if I wanted to," I said.

"It's cool, bro. All real niggas fall in love even if it is with their enemy," he muttered, looking out the window.

"Nigga, have you lost your mind? I'm not in love with shorty. We had sex so I could knock her ass out, and she shot me. That's it."

His head snapped in my direction. "You clapped them cheeks, bro?" He grinned at me.

"I'm not about to talk to you about that," I said.

"I mean, you already did, but it's cool." It got quiet before he turned around and smiled. "She got a friend? Or two?"

"Nigga . . ." I shook my head at him.

We pulled up to the complex soon after, and we got out of the car. Hussein followed me to the elevator, and we waited until it reached us to get in. We rode it to my penthouse. When the bell chimed, we stepped off the elevator.

"Hydiah?" I called out.

"Daddy!" she yelled out, and seconds later she came into view. I bent down to pick her up. "Don't leave me again."

"What's wrong, Hydiah?"

She shook her head. "Nothing. I would just like to go to Grandma and Grandpa's house if you're not staying here. That's all," she said before hugging me around my neck then reaching for Hussein.

He took her out of my arms before looking around to check to make sure she was good. "You trying to have a sleepover with Uncle Hussein or what?" he said.

She nodded, smiling. "Yes, I am. Are we going to blow the bed up?" she asked.

I shook my head because Hydiah loved that damn bed. She would much rather sleep on that one rather than hers just so she could jump on it. "I'm about to go back here. Hydiah, be good, baby. I love you." I kissed her cheek.

"I love you too, Daddy."

I left them in the living room, then headed up the stairs to my room where Nylah was with Haylee. She had her in between her legs while she slept.

"Why you got her on my bed like that? Put her in the bassinet," I told her, unzipping my jacket. I winced as I pulled it off. Nylah noticed the blood and jumped off the bed to run to me.

"What the hell happened, Hendrix?" she asked, running her hands lightly over the bandage.

"Nothing, I'm good. Put her in the bassinet, Nylah," I repeated, backing away from her so that I could head to the bathroom.

"Who is she, Hendrix?" Nylah inquired to my back.

I turned around and looked at her. "What are you talking about?"

"Whoever she is, I can smell her all over you," she said, crossing her arms against her chest.

I sucked my teeth. “Business is all it is. I don’t feel like doing this shit with you tonight. And what the fuck was wrong with Hydiah? Why did she act like that with you? She’s never done that before,” I asked, squinting at her.

She shifted her weight from one leg to the other before shrugging her shoulders. “I don’t know.”

I studied her for a second before nodding. “Yeah, okay.”

I shed the rest of my clothes before heading to the shower. She was off. I could tell by her body language. Baby mama or not, I didn’t play about Hydiah. And if she did something to her, we were going to have a serious problem. I didn’t mind being a single dad again.

Chapter 14

Lihanny Wright

I looked around the neighborhood as I watched the cars drive past. I had been sitting here for the last fifteen minutes waiting for this bus to come. At first, I was hesitant to do this, but I had the perfect plan. And I was going to go through with it by any means necessary. Hendrix might have had a soft spot for me, but I didn't give a fuck. I was done playing with this man, and it was about time he saw that. I was going to eliminate him just like I did with Malaki, and then I was going to take over. With no worries and no enemies, I was going to be the queen.

I sat up once I saw the bus pull up. Looking in the mirror, I checked to make sure I looked right before getting out of the car and walking to the little girl who was looking around for her father or possibly grandparents.

"Hi, Hydiah," I said, smiling down at her.

She stepped back some. "How do you know my name?"

"I'm a friend of your father's. I was told to come pick you up and take you out for ice cream." I was praying that that helped, but she crossed her arms across her chest and moved her weight to one side.

"I'm not supposed to go anywhere with strangers," she said.

"I'm not a stranger. Do you remember Malaki?"

She placed her finger on her chin before nodding and smiling. "Yes."

"Well, I'm his girlfriend. He and your daddy are on their way to the ice cream parlor to meet us."

"Are you sure my daddy sent you?"

I nodded. "I pinky promise," I said, holding out my pinky.

She stood there for a minute before smiling and nodding, locking her finger in mine. "All right, let's go."

She grabbed ahold of my hand. I looked both ways before crossing the street and heading to an old Nissan Altima I'd stolen. There was no way in hell that I was going to come out here with my Jeep so that somebody could identify it. That was also why I was wearing a short auburn wig and had glasses on.

I helped her into the car before getting into the driver's seat. Once I put my seat belt on, I turned on some music and pulled off.

"What kind of ice cream do you like to eat?" I asked, looking into the rearview mirror at her.

She smiled, showing her cute little dimples. "My favorite is strawberry with real strawberries and gummy worms on top."

"That's my favorite too. Sometimes I like to add a little chocolate," I said. That shit low-key sounded good right now.

"Me too. All my daddy eats are Oreos though. I don't like Oreos," she said, scrunching her face up.

"Yeah, I don't really like Oreos either," I said.

It didn't take long to get to Cold Stone on West Twenty-first Street. I placed the car in park, then climbed out with Hydiah right behind me. I opened the door for her and allowed her to walk in first. We got to the counter, and I nodded to the cashier. "Give her whatever she wants," I said just as my phone started ringing.

I pulled it out of my pocket, then answered, "Hello?"

"Bitch, have you lost your fucking mind? Where is she?" Hendrix hissed through the phone.

A smirk fell upon my face. "Oh, she's ordering some ice cream right now. Don't worry, she's fine."

"Lihanny, I will fucking kill you with my bare hands if you lay a hand on my daughter's head. All that Mr. Nice shit is over with."

I rolled my eyes as I looked at my nails. "Oh, pish-tosh. Nobody is going to hurt her. I want you."

"I don't give a fuck what you want. Tell me where you at so I can get my daughter."

"Give me about an hour or two. We're bonding right now."

"Bitch—"

I hung up the phone before he could say anything else. I ordered some ice cream too, then paid for it. We took our seats and started talking a little bit. I was waiting for Dez to call me back with the information about the house we robbed. We had to make sure all our tracks were covered because I had enough shit to worry about with the Feds.

Just as that left my thoughts, I heard the door chime, and when I looked back, I rolled my eyes. Roy was walking in with his son. When he spotted me, he nodded over to an empty table.

"Stay right here," I told Hydiah.

She swung her little legs and nodded as she took another scoop of her ice cream. I pushed my chair back and walked over to the table. I waited for him to say something but kept an eye on Hydiah.

"Listen, I've been meaning to call you. We have a big problem," he said.

"I don't like the sound of that," I said, finally looking at him.

"I told you that my boss is continuing the case with Malaki because he wants to find his killer and the connect. Well, they have a lead."

"Have a lead on what? Stop talking in code and just say the shit," I said, getting annoyed.

"They got a call a few days ago. Somebody witnessed you murdering Malaki."

"What!" I damn near yelled.

He looked around before turning his attention back to me. Before he could say anything else, I was going in on him.

"You dumb muthafucka. Why am I just now hearing about this? It's like you live under a fucking rock."

"Listen, listen. I'm just now hearing about this myself. I was going to call you as soon as I got home. I've been very busy," he said.

"I don't give a fuck! You work for me. When it comes to important shit like that, you are no longer busy until we figure out how to fix it. Who is the witness?"

He shrugged his shoulders. "That's something that can't be released until trial."

"You have twenty-four hours to give me a name, or I will kill everybody you love, including that sweet little boy over there."

"All right, all right. I will do my best, but they have a warrant out for your arrest. You're going to have to think of something fast."

I sighed and shook my head. I looked over at Hydiah. That was when something came to mind. I looked over at Roy. "What if I were to give you Malaki's connect?"

Chapter 15

Cassie Gold

A Few Hours Before

I paced back and forth in the police station, waiting for somebody to tell me something. I was scared shitless, and my ass was starting to regret agreeing to this bullshit anyway. Well, I didn't technically agree to snitch on my best friend. It was more like I was being forced to. Once Nigel found out what I did for Lihanny, he went ham on me. He had been beating my ass for years, but I never gained the courage to leave him. I loved him too much, and I didn't blame him for his actions. He had a fucked-up childhood with his father, who used to beat and rape him and his mother any chance he got. Nigel was just broken and needed somebody to fix him. And I liked to think that God brought me into his life to do just that. It was just taking some time.

The door to the room opened, causing me to look in that direction. Nigel was walking in with his boyfriend, Eugene. I knew it was weird, but I loved him, and this was what made him happy. At first, I wasn't feeling it because who the hell wanted to be with a bisexual man? But Nigel begged me to be okay with it. He said that he didn't want to lose me and that he was in love with Eugene, so he didn't want to lose him either. After a month of begging and pleading, I finally agreed to it, but only if we all got tested every six months. I knew what diseases gay men carried, and I wasn't trying to die because I wanted to make him happy. If my girls found out, they would be questioning a lot of shit, and I didn't have time for that, so nobody knew about it.

"What are they saying? Can I go?" I questioned, looking up at Nigel.

He shook his head. "You can't leave until they have Lihanny in custody."

My eyes bucked out of my head. "Wait, she's coming here?" I asked him.

"Yeah, they have a warrant out for her arrest. As soon as they bring her in for questioning, you can go," Eugene spoke up, looking down at his phone.

"No, no. I have to leave before she gets here. If she sees me . . ." I couldn't even finish what I was going to say.

If Lihanny found out that I was the one who snitched on her, she would have me killed the second I stepped foot out the door. They didn't understand how fucking crazy this girl was. How many connections she had in this police department. Everybody knew how close we were because we were always together. Sooner or later, she was going to get word about me being here, and after that, it'd be bye-bye, Cassie. Hell, she killed her fucking boyfriend and showed no remorse, and the only thing that nigga did was piss her off by fucking another bitch in her bed. Imagine what she'd do to me for snitching on her. Or have somebody do to me. I was a dead woman walking all because Nigel was hurt that I fucked a dead nigga for $20,000.

"She isn't going to see you. They are going to put her in a room, then bring you out," Nigel said, rubbing his hand up and down my back like that was supposed to soothe me.

It wasn't doing shit, so I moved forward and crossed my arms across my chest. "Y'all don't understand how connected this girl is. If she doesn't see me, somebody else will. I will be dead as soon as I get home. I shouldn't have agreed to this. I really shouldn't have."

"You're not going home, Cassie. You're going into witness protection. We are going to send someone to get you clothes from your house. Then you and Nigel will be escorted to a new home with officers watching until this is all over," Eugene said, finally looking up at me.

I rolled my eyes because they weren't understanding. If I testified against Lihanny, the second I walked out of the courtroom I'd be dead. I wasn't trying to risk my life for this bullshit.

"I don't want to do this anymore," I muttered, shaking my head.

"Why are you so terrified of her?" Nigel asked.

I looked at him. "Because she is crazy."

"I'm just not understanding why she would kill her boyfriend," Eugene said.

"Because she's a drug dealer, right, Cassie?" Nigel said, looking over at me.

I looked at him like he was crazy and shrugged my shoulders. "I don't know anything about that. She didn't say why she wanted to do it."

"Really, Cass?" Nigel shook his head.

"Yes, really, I don't know." He could get her killing him out of me, but I was done giving any other information.

"Well, just sit tight here, and we will get you when she gets here," Eugene said before kissing Nigel on the cheek then walking away.

I turned my nose up, then took a seat in one of the chairs that was in the room. My ass was fucking doomed. I didn't know why in the hell I let this man talk me into signing my own death certificate, because that was exactly what I was doing the second I walked into this police station. I felt it in my soul that I would be dead within the next few days. There were only two people who knew about this: Lihanny and me. Sooner or later, she was going to put two and two together, and I'd be done for. All because I wanted to make this gay nigga happy.

Chapter 16

Hendrix Brown

A Few Hours Later

"Hendrix, just relax. She already said she wasn't going to hurt her. Don't worry," my mama said.

"Y'all don't understand what this girl is capable of. Why weren't y'all at her fucking bus stop in the first place?" I said, kicking over the chair that was in front of me.

I was losing my fucking mind because I didn't know where Hydiah was. *That bitch better know how to fend for her fucking life, because I have a few bullets with her name on them.* I didn't give a fuck about the shit going on in the streets. My family was off fucking limits, fuck the codes. Niggas learned years ago that I didn't play when it came to my baby girl. She was my world, my firstborn, and I was ready to bust some ass. Especially Lihanny's. I had given that girl way too many chances, and she was showing me that she didn't give a fuck. I was ready to do the same thing though.

"Boy, you'd better calm your ass down. Now I understand that you're upset, so I'm going to let that slide, but the next time you fix your lips to curse at me, I'm going to beat your ass. Now play with it," my mama said, snapping me out of my thoughts.

I sighed, "I'm sorry, ma. I'm just stressed the hell out. Look, I need to get out of here." I stood up and headed for the door.

Wasn't shit going to get done with me sitting in there with them talking. I needed to get my baby back. I walked out of the house with my brother on my heels. I wasn't even going to stop him this time. I was going to pay her little friends a visit. They could either give her ass up or die. It was just that simple. When I climbed into the car, I quickly sped off before he could close his door all the way.

I pulled my phone out and tossed it over to Hussein. "Call Jerry. Tell him to meet us at the girl's house," I told him.

Nothing else was said as he did what he was told. The truck was so quiet, and it left me with all my thoughts and emotions running through me right now. I was pissed the fuck off that I wasn't able to protect my daughter. I was pissed that I allowed my lust for this bitch distract me from killing her ass a long time ago. I allowed a pretty face and a phat ass to distract me from what was important. Now she had my fucking daughter.

"We're going to get her back, bro. Don't worry about it," Hussein said, but I said nothing.

It took us twenty minutes to get to the house, and when I saw that the car wasn't there, I knew she wasn't either, which pissed me off even more. I repeatedly punched the steering wheel before getting out of the car. I needed to cool myself down before I did some reckless shit that ended me up somewhere that I didn't want to be.

Jerry pulled up to the house and hopped out of the car. "Boss, our people are on standby. They tracked the phone and found an address to where she was last," he said, handing me a piece of paper.

I took it from him and got back into the truck. "Jerry, stay here in case this bitch shows up. If she does, take her to the warehouse," I told him before speeding off.

"When we get here, all I need for you to do is take Hydiah and go get Nylah and Haylee, and then y'all go back to Mama's house," I told my brother.

"What if she got people up in there waiting?"

"If she does, then fuck it. I'll handle it. You do what I said, all right?" I looked from him to the road, waiting for him to respond to me.

He nodded. "All right."

Nothing else was said as we drove to the address. I didn't know why, but I was so fucking anxious to kill this bitch. I could have easily had a team there to take her out and get Hydiah, but I wanted to do this shit myself. Her pussy was good and all, but she had to fucking go. Tonight.

Considering that this bitch was all the way out in Suffolk, it took us a minute to get there. I parked down the street instead of in front of the house so she wouldn't see me coming. I turned the car off and hopped out with Hussein right behind me. Popping the trunk, I looked over at my brother.

"You know how to shoot?" I asked him, already knowing the answer to that question. If the military hadn't taught him anything, my father used to take us to the gun range all the time when we were kids.

"What type of question is that? Hell yeah, I know how to shoot."

Nodding, I lifted the compartment in my trunk, took the tire out, then lifted another part that I had built in for this particular situation. There were guns, vests, bullets of all kinds. Taking a vest out, I passed it to Hussein before putting the other one on for myself. After that, I pulled out two Desert Eagles and strapped them in the holster before grabbing the AK-47 and putting it around me. Once Hussein grabbed what he was comfortable with, I closed the trunk, and we headed to the house. It was dark outside even though it was only six o'clock, so nobody could see us as we jogged to the house with guns strapped to us.

"Go around back," I whispered to Hussein when we got close to the house. I didn't need for her to try to run away.

He nodded and jogged to the back of the house. I looked to make sure nobody was around before I grabbed the handle and twisted it open. Letting out a sound of relief because it wasn't locked, I made my way into the house and started looking around. When I didn't see anything in the living room, I walked down the hall to the kitchen, where I ran into Hussein.

He shook his head no, saying they weren't in the back either. I pointed to the stairs, but before we could ascend them, we heard sniffles coming from a closet downstairs. I looked at Hussein, and he looked at me as we stood on opposite sides of the closet. I counted down from three on my hand, and when I got to one, he opened the door.

Hydiah gasped when she came face-to-face with the guns we were holding. I put mine down and pulled her out of the closet and into a hug.

"You okay?" I whispered to her, and she slowly nodded. "She still here?"

She nodded again.

I kissed her forehead, then passed her over to Hussein so that he could take her out of here. Shit was about to get real bloody real fast, and I didn't want her to see that. Hussein scooped her up, and I watched them back out of the house. Once they were gone, I turned back around and continued my search for this bitch. When I found her, she was in the den, sitting in a chair, drinking a glass of wine. This bitch looked real fucking comfortable, too, with her feet up on the table.

"Nice of you to finally join me," she said, taking a sip of her drink.

"I'm glad you're getting comfortable before I put a bullet in your head," I said with my gun still aimed at her.

She smiled at me. "That's funny. I wasn't planning on being the one to die tonight," she said before picking up her gun and shooting in my direction.

Pow!

I moved behind the wall, dodging the bullet before I shot a couple rounds of my own.

Pow! Pow!

"I should've killed her dumb ass a long time ago!" I yelled in frustration before letting off two more rounds.

"Yeah, well, I'm not that easy to kill."

Pow! Pow! Pow!

When they stopped, I wasted no time coming from behind the wall and shooting in her direction, then going back for cover.

Boom!

The sound of a big-ass shotgun sounded before the wall I was behind was shot through, causing me to duck and move to another spot. Another two went off, and we were just going shot for shot. I was down to one round, and this bitch still wasn't dead. We were all over the first floor. There were holes in all the walls, and shit was broken everywhere.

"You're having a really hard time killing me!" she mocked.

Saying fuck it, I just started letting out everything I had as I moved in her direction. Once I was out, I tossed the gun to the side, and she came from behind where she was with a smirk on her face.

"Damn, you're all out, huh?" she said, gun pointed in my direction.

We were just three feet apart, and I knew if I just reached out and punched her in her face, it would be over. Her finger moved to the trigger, and before she could put all her weight on it, I tackled her ass, knocking the gun away from her. I climbed on top of her and started choking her out. She scratched and clawed at my face before her hand dropped, and I felt a piercing through my arm. I looked down to see that she had stabbed me in my arm with a piece of glass that was lying on the floor from a broken mirror.

"You bitch!" I yelled as she pulled it out and stabbed me again.

I tried to grab ahold of her hand to get the glass, but she punched me in the arm right where she cut me before pushing me off of her and trying to crawl to the gun. I grabbed her by her leg and pulled her back before reaching for the gun myself. As soon as I got my hand on it, she elbowed my ass right in the fucking nose. My shit instantly started leaking, and I knew right then that she had broken my shit.

The sound of sirens stopped us both in our tracks as our heads darted to the door then back at each other.

"Shit," she muttered, but it meant more than, "Oh, shit, the police are coming."

"You set me up," I said once I saw the look on her face. She knew they were coming. I read it in her eyes. She just didn't think she would be here when they did come.

"Kinda." She touched her neck where I had choked her.

"Fuck you mean, kind of?" Just that fast, I had forgotten about the fuck shit she did.

"Okay, so I kind of gave you up because I was being fished around by the Feds because of Malaki's murder." She looked away then back at me. "Look, we aren't going to get out of here if we are focusing on the past. We need to work together."

The sirens got closer, so I quickly got up, grabbing the gun and pulling her up by her arm at the same time.

"Let's go," I said, pulling her toward the back door.

She pulled back. "No. If we go that way, we're risking being caught. You don't think they're going to be waiting for us back there?"

I turned to her, putting the gun under her chin. "You're going to get us out of here, or I'm going to use you as a shield when these muthafuckas come. You're the reason we're in this shit, so you're going to get us out. Understand?"

Rolling her eyes, she nodded before pulling me upstairs. We went into a room, and she pointed to the bed. I ignored her and went into one of the drawers to grab something for my nose because my shit was still leaking. When I turned around, she had the mattress up, and all you could see were guns laid out.

"This is how we get out," she said before picking up a vest and putting it on.

"This is your plan?" I said, watching as she started to strap up.

She paused and looked at me. "You scared?"

I stared at her for a minute before following suit and grabbing whatever I could strap on me. Once we were good, we headed to the door.

"This is the FBI. We have the house surrounded. Come out with your hands up!"

She looked at me, and it caught me off guard when she kissed me. But I kissed her back, then pulled away.

"You ready?" I asked.

She nodded, smirking. "As ready as I'll ever be."

Chapter 17

Lihanny Wright

I looked across the van at Hendrix. The pissed-off look on his face kind of made me smile because I knew that I was the reason behind it.

The plan was to shoot our way out, but just before we could start letting shit blow, he got a call from someone, and they told him to surrender. Without question, he did, and now we were in the back of a police van heading to the jail in Norfolk. I was waiting for him to tell me the plan, but he hadn't said shit. He hadn't even looked up at me since we'd been up in here.

When I had that talk with Roy to get the police off my back, my plan wasn't to give him Hendrix. That was what I told him, but I lied. I was going to make sure that we were both gone before they showed up, but things kind of got out of hand. I sighed and rolled my eyes because this was something that I wasn't expecting to happen. I should have disposed of Malaki's body when I had the chance.

Hendrix looked up at me. "Come sit over here," he simply said.

My original thought was to say something smart, but we didn't have time for that. So I did as he said, and as soon as I did, something crashed into us, causing my head to fly back into the wall of the van.

"Ahh," I moaned out in pain as I moved my hands to my head.

A minute later, the door of the van slid open, and some big, bulky white dude stood there in a suit. I couldn't lie. White boy was fine as hell. He looked at me then over at Hendrix and nodded. "Sir."

Hendrix stood up and climbed out of the van. While the man took off Hendrix's cuffs, he looked over at me. "You coming or what?"

Without a second thought, I climbed out of the van, and the white man led us to a car that was parked behind us. I noticed that the car that crashed into us was still there. I was almost confused about how this nigga had two cars, but there was another nigga inside of the one that we were going to. Just as we were getting in the back, one of the officers slowly climbed out of the van and started shooting at us.

"Help! Help!" I yelled out before getting in the back of the car.

Hendrix got in and they sped off. "What the fuck was that?"

I shrugged my shoulders. "It's called acting, love. Don't worry. It'll make sense soon."

The dude who was in the front seat turned to the back to look at me with a smile on his face. "So you're Li? The one who keeps testing my brother? I can see why he hasn't killed you yet."

"Shut the fuck up, Sein." Hendrix shook his head.

"Where to, boss?" white boy asked, looking at him through the rearview mirror.

"Take us to the house in Chesapeake. We need to switch cars first. It'll raise suspicion if we're driving around in a car with bullet holes in them," Hendrix told him before looking down at his watch.

"I'd like to go home," I said, leaning my head back on the seat. My head was throbbing.

"Go home and get caught? I'm positive that they know where your ass lives," he said.

"No, they think I still live in the house out in Lakewood. I don't. I have a loft downtown. You know, the one you continued to break into."

"It's still not safe. If I could find it, so can they."

Sighing, I looked over at him. I was really confused as to why this nigga hadn't killed me yet. He'd had plenty of chances. Hell, if I were him, I would have killed my ass the first time I disrespected him. I didn't understand, but I wasn't about to question him on it. He was allowing me to see his weakness. And as I was his enemy, that was the last thing that he should have done.

As Hendrix instructed, we went to a junkyard called Two Chiefs to switch cars. It was like this nigga had planned out this whole shit, because there was a truck there waiting for us.

The rest of the way to wherever we were going was quiet. Nobody said anything. It wasn't long before we were pulling up to some nice-ass house in a neighborhood called Culpepper Landing. Everyone climbed out of the car and walked to the door. White boy pulled out a pair of keys and unlocked the door before stepping aside and allowing everyone to go in. I looked around, amazed at how nice this shit was. It was already furnished and all. If I made it out of this shit, I was definitely going to see about buying a house out here.

"All right, what's the plan?" the dude Hendrix had called Sein asked as he took a seat on the sectional.

"The plan is I kill her and give her to the Feds since that was her plan for me, right?" Hendrix held his hand out, and white boy passed him a gun.

"No. Well, yes, but it was never going to happen. I wasn't going to actually hand you over. We weren't supposed to be there when they showed up, but shit went south when you started shooting at me and shit."

"Bitch, you kidnapped my fucking daughter. The fuck you thought I was supposed to do?" He looked at me like I was crazy as he cocked the gun back.

"I didn't hurt her. Hell, I even took her to get ice cream. She's really sweet by the way. Anyway, all of this could have been avoided if you had just agreed to work with me. That's all I wanted, but your ass is so damn sexist that you couldn't even do that." I shook my head and took a seat on the chair next to Sein. He scooted over so that he wasn't so close to me. I rolled my eyes and shook my head.

"You should have just left well enough alone. Leave the drugs to the big boys," Sein said.

I turned my nose up at him. "Nigga, what are you, like seventeen? Stay out of grown folks' business."

He looked up at Hendrix. "Just kill this ho already."

I chuckled and shook my head. It was obvious that this nigga wasn't going to do it, or he would have done it by now. "All right, let's just face it. If I die, he won't be the reason behind it. Now, can we skip the act and the chitchat? Uncuff me. I need to go to the bathroom. I feel sick." I held my hands out, waiting. I probably had a damn concussion from how hard my head hit the wall of the van. I felt like I was going to throw up everywhere.

"She's playing you. As soon as you uncuff her, her ass is going to run," Sein said.

"Run where, stupid? I don't even know where I am, and I'm more than positive that my face is all over the news by now. Didn't I tell you to stay out of grown folks' business?"

Sein mugged the fuck out of me, and I just gave him a smile. Hendrix placed the gun on safety before nodding to white boy to uncuff me. As soon as he did, I took off to the bathroom and threw up everything that I ate today. Just doing that made my head hurt even worse.

"Dammit!" I fussed as I flushed the toilet, and then I went to the sink to rinse my mouth and wash my hands. The sound of my phone ringing in my jacket pocket made me jump a little because I'd forgotten that it was there. Pulling it out, I looked at it to see that it was Cassie calling me. Putting it on speaker, I set it on the lid of the toilet.

"What's up, Cass?" I placed some water in my hand and splashed it on my face.

"Li, you good? Nigel just called me and said that you were on the news."

"Yeah, I'm good," I replied, grabbing one of those mini towels to wipe my face off.

"Where you at? I can go scoop Lonny up, and we can come right to you," she suggested.

"I'm . . ." Before I could tell her, my phone beeped, indicating that I had another call coming through. "Hold on, Cassie."

I clicked over. "What is it, Roy?"

"What the hell was that? Why were you there when they arrived?" he asked.

"Nigga, last time I checked, I don't have to answer to you. It's the other way around. I wouldn't be in this shit if you had told me about the witness earlier, so don't question me about nothing that I'm doing," I spat. As soon as I got out of this jam, I was going to put a bullet in this nigga's head.

"That's why I called actually. We were briefed on your case. The witness is a friend of yours. Cassie Gold. She said you caught her sleeping with Malaki, and you killed him in front of her. She said you threatened to kill her next if she said anything to anybody."

My blood was fucking boiling. I just hung up the phone saying fuck the fact that Cassie was on the other line. Her bitch ass was probably sitting right in that fucking police station with them muthafuckas waiting for me to give up my location. I couldn't wait to see this bitch because I was going to ring her fucking neck, and that was on my daddy's life. This bitch had me fucked up if she thought that she was going to get away with snitching on me.

"Fuck!" I yelled as I slammed my fist into the mirror. Blood instantly started oozing out of my hand.

Turning to the door, I snatched the door open and saw all three of them standing there, looking crazy. Hendrix looked up at the mirror then down at my hand. "Did you just punch my fucking mirror?"

"This bitch is really crazy," Sein all but whispered.

Ignoring them both, I picked up my phone and walked to the kitchen. I could hear Hendrix telling Jerry to pick up the glass before he started following me. Dialing Lonny's number with my left hand, I paced back and forth, waiting for her to answer.

"Send me your location," she simply said before hanging up.

If I could trust anybody, it was Lonny, so I quickly dropped my location, then tossed my phone in the sink before running water on it. I knew that they were going to try to track my phone to see where I was. While water continued to run over my phone, I sighed. I couldn't believe that Cassie was talking to the fucking police. Like, this shit was really blowing my fucking mind right now. Now I saw why my dad never trusted people and always stayed to himself, because niggas were fucking snakes.

On top of me being pissed off, I was now feeling the effects of punching that mirror, and my head was still hurting like hell, which pissed me off even more.

"Yo, you need to run your hand under some cold water. You are getting blood all over my fucking floors," Hendrix said, walking up on me.

I backed away from him. "Not now."

"Fuck that. Put your hand under that fucking water, Lihanny." He roughly grabbed my wrist, forcing my hand under the water.

I wanted to cry so fucking bad because this shit was hurting so fucking bad.

"What happened?" he asked.

I sighed, "One of the bitches I thought I could trust with my life ratted me out to the police about Malaki's murder."

"How does she know you did it?" he asked, turning the water off.

I inspected my hand and saw that I had cut it up to the white meat. I winced in pain when I tried to make a fist. "I used her to set him up," I responded.

"Here you go, boss." White boy walked into the kitchen with a first-aid kit.

"Thanks. Come on." Hendrix grabbed a bowl from one of the cabinets before grabbing my left hand, and he led me over to the dining room table.

I took a seat on one side, and he sat across from me in another chair. I watched as he started working on my hand. Picking it up, he held it over the bowl, then grabbed the alcohol. "This is going to sting," he said before pouring it all over my hand.

"Oh, my God," I cried out.

"You're not so tough now, are you?" Sein said, coming into the kitchen. I looked over at him and rolled my eyes.

"You get in touch with Pop like I told you to?" Hendrix said, not taking his eyes off what he was doing to my hand.

"Yeah, he has Nylah and the girls there with him. I told him where we were, and he asked about her." He nodded in my direction.

"Probably wondering why you haven't killed me yet."

Hendrix looked up at me briefly. "He doesn't want me to kill you."

"I don't see why not," Sein muttered, and I shot him a look.

"Shouldn't you be in bed? I'm sure you have school in the morning."

He sucked his teeth. "I'm twenty-two years old, sweetheart. A grown-ass man."

"I'm sure you are."

"Sein, go back in the living room with Jerry." Hendrix began wrapping my hand up in gauze.

"So that's fine ass's name."

When I said that, Hendrix looked up at me like he wanted to wrap his hands around my throat. I smirked at him and blew him a kiss. He shook his head before finishing up. Once he was done, he picked up the extra stuff he'd laid out and went to dump out the bowl that had a mixture of my blood and alcohol in it.

Just as I stood, there was a knock on the front door. Hendrix placed the stuff on the counter before grabbing his gun and walking toward the door. I watched as he, Jerry, and Sein stood by the door waiting to blast whoever was on the other side.

"Don't shoot. It's my friend," I told them, heading to the front door.

Hendrix looked at me like I was crazy. "The one who's snitching?"

I shook my head before going to open the door. On the other side stood Alondra, with a bag in her hand, and Dezmond. I pulled them into the house before closing the door.

Dez mugged everyone as he pulled his gun from behind him. "Who these people?" he asked.

"Nigga, who the fuck is you?" Sein spat back.

"Both of you chill. Dez and Alondra, this is Jerry, Hendrix, and Sein. Now can y'all put the guns down?"

Alondra looked around at them, and then her eyes focused on Jerry. "You were sitting outside my house."

Instead of responding, he said nothing.

I looked over at Hendrix. "Can y'all put the guns away? They're cool."

"Didn't you just say one of your friends ratted you out? Is this her?" he repeated and nodded his head in her direction.

I sucked my teeth. "Why the hell would I bring her here?"

"Wait, who is he talking about?" Alondra asked, then looked down at my hand. "And what happened to your hand?"

"I found out that Cassie is talking to the police about me killing Malaki. And I punched a mirror."

"Wait a minute, you killed Malaki?" Dezmond looked at me, confused.

"Of course I did. Anyway, that doesn't matter. They are looking for us, and we need to figure out a way out of it." I walked away from them and went into the living room.

After they finally put their guns down, they came into the living room with me. Lonny sat on my right side while Dez sat on my left.

"How did Cassie find out about it, Li?" Alondra asked.

"I used her to do it, but I planned the shit out to a T. I have an alibi, so really, it's my word against hers. They know that."

"But you look guilty because you broke out of police custody, Li," Dez said.

I smirked up at him. "They think I was kidnapped."

"What?" Hendrix said.

"I made it look like I was kidnapped when I yelled for help." I shrugged.

I wasn't stupid. If they caught me, I was going to get hit with another charge for escaping. So I didn't escape.

"Damn, she's smart as fuck," Sein said.

"Either way, we need to get your name cleared. We have business to attend to, and we can't do that with you on the run."

"We need to switch shit up. Even if I do get off, they're going to be watching me like a hawk. So you'll be the face until I shake them," I told him.

"We still need to find some work. You haven't gotten through to that muthafucka yet?" Dez asked, talking about Hendrix. Some people knew who Malaki's connect was, and some people didn't. Dez was one of those who didn't.

"I don't know. Have I gotten through to you yet?" I looked up at Hendrix, causing Dez to look at him too, obviously putting it together.

"Wait a minute, is he . . ." Lonny started.

I nodded. "Yes, he is."

"Like I said, I don't work with bitches where my money is concerned. But that's neither here nor there. We got bigger shit to worry about."

Rolling my eyes, I didn't even fuss with him because he was right. We needed to get out of this situation with the police first. I stood up and began pacing the floor. I thought about my original plan, when I was going to give them Malaki's connect. I had a friend of mine who was willing to take the charge and accept a hefty amount of money for it. That was it.

"I'm going to turn myself in," I simply said.

"Then what?" Alondra said.

"Scott. Lonny, tell Scott the plan has changed," I told her, and she nodded, already knowing what that meant.

We met Scott in high school, and he was always known as the nigga who gave no fucks about anything. He was kicked out of school after he smashed a student's head into a school computer. After that day, he was known for lashing out at any given time. He was bat shit crazy, and everybody knew it. Scott's rap sheet was long as fuck, so everybody in the police station knew him. I went to Scott with a proposition. Recently, Scott's girlfriend gave birth to a baby boy. Because he had such a record, he couldn't get a job anyway, so he turned to the streets. He came to me, and I told him that if I had any run-ins with the law and could use him, in return I'd give his family a hefty amount of money. He was hesitant about that at first because he wanted to be there for his kid, but I assured him that I had a plan for that also. He trusted me so he agreed.

"You're talking in circles. What's the plan?" Hendrix said.

"Well, a friend of mine is willing to take the fall for me, and in return I'll give him five million."

"What is a nigga in jail going to do with five million?" Sein asked.

I looked over at him. "He has a family."

"All right, so what is he going to do?" Dez nodded toward Hendrix.

"I don't need a plan. I'll walk right out of there once I go in," he simply said just as his phone rang. Pulling it out, he shook his head before walking out of the room.

"All right, so what time y'all going in? And what time do I need to tell Scott to be at the station?" Lonny asked.

"Wait about an hour after I go in. I mean, considering that I have an alibi, they have to release me."

"Okay, and what are you going to do about Cassie?" Dezmond asked.

"I can't wait to see that bitch. I swear, I'm going to beat her ass," Alondra said.

She was just as pissed off about this whole thing as I was. Cassie was our best friend. We never expected some shit like this out of her. We'd always been three peas in a pod. And honestly, I wanted to know what the fuck she was thinking.

"No, we're going to wait it out. We need to continue to act like we don't know, because if we don't, I lose my inside person."

Lonny sucked her teeth and rolled her eyes, but I knew she was going to follow what I said. Hendrix came back into the living room and took a seat. "Jerry, I need you to go get Nylah and the girls and bring them here. Be careful, and make sure nobody follows you."

Nodding, Jerry stood and went out the door. Lonny looked at me. "Does he not speak?"

I shrugged my shoulders. "He only talks to him. But you guys need to get out of here. Y'all need to get back on regular routines as if y'all know nothing."

"Are you staying here? With him?" Alondra nodded in Hendrix's direction, and he just smirked at her.

"Yeah, I'm good. He hasn't killed me yet." I went to take a seat and stumbled a little bit, causing Dez to catch me.

"You good, Li?" he asked, helping me sit down.

"Yeah, I just have a huge headache."

"Maybe you need to get some sleep until it's time for you to go turn yourself in," Lonny suggested.

I nodded, and they stood up to leave. Once they left, I picked up the bag Lonny brought for me and headed up the stairs, leaving Hendrix and Sein down there. Once I found the nearest room, I closed the door and ended up passing out on the bed.

Chapter 18

Hendrix Brown

Later That Night

After Lihanny went upstairs, I left Hussein in the living room to make a couple calls. We were planning to do this at twelve, and I needed to be out of there by twelve thirty. I was surprised that Lihanny had a plan to get her out of the mess she was in. I couldn't lie and say that it wasn't a brilliant plan because it was. I just hoped once this shit blew over that she was going to find something better to do with her time. Shorty fucked herself up when she called herself snitching on a nigga. I was thinking about allowing her to handle Norfolk, and if she wasn't able to do it, then I was going to have Jerry handle her since I clearly had a hard time doing so.

"Daddy!" Hydiah called out to me, snapping me out of my thoughts.

I turned around just in time to catch her. "What's up, baby girl?"

"Jerry let me ride shotgun." She excitedly smiled.

I looked up just as Nylah walked into the kitchen holding Haylee's car seat. I walked over to her with Hydiah still in my arms and grabbed the car seat. Setting it on the table, I pulled the visor back and smiled down at her as she slept. She was knocked out, too, sucking on her thumb. After pulling it out of her mouth, I pulled the visor back down, then looked over at Nylah as she pouted like she was Hydiah's age.

I pinched her chin. "Fix your face. What's wrong?"

"Nothing, Hendrix," she sighed, pulling her phone out.

She just wanted me to baby her, but I wasn't about to do it. There was too much shit going on for her to be acting like she wasn't a grown-ass woman. So instead of feeding into her, I picked Haylee's car seat up and walked into the living room. Jerry and Hussein were sitting in there eating and watching *The Walking Dead*. I took a seat, placing Hydiah on her feet then putting the car seat on the floor in front of me.

"When y'all niggas order food?" I asked, taking Haylee out of her seat.

With all the shit that was going on, I hadn't even been able to care for or be around my baby girl. I felt bad as fuck that I wasn't around, but I was going to get shit straight real soon.

"Mama sent this with them. This shit good as fuck, too." Hussein nodded as he tossed a forkful of string beans in his mouth.

Just looking at it made my mouth water and my stomach growl. A nigga was hungry as fuck and hadn't even realized it until I saw this good-ass food. But I was going to eat after I was done fawning over Haylee.

"Daddy, she 'sleep," Hydiah leaned over me and whispered.

I looked over at her and smiled. "Yeah. She does that a lot, doesn't she?"

Hydiah nodded, then turned to look at the TV just as a zombie popped up. She screamed loud as hell, scaring the shit out of Haylee, and she immediately began to cry.

"Ay, turn this shit off," I fussed as I looked around for her pacifier.

I was a real live sucka as I looked at my baby frowning and screaming her lungs out. Once I found her pacifier, I placed it in her mouth, then stood and began bouncing around until she quieted down.

I looked over at Hussein then down at Hydiah, who was clinging to my leg. "You want to watch cartoons, Hy?"

She nodded. "*Trolls*."

"Put *Trolls* on, Hussein," I told him, and I ignored him when he sucked his teeth like he was a big-ass kid.

Hydiah took a seat back on the chair and swung her feet when *Trolls* came on the TV. I had to laugh at Hussein eating his food and fucking pouting. Nylah walked into the living room and looked up at me.

"Can I talk to you for a second?" She didn't even wait for me to give her an answer. She just went ahead and walked her ass upstairs.

"She must know about your little guest," Hussein said.

"Shut up." Walking over to him, I took his plate out of his hands and handed Haylee over to him.

Once I was sure that she was good, I went ahead and walked up the stairs. Nylah was standing in front of one of the doors, looking crazy.

"Yo, what you doing?" I asked her.

"Why is this door locked?" She pointed.

"It's occupied," I simply said before walking past her and going to the master bedroom. I took a seat on the bed and pulled off my shirt.

She walked in and closed the door. "Who's in there?" she inquired, raising an eyebrow.

"Is that what you wanted to talk to me about? Because if so, this conversation is over. It's been a long-ass day, and I'm not about to fuss with you."

"You are that disrespectful toward me that you would bring me to a house where you have another bitch lying up?"

Running my hands down my face, I looked over at her. All I could do was shake my head because she was about to piss me off. For Nylah to be so fucking beautiful, all she fucking did was nag. This was why I knew that we weren't going to be together for long, because I wouldn't be able to stand this shit every fucking day. It just wasn't possible.

"Why you just staring at me like I'm crazy?"

"I'm trying to refrain from disrespecting you, Nylah. What the fuck is your problem yo?"

"My problem is that you're acting like you don't have a fucking family, Hendrix. This is the third time you've seen your daughter since she was born, and it's been months. When I first met you, I didn't take you for a deadbeat-ass nigga, but lately that's all you been showing me you are."

"Man, g'on head with that bullshit yo." I waved her off.

"I don't even know why I came down here. I should have stayed my ass in Miami," she muttered, running her hands over her sleek ponytail.

Just looking over at her, I couldn't help but to lick my lips. She didn't even look like she just had a baby three months ago. Her stomach was flat in the high-waisted jeans and cropped top she was wearing. Standing, I walked over to her and pulled her into my arms.

"Look, I apologize for my absence. A lot of shit has been going on, and I can't be around like you need me to be until I get shit situated, Ny. By the end of the week, we will be back at the house in Miami, all right? I just need until Sunday, ma."

She looked up at me. "Sunday?"

I nodded before bending down and kissing her plump lips. "Sunday, and it's back to you, me, Hy, and Haylee."

"Okay." She stood on her tiptoes to kiss me again.

"All right now. Let's get the kids to sleep so we can have some fun in the shower. I missed yo' ass." I smacked her ass before grabbing a handful, causing her to giggle.

"Haylee is already asleep."

"Yeah, but Hydiah isn't. Go ahead and start the shower. I'ma go get her situated, and then I'll be back." I kissed the side of her face before releasing her.

Happily kicking off her heels, she walked toward the bathroom. Letting out a breath, I shook my head before walking out of the room. Instead of going straight downstairs, I pulled a set of keys out of my pocket and unlocked the room that Lihanny was in. Peeking my head in, I saw that she was knocked out in her clothes from earlier. Her ass was probably too tired to even get in the shower. I caught myself grabbing my dick at the thought of how tight and wet her pussy was when we fucked. Smirking, I closed the door, making sure to lock it before I went down the stairs.

It had to be about four in the morning when I heard noise downstairs. Looking to my left, my eyes fell on Hydiah, Haylee, and Nylah, who were all asleep. I was glad that I had a California king bed in here because all three of them slept wild as fuck, including Haylee's little ass. Hearing the noise again, I tossed the cover off of me and grabbed my gun from inside the dresser. Slipping on a pair of shorts and my slides, I walked out of the room, careful not to be so loud. I walked down the hall then down the stairs. When I got to the kitchen, I shook my head as I watched Lihanny walk around like it was her house. She was all in the fridge, pulling shit out. I licked my lips at the sight of her in a tank top with no bra and a pair of shorts that clung to her ass. Her hair was in a bun on top of her head. This girl was fucking fine.

"You loud as fuck," I spoke, scaring the shit out of her.

"You scared me," she muttered, picking up the fork she had dropped when she jumped. She rinsed it off.

"My fault. Your ass almost got shot though." I lifted my gun up before walking farther into the kitchen and setting it down on the island. I took a seat in one of the chairs.

"I didn't mean to be loud. I'm just hungry." She held up the bacon that she had in her hand before setting it on the counter.

Once again, the sound of food made my stomach growl. I didn't end up eating because I was too busy digging in Nylah's guts after Hydiah fell asleep, so a nigga was starving. "Ay, what you making?"

She closed the fridge after she had all her ingredients. "French toast, eggs, and bacon. Want some?" She looked over at me.

I raised an eyebrow. "Can you cook?"

Sucking her teeth, she turned on the stove. "Selling dope isn't the only thing I'm good at."

I shook my head and said nothing as I watched her work her way around the kitchen. She did her thing and we barely talked, but it wasn't long before she was placing a plate of food and some juice in front of me. Walking around the counter, she took a seat in the second chair so that there was one between us. After I said grace and thanked her for it, I started digging in.

"Is it good?" she asked.

I looked over at her, nodding as I stuffed more eggs in my mouth. "This shit is fire."

Smirking, she said, "Thank you. Now let me ask you something else."

I grabbed a napkin and wiped my mouth. I looked over at her. "What?"

"Are you going to let me work for you now?" Her eyes were trained on me.

I placed my fork down. "I'll answer your question if you answer this: why you so hell-bent on selling dope? There has to be something else you're good at and can make a profit at."

Sighing, Li picked through her food some before speaking. "Since you know who my father is, then you know who my mother is and what she used to make me do."

I nodded. Besides her saying it at the funeral, Pop used to tell me all the time that Patty sold her daughter out for money after Karter died. It was no secret. Hell, she used to brag about it herself all the time. Shit was sick and clearly so was she.

"After the first night, when she allowed my father's old worker to force himself on me, I used to cry when she'd ask me to do it again. One time, I threatened to tell my teachers about what she was doing to me, and she said, 'You think those people give a fuck about you? They don't care about your ass, Lihanny. I'm all you got, baby. *This* is all you got. You'll never be good for nothing other than a fuck, Li. That's all.' Since that night, I told myself that I was going to prove to her that she was wrong. I can admit that when Malaki forced me into this shit, I wasn't feeling it at all. I was scared out of my mind for one, but I played Patty's words back in my head over and over and over again. Once I got the hang of it, I realized that I was really good at this shit. Like I felt like this shit was meant for me to do. Not popping pussy for my mama for a couple dollars.

"It was like second nature to me. In the beginning, nobody thought I was serious. They saw me as a bitch trying to play in a game that I had no business playing in. They didn't respect me, and I didn't blame them, but I put everything I had into it. Eventually they saw that, and I felt like I was finally their equal. I busted my ass to show them that I was worthy enough. This shit is my life, Hendrix. Believe it or not, I'm the reason why the shit is as strong as it is now. You can ask anybody. That's why Malaki had to go. He was slacking and didn't give a fuck about anything. I wasn't going to allow him to destroy what I worked so hard to keep up, so he had to go. I'm great at what I do, Hendrix, a fucking beast. You reminded me of Patty when you said I couldn't do shit for you unless we were fucking or I was cooking. So I made it my mission to prove you wrong, and I'm succeeding, considering that I'm continuing to piss you off and I'm alive. A chance is all I'm asking for."

I chuckled but couldn't help but to respect what she was saying. "All right, I'm gon' do business with you. But I don't play about my money, ma."

"Neither do I. Why you think I've gone through all this shit?"

I nodded. "All right. After this shit blows over with the cops, we can get down to business."

Lihanny widely smiled before going back to eating her food. We finished off our food in peace. I was more than positive that she was racking her brain in excitement. I was hoping that I was making the right damn decision by doing this. I'd never allowed a bitch in my camp, but it was either do that or kill her. And since for some fucking reason I couldn't kill her, I had no choice.

"All right, I'm going to get ready to go." Standing, she took our empty plates to the sink.

I stood too. "Go where?"

"To the station. I don't think I should wait until the morning," she said as she washed the dishes she'd used for cooking.

"All right, then I need to go with you. Let me get dressed and I'll be down."

"No, I don't think we should show up together. It'll look suspicious, so I'll go first and maybe you can come in next in a couple hours. You don't want to alarm your girl and the kids, and you will if you just up and leave in the middle of the night." She muttered the last part.

I watched her intently with my arms crossed. She was doing everything to not look at me. Walking closer to her, I leaned against the counter, where I was at arm's length. I grabbed her wrist, stopping her from picking up another dish to wash.

"Put it down, Li, and come here."

Sighing, she did as I asked and took three steps so she was standing in between my legs. My hand moved to her face as I moved a piece of hair before cupping her chin. "Are you jealous?"

She scoffed and tried to move back, but I wrapped my arm around her waist and pulled her closer. "I don't have a reason to be. You aren't my nigga, and I'm not fucking with you like that."

My eyebrow raised as I smirked at her. "Damn, it's like that?"

"Yes. I don't mix business with pleasure."

"We aren't in business with each other yet, sweetheart."

I ran my thumb across her lips before grabbing the back of her neck and pulling her to me. Our lips connected immediately. At first, she was trying to resist, but she eventually wrapped her arms around my neck, pulling me closer. I pushed away from the counter and turned us around without breaking the kiss, so now she was leaned against the counter. My hands traveled to her sides as I picked her up and placed her on the island top.

Pulling away from her, I bit down on my bottom lip. My hands traveled inside her shorts. She looked up at me with low eyes as my fingers moved to her slit. I sat her up and slammed my lips against hers as my fingers plunged deep into her opening. She moaned loudly against my mouth. I wanted so badly to just bend her ass over on this counter, but I knew she was going to be loud, and I was already pushing it doing this while Nylah was upstairs. This was just going to have to do. I didn't stop my rhythm as I continued to push my fingers in and pull them out. She began to rock against my fingers with her head thrown back in pleasure. Seeing access to her neck, I immediately attacked it, licking and sucking all over her. I knew for a fact that I was going to have blue balls after this shit, but I didn't give a damn. Her pussy had a death grip on my fingers as she whispered in my ear that she was about to cum.

"Let that shit out, ma," I muttered, licking my lips.

Not long after, she was bucking and cumming all over me. Just to fuck with her, I pulled my fingers out, then bent down so that I was at eye level with that pussy. I moved her shorts to the side, then allowed my tongue access to her clit. She shuddered at the feel of my tongue on her since she was sensitive. She pushed me away weakly. I stood back upright and laughed at the sight of her looking like she wanted to fall asleep right now.

"Daddy," Hydiah called out to me softly.

"Oh, shit," Lihanny muttered as she quickly hopped off the counter and tried to fix herself.

I chuckled because she was making it obvious that we were doing something. It was a good thing that Hydiah was too young to understand what was going on.

"What's wrong, Hy? Why you up?" I hid myself behind Li for a second so I could fix myself. A nigga was hard as fuck, and I wasn't trying to walk to my baby girl like that.

Once I was good and I washed my hands, I walked toward her, waiting for her to answer my questions. She wiped her eyes before opening her arms for me to pick her up, so I did. She often did that when she was sleepy and wanted to be babied.

"I rolled over and you were gone." She looked over at Lihanny and smiled. "Hi, Li. When did you get here?"

I was surprised that she was speaking to Lihanny because the last time she saw her, she was kidnapping her ass.

"Hey, Hydiah. I've been here since last night, but you were asleep." Her eyes went to me as she unintentionally bit her lip.

"Can we get ice cream again soon? Maybe my daddy can come this time." Hydiah looked over at me.

I shrugged my shoulders. "It's up to Li. But it's late, Hy, and you should be in bed."

"You coming too?" she asked.

"Yeah, I'll be right there. I need to talk to Li for a minute. Go ahead upstairs." Bending down, I placed her on her feet.

She looked between the both of us, glaring like she knew we were up to something, before turning around and going up the stairs. Once she was gone, I burst out laughing.

Lihanny walked over to me and smacked my arm. "That's not funny. What if she had caught us? And how do you know that she isn't going to say anything to your little girlfriend?"

"One, it was funny seeing you sweat like that. And two, I'm a grown-ass man. I can handle Nylah. I don't think Hydiah likes her anyway," I said truthfully.

I knew from the moment they met that Hydiah wasn't feeling Nylah. And I felt that it was vice versa. I confirmed it when Nylah called my mama that one day and Hydiah was screaming in the background. They didn't fuck with each other at all, so Hydiah telling Nylah was the last thing on my mind. If I didn't tell her, she was never going to know.

"Mm, well. I'm about to go shower then get going. You got me all sticky." She rolled her eyes as she tried to walk past me.

I grabbed her by her elbow, pulling her back, then cupped her face and kissed her lips a few times. When I pulled away, her eyes were still closed, causing me to smirk. I kissed her once more before tapping her ass. "I'll see you when I see you."

Chapter 19

Lihanny Wright

Three Hours Later

"Thank you." I passed the twenty that I had on me to my Uber driver as I stepped out of the car.

He gave me as smile before pulling off. Turning around, I took a deep breath before I walked into the police station. As soon as an officer spotted me, he pulled out his gun and pointed it at me.

"Turn around and put your hands behind your head," he said, gaining everyone else's attention as well. "Turn around!" he yelled again.

I did as he said and placed my hands on my head. A second later I was thrown to the ground, and they placed my hands behind my back before handcuffing me. They were tight as fuck, but I knew that they were doing it on purpose. So I stayed quiet as they stood me up and walked me to the back. He opened one of the doors and pushed me inside the room, making me stumble. Turning around, I glared at him as he smirked at me.

"Paul Bundy." I read the name on his tag aloud to him. His smirk was no longer there, but mine was because I was going to be paying him a visit as soon as my name was cleared.

He slammed the door shut, and I rolled my eyes before taking a seat. I sighed as I looked around. I hoped that they sped this shit along because I had other shit to do. Like get at Cassie's snitching ass. I couldn't wait to beat that bitch to a bloody pulp, and I wanted my fucking $20,000 back, too. If she didn't have it, I was going to put that bitch in a wheelchair. She had me fucked up to the highest extent. I was still bugging off the fact that she went to them like her ass wasn't in on it. She'd just better pray that I was released, I knew that much.

I was in here for a good twenty minutes before the doors opened and in walked a detective, I assumed by the suit he was wearing. He walked in and took a seat across from me with their signature manila folder. Placing it on the steel table, he sat up and just stared at me. I didn't understand what he thought he was doing, but I played his game. Leaning back, I intertwined my fingers and set them in my lap as I waited for him to speak.

After a few minutes, he opened the folder, then looked up at me. "Leonny Wr—"

"It's Lihanny," I corrected him, already getting annoyed. I hated when people pronounced my name wrong like they didn't learn how to sound out words in the first grade.

"Lihanny Wright. Girlfriend of the late Malaki Edwards. You know what's strange?" He looked up at me. "You don't strike me as a murderer."

I looked at him sideways. "Who said I was one?"

Chuckling, he closed the folder before folding his arms on the table. "Cut the shit, Lihanny. We have an eyewitness saying that they saw you murder him in your bedroom."

I raised an eyebrow. "How is that possible when I was staying in a hotel the night he was killed? I mean,

I was told they gave you the cameras willingly. Am I wrong?"

"No, but—"

"So if y'all saw I was where I said I was, and the workers even said the same, why am I being accused of killing my boyfriend?"

"Because we have a witness th—"

"Clearly they're lying. I don't understand how y'all just believe anybody." I shook my head and scoffed.

He sighed, showing signs of frustration. I wasn't allowing him to get a word in, and it was pissing him off. That was what I wanted. I knew that they didn't have shit on me, and he knew it too. They were handed hardcore evidence that showed that I was in the hotel until I ran out the next morning when Dezmond called about Malaki. Yes, they had Cassie, but they couldn't hold me to that. I knew what I was doing when I decided that Malaki had to go, and I also knew that I covered my tracks. I couldn't be pinned to his murder if they had me on video killing him.

"Tell me what happened when you and Hendrix Brown were being transported."

"Someone ran into us and took us out of the van. Both of the officers were down, but when I saw one of them was alert, I yelled for help. I don't know who it was, nor did I see any faces because they had on masks."

"Who would want to take you?"

I shrugged my shoulders.

"Where did they take you?" he asked.

Again, I shrugged my shoulders. "They knocked me out as soon as I got in the car."

"So you don't know who took you or where they took you?"

I shook my head no.

"What about Hendrix? Do you know if the people could have been there for him? Where is he now?"

"I don't know. I don't even know him like that, to be honest," I replied.

"We were told that you have some ties to him. Is it sexual or business?"

I scrunched my face up in disgust. "For God's sake, my boyfriend just died. Sex is the last thing on my mind," I lied.

Hell, I had been thinking about Hendrix dicking me down since I left the house. I was horny as fuck right now, too, which was why I was ready to get the hell out of here. Looking up at the clock on the wall, I knew that Scott was going to be walking in these doors real soon. Now that I thought about it, I really didn't need Scott, because they had nothing on me. But I knew that they were going to continue to sniff around if he didn't show up, and that was the last thing that I needed.

"So explain to me about the bullet holes that were all throughout the house."

Before I could answer his question, the door opened, and I almost smiled at the sight of Roy standing there.

"Miss Wright, you're free to go," he said.

"Wait, no. How is she leaving?" The detective—I realized I didn't even know his name—stood and made his way to Roy.

"Someone just walked in and confessed to killing Malaki," Roy all but whispered in his ear.

"Can you take these off of me please? They're really tight." I lifted my hands up.

Roy nodded before pulling out a set of keys and uncuffed me as the other detective stood there in disbelief. I wanted to laugh so fucking bad, but I had to stay in character until somebody came and got me.

"What about her breaking out of police custody? There's a witness, for Chrissake."

"She didn't break out, Eugene. Somebody took her. Abraham confirmed that."

I assumed he was speaking about the officer who was there during the accident.

I looked over at the detective. "Eugene, is it? Thank you for your hospitality." I gave him a small smile before walking past them both and heading to the front.

My eyes landed on Scott, who was sitting in a chair looking calm as ever. His eyes landed on me, and I gave him an unnoticeable nod. As I was walking out, Hendrix was walking in, looking good as fuck. He had on one of those suits that he always wore. This nigga was dressed like he wasn't here to turn himself in. Behind him was Jerry, and of course, Jerry was in a suit as well. We didn't say two words to each other as we went our separate ways for now.

One Month Later

Wham!

"Where the fuck is my money?" I sent a chair across this nigga's face.

I knew off rip that I was going to have a problem with this muthafucka because he was one of Malaki's friends. From the jump, this nigga had been doing slick shit, thinking that I wasn't going to find out or that I didn't notice. But little did he know, I had Dezmond trailing that nigga every day to see how far his ass would go. Tonight, when Dez went to go pick up the money, this nigga didn't have none of it. $100,000 was gone, and he was acting like he didn't know where the fuck it went. So I was going to beat him to a bloody pulp until he spoke the fuck up about where the hell my bread went.

Wham! Wham!

He fell back from the force of the chains. I looked down at my purple red bottoms, which were now covered in his blood. Walking over, I bent down and grabbed him by his dreads. His face was no longer recognizable. It was all covered in blood and bruises. He groaned as I lifted his head up by his hair. Dropping the chains, I stared down at him as he tried to speak.

"P . . . please."

I shook my head. "Don't beg. You look pathetic. You don't have my money, so you will suffer the consequences."

He frantically shook his head as I picked the chains back up and wrapped them around his neck. I continued to wrap them around, then pulled them back as tight as I could. I watched as he struggled and coughed up blood before he finally stopped moving. I held on a little tighter for a little while longer before I finally let go.

"Damn, that was gruesome," Dez said as he walked over to me.

I unwrapped the chain before standing. Walking over to the sink that was in the warehouse, I tossed the chains in there to rinse them off and to rinse off my hands.

"Call someone to clean that up," I told him, grabbing a towel so that I could dry my hands.

"All right, but you have a phone call." He held up my phone.

Wiping my face, I took the phone from him, then put it to my ear. "Hello?"

"Meet me in an hour at the Feather 'n' Fin on Princess Anne Road."

I'd know that voice anywhere, but I hadn't heard it since the night I turned myself in. He hadn't been in touch with me since, not even for business. I was glad that I had a rainy-day stash because if not, shit would have been drier than a desert. I hung up the phone.

"We will be getting a shipment soon, so prepare them for it. Shut down the house on Park Place, and don't let them niggas leave until I find out what the fuck happened to my money. Call me if you get any info," I told him.

"Will do," he assured me.

I left the warehouse and headed straight home so that I could shower and then go meet this nigga. I was glad that it was late because I was covered in blood, and I was so pissed off that I didn't think to bring any extra clothes, which was a rookie move. I was just blown the fuck away about how $100,000 could disappear and nobody knew where the fuck it went. All I knew was that if niggas didn't start talking, there were going to be a lot of bodies dropping. That was for damn sure.

Once I made it home, I quickly went up to my apartment and hopped in the shower. I made sure to quickly rinse my hair, too, since I knew there was probably blood in it because it was flying all over the place. My shower lasted about ten minutes longer than I wanted it to because I didn't want to get out. I quickly dried off and placed my hair in a big-ass bun. Going into my drawers, I pulled out a pair of gray and yellow tights and the matching jacket. I opted for a pair of boy shorts and a sports bra because I knew that as soon as I got back in the house, I was going to drop these clothes and climb into my bed. Once I was dressed, I put on my yellow Nike Prestos and was out the door.

It didn't take long for me to get to the Feather 'n' Fin, but I decided to sit in my car for a little while. Looking down at my watch, I saw that it was just hitting twelve. And since it was the weekend, they closed down at two. My eyes danced around the inside until I saw Hendrix sitting at a table with Jerry. He was looking good as fuck dressed down in a sweat outfit and some Jordans on his feet. He had a hat on his head to the back. And all I could think about was him wearing that while he was hitting it from the back.

Opening my glove compartment, I fished around until I found my shades, then placed them over my eyes. Since Jerry crashed into the van last month when we broke out, my eyes had been really sensitive to light. So I had been wearing these glasses to keep it from glaring in my eyes. Sighing, I climbed out of my Jeep and walked inside. As soon as he saw me, he looked down at his watch. I knew that I was ten minutes late, but I didn't care. I was low-key in my feelings about this nigga ducking me for a whole month. And I didn't know how to get in touch with him, so it wasn't like I could reach out.

When I got to the table, Jerry stood with his plate of food and went over to the next table. Hendrix nodded to where Jerry was just sitting.

"Sit," he said.

I placed my wallet, keys, and phone on the table before taking a seat. Leaning back in the chair, I just stared at him as he did the same. It was like he was trying to stare into my soul even through the glasses, and I was doing the same. I was annoyed, and I felt as if he knew that.

He tried to remove my glasses, but I moved away from him and shook my head. "The light is too bright. It'll hurt my eyes," I simply said, and he just nodded.

"Hungry?" he asked just as one of the workers called out an order.

Hendrix stood up with his receipt. After accepting two containers of food and two drinks, he walked back to the table and placed the food down. He set one container in front of me along with a drink before sitting back in his seat. I wasn't really hungry since I didn't have much of an appetite. So I watched him lift the lid on his container, pick up the hot sauce, and drown his chicken and fries in it. He began eating his food, nodding in approval. This nigga was crushing, I mean, straight fucking that chicken up. It was funny as hell because he was eating as if he hadn't eaten all day. But I was annoyed and ready to go, and he still hadn't said shit about why he asked me to come.

Hendrix opened his container of macaroni, and the smell of it immediately filled my nose. But that wasn't a good thing, because it instantly made me nauseated. Getting up, I left my stuff as I ran out of the restaurant and threw up all in the grass. I continued to release everything in my stomach until I was just dry heaving. Standing up, I turned around and was met by Jerry. He had a cup of water in one hand and a napkin in the other.

"Thank you." I poured some water in my mouth and gargled it before spitting it out then wiping my mouth with the napkin.

Once I was done, Jerry pulled a piece of gum out of his pocket and handed it over to me. Nodding, I chewed it, then disposed of all the stuff before going back in and sitting back down. I pushed the container of food that was in front of me away as I leaned back in my seat.

"You good?" he questioned, sipping his drink.

"What did you call me here for? To eat? To just stare and not say shit?"

I was tired as fuck, and he was playing. He had better say something because I was seconds away from saying fuck it and walking out. But I knew that we needed this shipment because we were running dry. I just wished he'd stop playing games and get to it.

"I asked you a question, Lihanny. Are you good?" he repeated, glaring at me.

The way my name rolled off his tongue had me getting hot. I hadn't heard it in so lo . . .

Something was wrong with me. I straightened up and nodded. "Yes. I'm fine."

"Cool." He went back to eating his food, and I threw my hands up in disbelief.

Five minutes later, he was closing his container and getting up to throw it in the trash along with his empty cup. Hendrix came back to the table and sat back down. Folding his arms, he leaned back, just looking. "Monday at four a.m. Nothing has changed. Same date, same amount. One fuckup and you're out."

"Got it." I collected my things and stood up, preparing to leave.

Hendrix grabbed my hand, stopping me in my tracks. "Where you going?"

"Um, home?" I said more as a question because I was confused.

"Nah, this isn't over. I still have"—he looked down at his diamond Rolex before looking back up at me—"two hours until I go back home."

"Okay. That has to do with me how?"

"You can keep me company." Letting me go, he picked up the straw on the table and stuck it in the drink that was for me. "Sit." He nodded.

I sighed, turning in his direction. "Hendrix, I'm extremely tired, and I have had a long day. I got what I came for, and now I'm ready to go. So I'll see you when I see you." Turning on my heels, I walked out and headed to my car.

Opening my door, I hopped in the driver's seat just as my door opened on the passenger's side. I looked over and sighed at the sight of him.

"What are you doing?" I leaned my head back on the headrest.

I really wasn't in the mood for his shit. I was tired, my feet were hurting, and my stomach was killing me. He was doing too much for someone who said fuck me a month ago.

"With you. I told you that I have two hours before I left, and I plan on being in your presence until then. So drive."

Adjusting his seat, he got comfortable while he waited for me to start the car. Rolling my eyes, I started my Jeep up and pulled out of the parking lot. The ride back to my house was silent. He occasionally texted on his phone, and then Hydiah called him, wondering where he was. Just as he was hanging up his phone, mine rang in the cup holder.

Hendrix grabbed it before I could. "Focus on the road," he said before picking it up.

I sucked my teeth and shook my head. "Who is it?"

Ignoring me, he spoke to whomever was on the other end of the phone. "Yo? Yeah, she's right here. She driving, and I love my life. So I can't put her on the phone."

"Hendrix, put it on speaker." I looked between him and the road.

He looked over at me before doing as I said. "Don't take your eyes off the road, Li."

Ignoring him, I looked down at the screen, seeing who it was. "Dez, what's up?"

"Found your money, ma. Well, most of it. There's about twenty Gs missing."

"Where you at? I'm coming to you," I told him.

"I'm at the house on Debree."

"I'll be there soon," I assured him, heading there.

Hendrix hung up the phone, but instead of putting it down, he started scrolling and shit. "Who the fuck is Q?"

I shrugged my shoulders. "A friend of mine. Why?"

"Why my ass. Where you meet this nigga?" he chastised me as he continued to scroll.

I looked over at him and smirked at the mug on his face. "It's none of your business where I met him. Stop going through my phone." I reached for it, and he popped my hand.

"Put your hands on the wheel, and stop playing with me, shorty. Where you meet this nigga?"

I shrugged my shoulders. "Why does it matter? Don't you have a whole family?"

He sucked his teeth. "Man, you bugging the fuck out. You better hope that I don't see this nigga. I don't know what the fuck you got going on." Hendrix shook his head.

I didn't even respond to him as I pulled up to the house. Dezmond walked out with two duffle bags in his hands. I placed the car in park, then stepped out, closing the door behind me. I met him halfway. I allowed him to put them in the back seat.

"Where was it at?" I asked, leaning against my Jeep.

"In the wall of the house. I spoke with Otis, and he said Jax was on some funny shit, so he took the money from the floor and put it in the wall. He said when he counted it, there was only eighty thou. He doesn't know where the rest of it is, but everybody in there is willing to put something up to come up with what's missing."

I nodded. "He didn't say what Jax was doing?"

Dez shook his head. "Nah. He said the nigga was just acting weird, and it felt off."

"All right, well, make sure you shut this shit down. We will talk about opening up another one around here before the shipment comes. Tell Otis to hit me up, too. I need to speak with him, and whenever they come up with the money, let me know," I told him.

"Fa'sho." He looked into the Jeep before smirking over at me. "I see your nigga back."

I rolled my eyes. "Not that it's any of your business, but he's not my nigga. I'm about to go home once I get rid of his ass. Don't forget to hit me up, Dez." I pointed my finger at him before starting for the driver's side.

"I got you, Li."

"And tell Lonny I said to call me. Y'all niggas can't keep a secret for shit." I laughed, and he gave me a big-ass smile before waving me off and going into the house.

I found out recently that they had been messing around. I knew the shit was going to happen sooner or later, but I was in my feelings that neither of them thought to tell me. Like, they were my best friends. It was cool though because I was happy for them, but I was definitely going to get in Lonny's ass about it when I saw her.

"You got problems?" Hendrix inquired when I got back in the truck.

"Nothing that I can't handle." Putting my seat belt on, I placed the car in drive and pulled back into traffic, heading home.

For the rest of the ride, Hendrix continued to go through my phone, questioning every damn body in my contacts. I found it amusing how jealous he was acting. This nigga was really mad, and the fact that I was ignoring his ass was pissing him off even more. We made it to my house in about ten minutes since I was down the street. I unlocked the door to my loft and tried to close the door on his ass, but he was right on my damn heels.

"Damn, Li, why you acting like you didn't miss a nigga?" He walked up behind me as I kicked my shoes off at the door.

"Who said I was acting?" I shot back, taking off my glasses after I dimmed the lights.

Chuckling, he wrapped his arm around my waist from the back, pulling me to him. Now this nigga's dick was all up on my ass. I was getting annoyed because the shit was turning me on. I tried to push away, but he wasn't having it.

"You didn't miss me?" He bent down and pressed his lips against my ear. "Huh?"

"Nah," I lied.

For the whole month I had been waiting for that nigga to hit me up. Whether it was about business or not, I yearned to hear his voice, and I got nothing. I didn't even know why I was expecting him to anyway when he had a whole family to worry about. I just thought that there was a connection there, but that was what my ass got for messing with this nigga in the first place.

"You did. That's why you in your feelings about me not hitting you up," he said like he was reading my mind. "I missed you too." Kissing my cheek a couple of times, he grabbed my hand and led me to my bedroom.

Sighing, I pulled away from him just as we got by the bed. "Nigga, I told you I wasn't feeling good, so what makes you think that I'm about to have sex with your ass?" I raised my perfectly waxed eyebrow at him.

Hendrix looked me up and down, licking his sexy-ass lips. "Who said I was trying to hit? We were going to lie down until it was time for me to go."

My face softened a bit before I undressed without saying another word. As I was climbing into bed, he took his shoes off and did the same. I scooted damn near to the end of the bed so that we weren't touching. But he pulled me to him and wrapped his arms around me so that I couldn't move. I couldn't lie and say that it didn't feel good because it did, but I knew it was only temporary. This nigga was going back to his family in an hour or so. As much as I wanted to get up and make him leave, I couldn't. So I just lay there, basking in the moment. And it wasn't long before I was knocked out.

Chapter 20

Lihanny Wright

The Next Morning

"Getcho ass up, ho!"

I closed my eyes tighter at the bright-ass light that was beaming inside of my room. Grabbing a pillow that was next to me, I placed it over my face. "Alondra, if you don't get the hell out of my room . . ." I groaned.

"Bitch, it's almost two in the afternoon. Wake up," she said. Then a second later, my covers were being snatched away from me.

Taking the pillow off my head, I mugged the fuck out of her. "I want my damn key back."

"Yeah, yeah. Get yourself together. We're going to get some food, then get your hair and shit done. You look a mess." Turning on her heels, she headed out of the room taking my blanket with her. "Don't make me have to come back in here!" she called over her shoulder before my room door closed.

Sighing, I lay there for a good five minutes before fighting the air, then sitting up in my bed. I stood up and stomped my way to the window to close my curtains because the light was killing me. After stretching, I undressed where I stood, then walked into the bathroom that was in my room. While the shower ran, I washed my face and brushed my teeth. I stood there in the mirror looking at myself before turning sideways and placing my hand on my stomach. I slowly rubbed across it before turning and hopping in the shower. The water ran down my hair and face as I cleared my mind. The shower was my safe haven. When I crossed the threshold entering the bathroom, all my problems fell off my shoulders. And as soon as I stepped back in my room, they were weighing me down again. So I savored this time and stayed in the shower for well over forty-five minutes before Alondra came banging on my door for me to get out. I washed three times before turning the shower off. After drying off and walking into my bedroom, I went straight to the closet to see what I wanted to wear.

"Lonny, what it feel like outside?" I asked, thumbing through the many outfits I had.

"Girl, hot as fuck," she replied, walking into the room with two smoothies I was sure she'd just whipped up for us. I thanked her for mine, then set it on the dresser. I wasn't really in the mood to get dressed up, so I decided on a white tube top and the matching spandex shorts I'd bought from Fashion Nova. I dropped my towel and put on lotion, then put on some deodorant. I quickly put my clothes on, then sat on my bed and grabbed my smoothie.

"We are going to spend the day relaxing because all the shit you are taking on is having you look like nobody loves you," Alondra said as she typed away on her phone.

The way she was smiling, I knew she was talking to Dez. Well, she better have been, or I was snitching my ass off.

"Girl, I don't have time to relax. Money needs to be made," I told her, taking another huge gulp. This shit was so good.

I always told Lonny she needed to go into the smoothie-making business because her shits were good as fuck. If she got serious about it, niggas would be like, "Tropical

Smoothie who?" But her ass was always playing. I told her if she didn't, then she needed to give me the recipes and I'd gladly do it.

"Dez is handling all of that. He says to tell you that he has the money and don't go near anything business related," she carried on.

I chuckled and looked back at her. "How that nigga gon' tell me not to come near my business? I'm his boss."

I watched as she typed away on her phone. I assumed she was telling him what I had said because about two minutes later, she looked up at me and said, "He said not today. He's your boss, and you will be escorted out of all establishments."

I laughed at that also because I was dying to know who was going to escort me out of any place that I entered. I knew Dezmond was up to something, and I didn't even have the energy to go back and forth with him about it. So I was going to take this one day, then get right back to it tomorrow. After finishing up my smoothie, I ended up stealing Lonny's, then finished getting ready.

"Okay, let's go," I told her once I slipped my feet into my flip-flops and placed my shades over my eyes.

She looked me up and down, and her eyes stopped on my stomach. Rolling my eyes, I walked in front of her, leading the way out of the apartment. Lonny followed out right behind me, and we wasted no time going downstairs and getting into her car.

We went to get our hair done first. I was only going to get a blowout and flat iron, but our stylist convinced me to get a yellow long and wavy lace front. After that, he did my eyebrows, then went ahead and did Alondra's hair next. She went all out too, getting a platinum blond bone-straight lace front. Once he did her eyebrows, we got back in the car and headed to get our nails and feet done.

It didn't take us long to get to Q P Nails in Janaf Shopping Center. We had been coming here since we became best friends. We had never allowed anybody other than Kim to hook us up because she was a beast and everybody else in this shit was rough as fuck.

When we walked in, Kim immediately waved us over. "Mani, pedi?" she questioned, pulling us in for a hug.

"You already know," Lonny replied just as my phone chimed in my hand.

I looked down to see Daddy flashing across my screen and got confused as hell.

"Li, come on," Lonny called out to me, causing me to look up.

I walked to the back where the chairs were for the pedicures and took my seat. As Kim got our water ready, I got situated in the seat, then opened the message.

Daddy: Good morning, beautiful. How you sleep last night?

My mind immediately went to Hendrix, causing my eyes to roll but a smirk to appear across my face.

"Who you over there texting who got you smiling so hard?" Lonny peeked over at my phone.

Ignoring her, I changed his name in my phone to PLUG before responding.

Me: Who is this?

PLUG: Don't play me, Lihanny.

Me: Does it sound like I'm playin'? You about to get blocked!

PLUG: Block me and I'ma fly back up there and put my foot in your ass.

"Where ya other friend?" Kim asked as she pulled my feet out of the water and started working on them.

I looked over at Lonny, and she just shook her head. Before Cassie ratted me out, the three of us came here together. But fuck that ho, and I meant that with every fiber of my being.

"She died," I muttered, and Lonny burst out laughing.

Kim looked up at her like she was crazy before going back to doing what she was doing.

Me: Dezzy, how's everything?

I couldn't resist checking on my shit. It felt weird as fuck being somewhere other than handling business. While I waited for him to reply, another message came through.

PLUG: Don't test me, Li. WYD

Me: Minding my business. Where's your girlfriend? You sure have a lot of time on your hands to text me.

PLUG: The mother of my child is out shopping, and I'm in the crib with my girls. Now answer my question.

Me: Tell baby girl I said hi, and I'm at the nail shop. As I said, minding my business.

"Bitch, if you text Dez again, I'm taking your phone." Lonny glared at me.

Sucking my teeth, I closed out my messages, then went to scroll on my Instagram. I did a quick boomerang of me and Lonny before going to check my DMs. Of course, there were a lot of thirsty niggas sending some creepy-ass shit. But one female name caught my eye, and I immediately clicked on it.

LuvBlair: I've been looking for you forever (crying emojis).

Before replying to her, I clicked on her profile, and I swear I wanted to cry. Blair was my favorite cousin on my father's side. When my dad passed away, her mother and father moved her away. Being that Patty hated my aunt and uncle, they never called to avoid having to deal with her. I was so heartbroken when they told me they were moving away. I felt like my entire world was falling down. Blair was my best friend when I was younger. We were more like cousins than sisters, and it killed me to be separated from her. I tried to look for her for years, but I always came up with nothing.

Quickly wiping the tear that fell away, I went back to our messages and responded to her.

Me: OMFG! Blair Bear

A message from Hendrix came through, but instead of responding right away, I waited for Blair to text me back. I was sure it was only five seconds later when I got impatient and sent her my number and told her to call me. Just as she was beginning to text me back, the bell chimed from the door of the shop opening. Instinctively, I turned my head to see who it was, and my body got hot as fire seeing Cassie standing there with two other bitches. Kim looked up and had to do a double take because she was confused since I had just told her that Cassie was dead.

"Lihanny, don't. She's going to get hers, but this is not the time or place for that," Alondra tried to reason with me, but I wasn't hearing her.

All I saw was red as I looked at this rat-ass bitch. My temperature went to 500 as I thought about all the times I broke bread with that ho. The times when I allowed her to cry on my shoulder, sleep in my bed, wear my fucking clothes, et cetera. She knew how much loyalty meant to me, and she still decided to walk her happy ass into the police station and open her lips. A smirk appeared across my face as I thought about ways to torture this bitch. Maybe I should cut her fucking tongue out and sew her lips shut. Yeah, that shit sounded nice as fuck.

I watched as she made her way to the back. As soon as she realized it was us, she was damn near skipping her happy ass over like I fucked with her like that. I hadn't seen this bitch at all since I found out that she was the reason the Feds were sniffing places where their noses didn't belong. I knew if I saw her, I was going to drag the fuck out of this ho before I slammed her head into a brick wall. When I got my hands on this ho, I was going to do this bitch filthy, and I put that shit on Patrice Wright!

"Li! Hey, girl," she spoke before looking over at Lonny. "I thought you told me she was out of town with family."

Lonny rolled her eyes at her, clearly annoyed at her for messing up our peaceful day. Cassie looked surprised at the gesture before turning her attention to me. "I've been trying to get in touch with you. But every time I call, my phone goes to voicemail, and you're not staying in your old apartment anymore. What's been up?"

I gave her the most stank face that I could muster up. We had to go before I put my hands around her throat.

"She's not in the mood, Cassie. Leave her be," Lonny spoke up.

PLUG: Go home. Don't start no shit.

I read the message before looking around to see if he was stalking me or some shit.

"What the fuck did I do? Why y'all acting fake?" Cassie said with an honestly confused look on her face.

I cocked my head to the side as I looked at this bitch like she was crazy. Looking down at Kim, I respectfully removed my feet from her hands and slipped them into my shoes. Alondra pulled her feet out of the water, quickly drying them off then putting her shoes on as well. I took a $100 bill out of my purse and handed it to Kim. I wasted no time after that punching Cassie right in her mouth and instantly knocking her on her ass.

"Bitch, don't ever fix your lips to say shit else to me. Your best bet is to stay the fuck out of my way. You gon' get yours. Believe that, ho." I stepped over her and headed out of the shop.

"Fake-ass bitch." Lonny looked at her disgustingly before following me out. "I should have whooped that ho's ass." She sucked her teeth.

Before I could say anything, my phone rang. I rolled my eyes and declined the call before hopping in Lonny's car.

"Bitch, let's go to Logan's. I'm hungry as fuck." I rubbed my stomach as I went back to my DMs.

LuvBlair: I'm at work, but I will call on my break in fifteen minutes. I need to get you down to Miami for a week. We need to catch up.

Me: I'm definitely down. We will talk more when you call.

"Hmm. I bet you are hungry. After we eat, I'm taking you to buy a pregnancy test. Your stomach is poking, and you and Hendrix were fucking like rabbits."

My mouth dropped as I looked over at her. "Bitch, I'm not pregnant. It's stress weight is all. Don't wish that on me."

Lonny laughed as she pulled into a parking spot at Logan's. It was in the same shopping center, so it took us no time getting there. "Bitch, who you think you fooling? I know a pregnant bitch when I see one." She placed the car in park and turned it off.

"Ho, who have you seen pregnant? Please tell me." I crossed my arms across my chest, waiting for her response.

"You acting like the whole of Norfolk isn't pregnant, ho. Don't play." We burst out laughing before getting out of the car.

She wasn't lying. Norfolk bitches stayed pregnant. Everywhere you looked there was a pregnant ho walking around. A man coming out held the door open for us. We walked in and waited in the line to be seated.

"If I'm pregnant, I'm going to die, bitch. I swear." I shook my head and ran my hands over my hair.

"You might as well drop down right now then." Lonny smiled.

I just shook my head as my eyes ran over my knuckles. I didn't even feel the pain, but I could see that they were a little bruised.

"Your table is ready," a young girl called out to us.

I stood up, and we followed her to our table. As soon as she set that bread down, my mouth watered. That shit looked and smelled so fucking good. I couldn't help but grab one and bite into it. I moaned at the taste, closing my eyes and all.

"This shit is bomb as fuck," I muttered to myself.

"This bitch is fucking fat," I heard Lonny say.

I opened my eyes to her recording me, and I burst out laughing, then flicked her off. "Bitch, fuck you."

She rewatched the video before posting. Our waitress came over and took our drink order before leaving again. I placed my phone on the table. "So you and Dezmond. I saw that shit coming."

Alondra smirked. "He got some bomb-ass dick." She burst out laughing when I turned my lip up at that comment.

"I don't want to hear that. He's like my brother."

Lonny shrugged her shoulder before grabbing a piece of bread and taking a bite out of it. I got her ass back with a video because she was worse than me. This bitch was acting like she was having an orgasm.

"Bitch, you hungry as fuck, aren't you?" I laughed as she threw her last piece of bread at me, and I caught it in my mouth.

"Miss Lihanny."

My head spun in the direction of Jerry's voice. There he stood, in a suit of course, holding out a phone in my direction. "For you."

"Bitch, you in trouble," Alondra said just as our waitress came back to take our order. I told her to order for me also.

I grabbed the phone from Jerry and placed it to my ear. "What do you want?"

"Your ass ain't seen me calling you, Lihanny? I told you not to start no shit in that damn salon and you did anyway."

"Because I'm grown as fuck, and you're not my father," I replied, picking up another piece of bread.

"Why you like testing me yo? Don't even worry about it. I'ma show your ass something. I'm on my way."

Before I could reply, I was met by three beeps, indicating that the phone hung up. Shrugging my shoulders, I passed the phone back to Jerry.

"You want to join us, white chocolate?" I smirked at him.

Instead of replying to me, he turned on his heels and walked out of the restaurant. I looked over at Alondra, and we both burst out laughing. We talked until our food came back, and then Blair called me about us coming down to Florida to visit. I was all for it, too, so we started putting plans together. After we ate and paid, we got back in the car. As soon as I sat down, I was knocked out a minute later.

"Lihanny." Alondra shook me, causing me to lift up and look around.

"Damn, we got here fast as hell," I said, collecting my things.

I reached down to get my bag off the floor and noticed a Walgreens bag next to it. My head turned to Alondra, and she was wearing a big-ass smile.

"Bitch, I'm not taking that shit," I said.

"Yes, the hell you are. So let's go." Alondra snatched the bag up and got out of the car.

I sighed before slowly sliding out of the car behind her. She shook her head at me as I lagged on. I was not ready for this bullshit to tell me what I already knew. I told myself that I didn't want to know. If I had gotten any bigger, then that would have been the reason behind it. But her ass was going to bully me into taking this dumb-ass test. Lonny unlocked my apartment with the key that she had. As soon as I closed the door behind me, she pulled four tests out of the bag and shoved them in my hand.

"I hate you," I told her over my shoulder as I headed to the bathroom.

"I know," she responded. "Oh, and I called Stina to come do our nails. She will be here soon," Lonny called out after me.

I threw up a thumbs-up so she knew that I heard her as I walked into the bathroom that was in the hallway. Closing and locking the door, I placed my back to it and took deep breaths to slow down my racing heart rate. I was nervous as fuck. I didn't need kids right now. Especially by Hendrix's ass. He was for sure going to blackball my ass then. My life was over.

Relax, Lihanny. You don't even know the results yet. Just chill out. You good, girl. You not pregnant.

I coached myself before walking to the toilet and handling my business. After I was finished, I placed all four tests on the counter, flushed the toilet, then washed my hands. For the next three minutes I paced back and forth in front of the mirror, staring hard as fuck at those pregnancy tests.

Knock, knock!

I damn near jumped out of my skin hearing Lonny knock on the door. Sighing, I unlocked it and opened it up. She looked over at me before her eyes fell on the tests. The sight of her eyes bulging out of her head told me that the shit was positive. I didn't even look at them. I just walked out of the bathroom and into the living room where Christina, our nail tech, was setting her stuff up.

"Hey, girl," she spoke, and I gave her a subtle smile before speaking back.

A few minutes later, Lonny came back into the living room with a smile on her face. My eyes rolled so hard her way I thought they were going to get stuck. She laughed at me before going to sit down in front of Stina to get her nails and feet done, since Cassie showing up had stopped her from getting her feet done. My mind was everywhere but in this room as Lonny tried to start a conversation with me. A bitch wanted to cry so bad, but I wasn't going to do it. It wasn't the end of the world.

Bitch, yes, the fuck it is. Hendrix is really not going to let you live after he finds out about this shit.

I rolled my eyes at my thoughts. I was going to be good because Hendrix wasn't my nigga, nor was he my father. He couldn't tell me what to do. And if he tried to blackball me, I'd go find somebody else to cop from. I was the queen of the trap, and I would always make shit happen.

Chapter 21

Hendrix Brown

Eight O'clock That Night in Miami

I looked down at my watch then over to Haylee, who was knocked out on the couch. Hydiah was right next to her, snoring her ass off, which caused me to smirk. I was waiting for Nylah's ass to walk into this house so that I could get on my jet and head to Virginia and I could show Lihanny not to fuck with me. That girl was so damn hardheaded and a fucking headache. I left Jerry there to watch over her until I returned, which was how I knew about her knocking that Cassie bitch out in the nail shop. As soon as I hung up the phone with her, I had Jerry call and get the jet prepared. I planned to leave within the next fifteen minutes whether Nylah walked through those doors or not.

"Fuck it." I went to the back room and grabbed the girls an overnight bag. I mainly packed Haylee's clothes since Hydiah had hella shit at my parents' house.

Once I got all of their stuff together, I went back in the living room and got them situated. With Hydiah on my left shoulder knocked out, I was holding Haylee's car seat with my right hand. The door opened, and there stood Nylah looking like she was about to fall over. The shopping bags she had in her hands fell to the floor as she stumbled into the house. She looked up at me, and when she noticed I had the girls in my hand, she frowned.

"W . . . where you going?" she slurred.

"Back to Virginia," I told her, heading to the door.

She stepped in front of me, damn near about to trip over her feet. "Oh, you're going to go lie up with that bitch."

"Go lie down, Nylah. You're drunk as shit," I calmly told her.

"I'm not drunk, nor am I going to go anywhere. But what you're about to do is give me my baby, because I refuse to allow you to have her around the ho you been fucking there." She reached out for Haylee's car seat, and I stepped back.

"Nylah, go somewhere yo, before you piss me off."

"I don't give a fuck about pissing you off! You got me fucked up if you think you're going to take my baby with you to play house with that bitch!" She pushed me back, causing me to stumble back a little.

Her elevated voice and me almost dropping Hydiah caused her to wake up. She rubbed her eyes and looked over at Nylah with a frown on her face.

"Go in your room until I call you, baby," I whispered in her ear before leaning down and putting her on her feet. She immediately took off to her room.

I placed Haylee's car seat on the chair, and then when I turned back to face Nylah, I wrapped my hand around her neck. She immediately grabbed my wrist and looked up at me with fear in her eyes as I glared at her.

"Don't you *ever* in your fucking life put your hands on me when I have my kids in my arms or period. You are losing your damn mind, Nylah, and I'm going to need you to find it. And fast." I pushed her back, releasing her, and then I watched as she fell back on the floor, choking and trying to catch her breath.

"How could you do this to me?" she cried as she rubbed her throat.

"I ain't do shit to you, sweetheart." I picked Haylee's car seat back up. "Come on, Hydiah!"

A minute later, she came running down the stairs. Her eyes went down to Nylah, and I could have sworn I saw her smirk. She skipped her little self to the door, and I just shook my head and followed her out. I strapped them in the car, then got into the driver's seat, heading to the airstrip.

"Come on, li'l mama. What you doing all that crying for?" I looked down at Haylee's watery eyes. She stared back at me with a frown on her face.

"Maybe she's hungry, Dad." Hydiah looked back at me as she bit into her nuggets, then turned her attention back to the TV.

"Yeah, you might be right."

"What in the hell."

I smirked as my head turned to the direction where Lihanny was standing. She was standing by the chair in a sports bra and some shorts with some damn sunglasses on her face. Her hair was wrapped in a Louie scarf, and I couldn't help but to lick my lips at the sight of her. "Good morning, sleepyhead."

"Hi, Li." Hydiah turned around for a second to wave.

"Hey," she muttered, then looked over at me. "What the hell are you doing here, and how did you get in?"

"I told you I was coming, and how I got in doesn't matter. The fact that I'm here does. Now bring your smart-mouth ass over here," I told her as I tried to get Haylee to quiet down some.

"Hendrix, it's six in the morning and I'm tired as hell. I'l—"

"Come. Here. Lihanny." I sternly looked over at her.

She pressed her lips together like she wanted to say something but refrained from doing so. Walking over to the couch I was sitting on, she took a seat at the end, crossing her feet and tucking them under her. My eyes couldn't help but travel to her meaty thighs, which were on display since she was only wearing some small-ass shorts.

With Haylee in my arms, I leaned down to grab her diaper bag. "You're hardheaded as fuck, you know that?" I spoke as I made Haylee's bottle.

"I've heard it many times before," she muttered.

I leaned back and got Haylee comfortable in my arms before I placed the bottle in her mouth. As soon as she was eating, she was quiet. I looked over at her. "And why the hell do you have on those damn glasses?"

"Because this light is bright as fuck, and it's making my head hurt." She sighed.

"You been feeling like that since the accident, huh?" I waited for her to answer.

She slowly nodded her head, and I just shook mine. "Baby girl, you might have a concussion. You need to go check that out ASAP. That accident was a month ago. It could have gotten worse."

"I don't like hospitals, but can you tell me why you're in my house so early?" Standing, she walked over to where the switches were for the living room and dimmed the lights so she could take off her glasses. After doing so, she walked back to the couch and sat down.

"My flight landed a few hours ago. We been here for a minute. You're just now hearing us though because Haylee started crying." I looked down at her as she sucked away on the bottle with her eyes closed. That was why she was so fussy. Her little ass was tired and hungry as hell.

"She's beautiful," Li said, looking down at Haylee.

"'Preciate it. But check it. When I tell your little ass to do something, you do it. There's a time and place for everything, and you shouldn't have hit that girl like that," I told her.

Lihanny was a damn firecracker, and that shit was going to get her in trouble one day. That was why her hardheaded ass needed to listen to what I was telling her.

"When have you ever known me to listen to shit that you have to say? That bitch is lucky that all I did was punch her in her shit for the foul things she pulled."

"You don't know what or who she is connected to. That could have been a setup waiting to happen. You gotta know that them muthafuckas are pissed off because you were let off for Malaki's murder. You don't think they're going to try to find the smallest shit to put you behind bars? Even something as simple as an assault charge?"

Lihanny sat there and thought about what I said. The night I went in there to clear shit up, I found out some information. That was why I had been MIA for a month, because I was handling shit to make sure Lihanny couldn't be touched. I didn't need her having any run-ins with the law now that she was handling shit out here officially.

"Yeah, I guess you're right. But she did deserve that and much more. And she will be getting it real soon. Her and her bitch-ass, faggot-ass boyfriend." She scrunched her face up.

I chuckled and shook my head at her cute ass before looking down at Haylee, who was knocked out with the bottle hanging out along with a small part of her tongue. Pulling it all the way out, I placed it on the floor before laying her on the blanket that was placed between Lihanny and me.

"Daddy, I'm sleepy," Hydiah said, coming to stand in front of me.

I nodded to the love seat that sat to my left. "Go lie down, mama."

Lihanny pulled off the blanket that was laid on the back of her couch and handed it over. "Here, she can use this."

"Thank you." Hydiah grabbed the blanket from her, then walked over to the couch and climbed on it. Seconds later, once she was comfortable enough, she was knocked out.

I chuckled lightly and shook my head before turning my attention to Lihanny. She was staring at me with a nervous expression on her face. Her eyes quickly moved away once I was looking back at her.

"Why you look nervous?" I leaned my head back on the chair, watching her.

"I don't know what you mean." Her eyes slowly moved until we were staring into each other's.

"You look like something is bothering you."

She shook her head before looking somewhere else behind me like she was contemplating whether she wanted to expose what she was hiding. I used my hand to turn her attention back to me after she had looked away again.

"Your vibe is off, ma. What's up?"

"Nothing, I'm just tired," she lied. I knew her ass was lying because she looked away when she said it. Lihanny had always been the type to stare anybody in their eyes no matter how intense or intimidated she felt.

"Lihanny," I said sternly.

"It's nothing. I'm just thinking about my cousin. I just got back in touch with her. We haven't spoken or seen each other since we were kids."

I searched her face to see if she was lying. I could tell that the statement she just revealed was true, but I could also tell that it wasn't what she was just looking so uneasy about. But I decided not to push her.

"All right. So why haven't you seen your cousin or spoken to her in so long?" I questioned.

She sighed and laid her head back on the couch. "After my father passed away, my aunt and uncle moved away, taking Blair with them. They never got along with my mother, so me going to visit them was out of the question. Because we were so young when it happened, we didn't have any type of contact information to exchange." She sighed and got quiet for a second before starting to speak again. "It was like, as soon as they moved away, shit went left real fast. My aunt and uncle were my safe haven. I always felt like Patty knew not to do anything crazy because my aunt was really protective of me, and she would beat Patty's ass if she were to do anything foul. Patty knew it too, which is why she had a fucking field day when they finally moved away. But it's whatever." She shrugged.

"You know you do that a lot," I said, studying her suddenly confused face.

"Do what?"

"Downplay situations and shit to keep your feelings intact. You don't have to do that shit with me. I see right through it," I told her.

She glanced at me before looking away. I felt like she knew that I saw through her tough act. Anybody who studied her well enough could figure out that her past life took a serious toll on her. Her mother took a toll on her. Her father's death took a toll on her. Her cousin moving away took a toll on her. Her aura said she was crying for help. But because of the person she was, she would never admit that.

"I'm tired." She yawned before standing.

For some reason, my eyes were immediately drawn to her stomach. She stretched, and her shorts were no longer covering up her belly button, which gave me a full view of the pudge she was sporting. I didn't know whether it was from her ass eating a lot or if it was something else, but I was definitely going to address it tomorrow.

"What you gotta do later?" I asked.

She looked down at me after readjusting her shorts. "Business to take care of is all. Y'all can take the guest room. I'm sure it will be way more comfortable than these couches."

I nodded before picking Haylee up from the chair. I walked past Li and headed to her room instead of the guest room. Once I laid Haylee down in the middle of the bed, I walked back to the living room to pick Hydiah up so that she could sleep in the guest room. Lihanny followed me and watched my every move. I just knew she was going to curse me out for doing the opposite of what she said, but instead, she walked into her room with me hot on her heels and got in the bed.

"The only reason I'm not going to say anything is because I'm sleepy as hell," she spoke as she got comfortable.

I chuckled, kicking off my shoes and sweatshirt. "Nothing you said would have meant shit anyway. You should know that by now." I pulled the blanket back and got in the bed on the other side of Haylee. She stirred for a quick second before relaxing. I smiled a little bit just looking at her.

Once I got comfortable, Lihanny turned so that she was facing me. Her eyes were closed as I just stared at her. Like she knew that I was being creepy as fuck just watching her, she turned around, and I chuckled before putting my arm behind my head and falling into a deep slumber.

Chapter 22

Lihanny Wright

Ten O'clock That Morning

The sound of my alarm on my phone going off caused me to groan loud as hell. I was not ready to get up because I was still sleepy as hell. Hendrix waking me up at six in the morning messed up my sleep schedule. And I was for sure going to have a conversation with the front desk about letting this nigga up here in the first damn place. Them niggas were supposed to buzz me before they let anybody in here, but it seemed like the rules didn't apply to his ass. I yawned and looked over to the other side of my bed where I expected to see Hendrix and his baby lying. I wasn't even surprised to see that neither was there. His ass never stayed for me to ever wake up to him.

Hearing my alarm go off for the second time caused me to snatch off my blanket and swing my feet over the bed. I grabbed ahold of my forehead, feeling it already start to slowly pound. Standing up, I headed straight to the bathroom to get my hygiene together. Thirty minutes later, I was walking out and heading over to the chair in my room where I had my outfit laid out. I was going to be busy all day today. I had to meet up with Dez before I headed to the courthouse for Scott's hearing. They were going to sentence him, so I needed to be there on behalf of Malaki's bitch ass so it wouldn't look suspicious.

I put on my royal blue sleeveless pants romper and my gold sandal heels. Taking off my head scarf, I combed down my lace front, then put a couple of pieces of jewelry on along with my sunglasses. I grabbed my small purse and my phone, then headed to the front of my apartment. Once I spotted my keys, I was out the door and going down the elevator. When I got to the lobby, I walked up to the front desk.

"Hello, how can I help you?" the desk clerk asked as she looked up from a paper she was reading over.

"Is your manager here?"

"Um, yes. But maybe there's something I could help with."

"Maybe not. Could you tell your manager to come to the front please?" I lifted up my phone when it vibrated from a call. "Please hurry up. I have somewhere to be," I told her before taking a couple of steps back to answer the phone. "Hello?"

"Where you at, Li?" he asked.

I watched intently as the girl walked to the back before I replied, "Handling something at my apartment. I'll be there soon. What's wrong though?"

"Nothing is wrong. I was just trying to make sure your ass was up and moving around."

"Oh, yeah. You know I have to go to court at eleven thirty for Scott, but I'll be there in fifteen minutes," I told him before hanging up just as a fine-ass dark-skinned nigga with a bald head walked to the front desk.

This nigga was fine with his full-grown mustache and beard. He wasn't dressed like a manager should be, but that was neither here nor there. I walked a few steps up until I was at the counter.

"What seems to be the problem?" he inquired, looking me up and down.

I had to wipe the side of my mouth because I swear a bitch was drooling. "The problem is whoever was working around five or six o'clock let a strange man in and gave him a key to my apartment. I moved here for the privacy policy that y'all have, but obviously somebody missed that passage in the rule book. I am supposed to be notified before anybody who isn't on my list is sent up to my apartment let alone given a key to. I could have been dead as a damn doorknob up there, so I want whoever it was working at the time fired."

Without saying a word, he walked away from me for a second to grab a sheet of paper that was pinned to the bulletin board. Studying it for a second, he played with his beard before looking back at the girl who was standing next to him.

"You're fired," he said before walking away without another peep.

The bitch looked at me like she wanted to jump stupid, but instead, she rolled her eyes before going to the back as well. I smirked and shrugged my shoulders before turning on my heels and walking out the door. As soon as I hopped in my Jeep, I pulled off and headed to Dez.

I pulled up to the courthouse in downtown Norfolk at 11:15. After parking and making sure I was good, I climbed out of my Jeep and walked up the stairs. When I walked in, I immediately spotted the lawyer who was representing Malaki's interests. She spotted me and walked over, pulling me into a hug.

"Hey, Lihanny, how are you doing?" she asked after pulling away.

I took off my sunglasses before giving her a small smile. "I'm all right. I just want this to be over with. I can't get the closure I need with this case dragging along like this." I sighed then looked down at the floor.

She rubbed the side of my arm. "Aw, don't worry, sweetheart. Today you will get the closure you deserve. Come on." She nodded in the direction court was being held.

I rolled my eyes once she had turned her back on me before following her to the courtroom we were going to be in. The first people I spotted when I walked in were Malaki's mom and sisters. I placed my glasses back on my face so they wouldn't see me when I rolled my eyes at their annoying asses. I never liked these bitches. They stayed talking shit about me to Malaki when we were together but stayed in my face smiling and shit. I was never the one to be fake, so I called them on their shit on multiple occasions.

My eyes went to the left where Scott's girlfriend was sitting along with his mother, brother, and younger sister. I didn't know whether Scott had informed them of the plan, but right now wasn't the time to address them. I went to take my seat in the row behind Malaki's family but on the far end. His mother looked over at me with a somber expression on her face. I swear if we were in any other place but here, I would laugh in her fucking face. Malaki used to always come to me about the shit his mother used to say about him. She badmouthed him to every fucking body she could get to listen, but now she was sitting here like she actually gave a fuck that he was dead. *Bitch, please!*

The doors opened, and in walked Scott with two officers next to him. He looked directly at me before his eyes fell on his family. Once he was seated, the bailiff spoke.

"All rise!"

We stood as the judge walked into the courtroom and took his seat. As soon as we were instructed to take our seats, the sentencing began. The jury had already found him guilty of first-degree murder, so right now we were waiting for the judge to sentence him. I looked over at his girlfriend, who looked like she was about to shit her pants as she bit her nails. I felt bad for her because that told me that she knew nothing of this whole plan.

"Mr. Adams, you were found guilty of first-degree murder. I hereby sentence you to twenty-five years to life with no parole. You will finish out your sentence in Greensville Correctional Facility."

Scott's family cried out in sadness as Malaki's family stood to object.

"Just life? This man deserves the death penalty for what he did to my baby. My baby didn't deserve what he did to him! I bet if my baby were white and this motherfucker were black, he would have gotten the death penalty then. Fuck y'all and this white privilege bullshit!" his fake-ass mama cried before snatching her stuff up and stomping out of the courtroom.

I rolled my eyes and shook my head at her. She looked dumb as hell being extra. After the judge walked out and Scott stood to leave, I stood too so that I could get a few minutes with him before they took him back to his cell. When he looked my way, I gave him a slight nod before walking out of the courtroom.

I ran right into Roy as I headed for the doors. He already knew to meet me in my Jeep so that we could come up with a plan to get Scott out of there undetected. I walked down the stairs and climbed in my Jeep. Pulling off, I drove to the back of the courthouse and parked my car. I responded to a few messages from Lonny and Dez before Roy climbed inside of my Jeep.

"The officer who is taking him back to the city jail should be walking out in a minute," he said as he looked around to make sure nobody was watching us.

"I need the information for his transportation," I told him.

He nodded. "I can get that for you. Just give me a few days."

I shook my head. "No, not a few days. I need it by tomorrow, Roy. This plan has to be flawless."

Sighing, he reluctantly shook his head. "Okay, fine. I'll get the file on it when I get into the office. You have to be careful with this, Lihanny. If anyone were to find out about this, our asses are grass. They are still iffy as hell about this whole thing because of Eugene's eyewitness."

"Eugene? That's the one who questioned me, right?"

Roy nodded. "Apparently he has some kind of relation to Cassie and her boyfriend, which is why he is still sticking his nose into places where it doesn't belong."

I kept quiet as I processed everything that he was telling me. I was really about to say fuck what Hendrix was talking about and handle all three of them muthafuckas myself. They were causing unnecessary problems that I didn't need right now.

"I'll figure that out. Your main priority is to find a way to get Scott out of there without them asking questions."

The doors to the courthouse opened, and out walked Scott along with an officer. I climbed out of my Jeep to meet them halfway.

"How are you holding up?" I asked, leaning on the front of my Jeep.

He shrugged. "Jail ain't nothing new to me."

I nodded before looking him in his icy blue eyes. "You won't be in here long, all right? By next month, you will be reunited with your family on a private island somewhere. I got you. You just gotta trust me."

I was always known for keeping my word. That was very important to me because that was what my father instilled in my brain when I was a young girl. Your word was your everything, and without that, muthafuckas would always be looking at you sideways.

"If I didn't trust you, I wouldn't have gone through with this, Li." He smirked.

I gave him a smile. "All right. When you speak with Andrea, let her know that I'll be by soon to give her what is owed. Keep your head up, Scott."

"Always," he replied before he was led over to the police cruiser that was waiting.

I watched as he got inside the car, and then they pulled off. I turned to Roy. "Tomorrow, I'm expecting a call from you."

Roy nodded, indicating that he understood before walking away. I hopped into my Jeep and pulled off.

Chapter 23

Hendrix Brown

Nine O'clock That Morning

The sound of Haylee's light whimpers pulled me out of my sleep. I looked over at Lihanny, who was now facing us, but she was knocked out. Quietly, I grabbed Haylee's pacifier and stuck it into her mouth. Picking her up, I slipped my shoes on and grabbed my sweatshirt before going into the guest room. Hydiah was up like I knew she would be, watching TV.

"Come on, Hydiah, go put your shoes on so I can take you to Papa's house," I told her.

She jumped up immediately and went into the living room. I placed Haylee on the bed so that I could put my sweatshirt and shoes on correctly. Once I was put together, I picked her back up and walked into the living room, where Hydiah was picking up Haylee's diaper bag. After I placed her in her car seat, I made sure everything was straight at Li's house before we left.

When we got downstairs to the lobby, I gave a smile to the girl who was at the desk. She was the one who let me in and gave me a key to Lihanny's apartment after I promised to call her, which was a lie, but she didn't need to know that. I walked out of the building and got the girls situated in the back before hopping in the front and going to my parents' house. I stopped at McDonald's along the way to get Hydiah something to eat. I knew my mama was going to trip about letting her eat that this early in the morning because she didn't believe in fast-food breakfasts, so I told her to eat it in the car.

I finally pulled into the driveway and sat there for a few minutes so that Hydiah could finish her food. Once she was done, I wiped her face clean, then helped them out. Before I could knock on the door, it was being swung open.

My mama had a strange look on her face, which caused me to stop in my tracks. "What's wrong?"

Ignoring me, she grabbed Haylee's car seat. "Hydiah, go upstairs, brush your teeth, and wash your face, then get in the bath. I'll be right up there, and then you can help me make breakfast," she said, moving farther into the house so that we could walk in.

"I already had breakfast, Nana. Daddy bought me McDonald's," she blurted before taking off up the stairs.

I threw my hands in the air and shook my head. "Damn, Hydiah. How you just going to snitch on me like that?"

My mama glared at me. "I'm going to kick your ass, Hendrix. What I tell you about feeding my baby that poison? Especially when you know you're coming here?"

"She was hungry, Ma," I said, following her to the kitchen.

"Nigga, I got food in my damn house," she fussed, turning to me like she was ready to knock me out.

I stepped back and threw my hands up in defense. "G'on now, old lady. Don't make me drop-kick you in he—"

My smile dropped and my voice got caught in my throat when I saw my ex and daughter's mother sitting at the dining room table. My father was in his seat at the head of the table, and Hussein was next to him, smirking.

"What the hell are you doing here?" I folded my arms across my chest.

She nervously looked around before standing.

"Damn," Hussein said before my pops smacked him in the back of his head.

I couldn't even be mad though because Savannah was still fine as hell. Her rich vanilla skin tone was blemish free, and her natural red hair was not in her signature deep curls. She had it pulled back into a ponytail. Savannah stared at me with her big green eyes as she bit on her perfect pink lips. My eyes traveled to her body, which I'd mastered and shaped. When I first met Savannah in high school, she was like every other white girl with no ass. But I took her virginity, and that ass got fatter the more we fucked. Her getting pregnant and having Hydiah just filled her out more. And now she had a full-grown black-girl body. She looked good, but that was neither here nor there.

"Come on, y'all. Let's give them some privacy," my mama said, walking out of the dining room.

I could have sworn I heard both my brother and pops suck their teeth with their nosy asses, but they got up and followed her, sliding the doors closed. Once they were gone, I turned back to Savannah, waiting for her to open her mouth and say something.

"Um, I was wondering if we could, you know, talk?" she stumbled.

"Talk about what, Savannah? Have you lost your fucking mind coming here? Hydiah is right upstairs yo," I barked.

She jumped at the slight bass in my voice, taking a step back. "Yes, I know. But I didn't know how else to find you. You won't answer me anytime I call."

"That's because I'm too busy for your bullshit. What you need yo? You gotta get out of here before Hydiah sees you."

She looked at me like she was offended by me saying that, but I didn't give a fuck. She had been missing all of Hydiah's life, and now she wanted to come back here and expected us to welcome her ass with open arms. It wasn't fucking happening.

"Why are you saying it like that's such a bad thing?"

"Because it is. You haven't seen her since her ass was born, Savannah."

"I didn't have a cho—"

"You had a fucking choice! So don't let that bullshit fly out of your mouth. You chose to stay with your fucked-up-ass parents instead of with your fucking child! I was going to take care of you, but you wanted your parents' approval more than you wanted your own fucking child, so don't come stand in here and spit that bullshit to me."

She was pissing me the fuck off. I could never respect any female who put her child second to any fucking body. I didn't give a damn what the situation was. You brought them into this fucked-up world, so it was your responsibility to be there for them no matter what the next muthafucka thought about it.

She stared at me and sighed before backing up and taking a seat again. When she leaned back in the chair, I noticed something on her neck that I didn't notice before. I walked closer to her, and she flinched when I grabbed her chin so that I could get a better look at her neck.

I gritted my teeth at the big-ass print that was around her neck. With Savannah being white, that shit was noticeable as hell, and I could tell that it wasn't an old bruise because the shit was bright as fuck.

"Who did this to you?"

She grabbed my hand, trying to pull away from me, but I lightly smacked her hand away. "I'm not going to ask you again, Savannah."

Her eyes fell on mine, and I immediately noticed the tears that welled up in them, waiting to fall. “My husband.”

“Is that why you came here? To get away from him?”

Savannah’s head dropped, giving me her answer. “I didn’t know where else to go. My parents practically sold me to him so that they could do business with his family.”

“Do they know that this nigga is putting his hands on you?”

She looked up at me, and the tears were falling down her face rapidly as she nodded then began crying in her hands. “They practically handed me over to the devil, Hendrix. I don’t know what to do or where to go where he won’t find me,” she cried.

I released a deep sigh before running my hands down my face then looking back at her. As much as I wanted to say fuck her for abandoning my baby girl, I couldn’t just turn my back on her when she was calling out for help. I was familiar with too many abuse stories, and with her being the mother of my child and my first love, I had to do something.

“All right, look. Where you staying at now?”

She wiped her face with her hands and sniffled a couple of times before she finally answered. “Nowhere right now. I just got here an hour ago and came straight here.”

“Did you drive here?” I asked.

“No, I took the train. I withdrew as much as I could from the account he gave me because he could track me through my cards and the car he bought me, so I left it. But if he talks to my parents when he realizes I’ve left, he will know where to find me.”

“All right, look, I’ma put you up in a room until I figure some shit out. I got some errands to run, but I’ll send somebody over to take you to get whatever you need. Until then don’t come back here. I’m not trying to risk Hydiah seeing you.”

She slowly nodded. "All right."

"I need to get myself together. I got some shit to take care of. Just stay here until I come get you," I told her before turning and walking out of the dining room.

When I slid the doors open, I shook my head at my family as they tried to rush back to their seats. I chuckled, closing the doors behind me and heading for the stairs.

"I'm about to shower. Don't let Hydiah see her."

"Boy, don't tell me what to do. You don't run nothing around here," my mama fussed as she fed Haylee.

I smirked at her and just continued to go up the stairs because I knew that she wasn't going to allow them to see each other. I went into my old room and grabbed the shit I needed to take a quick shower. The sound of my phone ringing snapped me out of my thoughts. I peeked over at it and saw that it was Nylah calling me. My mind immediately drifted to Savannah and the bruises that she had on her neck, making me feel like shit for choking Nylah last night. Although she went overboard like crazy by pushing me when I was holding the girls, she didn't deserve that.

"Yo?" I answered.

"Um, hey."

I sighed, "Look, my bad for putting my hands on you, Nylah. You didn't deserve that, nor did I mean to disrespect you that way."

She cleared her throat. "I'm sorry too. I was drunk, and I wasn't thinking."

"Look, I'll be back there sometime tomorrow morning. We're going to have to have a talk because this shit can't keep going on like this," I voiced.

"Yes, I agree. How are Hydiah and Haylee doing? I miss my baby."

"They're good. I'm about to run a few errands, so they are with my mama until I'm done. But we will be back soon. I gotta go though, so I'll hit you later."

"Okay," she said softly before hanging up. I tossed my phone back on the bed before going to take my shower.

"I'll be back. Put her up in a room," I told Jerry before climbing out of the truck and walking inside of the Marriott Downtown Waterside on East Main Street.

I greeted the front desk clerk before heading to the elevators then going up to the conference room. When I got there, I walked in and immediately felt like the vibe was wrong. I trained my eyes on Garrett then Wilson, trying to see if I could read them. They were both nervous like a muthafucka, and I already knew that there was going to be some shit. So instead of taking a seat, I stood by the door and folded my arms across my chest.

"Y'all got my money?"

They looked at each other before turning to face me. Wilson was the one to speak up first.

"Okay, so we—"

I put my hand up, stopping him midsentence. "Yes or no?"

"Well, yes, but not all of it," Garrett blurted out.

I pulled my gun from behind my waist and placed it at my side. "Why not?"

"I mean, we have most of it. It's just that we came across a bump, and we needed to use some to get the Feds off our ass," Garrett started.

"That doesn't have shit to do with me. One of y'all muthafuckas aren't going to leave this room. And the other one is going to get the rest of my fucking money. Choose." I pointed the gun between them both.

They looked at each other. "Kill him. He was just going to take his family and skip town!" Garrett blurted.

I looked over at Wilson, and he looked like he was about to shit himself. I turned my gun on him, and he closed his eyes, accepting his fate.

Pow!

I watched as Wilson's eyes slowly opened. He looked over at Garrett and jumped back at the sight of his body slumped over. I didn't like snitches. Nor did I fuck with anybody who would turn on their own partner.

"You have twenty-four hours to get me my money, or you will be buried right next to him. Along with your family. And if you even think about running or going to the police, it's over for you. Got it?"

He nodded frantically. "Yes."

"Get out."

He quickly rushed past me and out the door. Two of my guys I had waiting outside walked in to take care of the mess. I handed them the gun, then grabbed the duffle bag that was on the floor and walked back down to the elevator.

"Where to, boss?" Jerry said, taking the duffle bag from me once I got outside.

"Take me to Smokey Bone on Virginia Beach Boulevard." I pulled my phone out of my suit jacket to check a message that I had from Lihanny.

Baby Girl: Hurry your ass. I'm hungry AF.

Me: Be there in 15 & your ass is always hungry.

Baby Girl: Fuck you.

I chuckled and shook my head. "Did you get Savannah up in a room?"

"Yes, sir. Room 416."

"All right, we need to make sure she's on the jet tonight when it's time for us to go."

I didn't know what I was thinking taking Savannah with me to Florida, but I needed to keep tabs on her. I didn't trust her ass for shit.

"Wait a minute, Jerry. Turn around and go get her," I told him.

I didn't know what I was thinking leaving her ass alone. I didn't know if she was on some funny shit, so I needed my eyes on her. I could admit that she looked genuinely scared as she talked about her husband, but Savannah took drama in high school. So it could be a front.

"Call Hussein, too, and tell him to meet us at Smokey Bones," I told him.

I never rode around dirty for too long. And I was about to have almost $3 million in my presence. That was just too much of a risk for me to take. So I was going to have Hussein take it to the house.

Jerry pulled back up to the hotel in no time since we were right around the corner from it before I told him to turn around.

Baby Girl: You got 5 minutes before I start eating without your ass.

Me: Go ahead and eat, fat ass.

Baby Girl: You love fucking my fat ass though.

I laughed out loud at her response and opted out of replying. Jerry came walking back out a few minutes later with Savannah hot on his heels. He opened the door for her, and she climbed in next to me.

"Where are we going?" she asked.

"To get something to eat. You hungry?"

Jerry got in the driver's seat and drove off. Savannah nodded. "Starving."

"All right, cool."

We pulled up to Smokey Bones about twenty minutes later since traffic was light. I climbed out of the car on one side, and Jerry opened the door for Savannah. We walked in, and I immediately spotted Lihanny because of that bright-ass hair she was wearing. I walked in her direction and shook my head at the sight of her fucking some ribs up. She looked up at me with a frown on her pretty-ass face.

"Took you long enough," she said, putting the rib down and wiping her hands on the napkin that was in her lap.

I pulled out a seat for Savannah, then took my own. "Keys," I said to her as Jerry walked next to me to pick them up.

"Aw, Jerry, is this your little girlfriend? She's cute," Lihanny said, picking her keys up from the table and passing them to Jerry.

Jerry looked at her and shook his head before taking the keys from her and walking out of the restaurant. She looked over at Savannah, who was reading over the menu.

"Why is he so damn quiet all the time?"

Savannah looked over at me before looking back at Li, not saying nothing.

"Oh, you a mute too?" Li said.

"Li, chill." I shook my head.

"I'm not a mute, and Jerry isn't my boyfriend." She peered over at me. "Did you really bring me on your date?"

"Date? Girl, this isn't a damn date. We're business partners, boo. We are here to discuss business," Li said.

Savannah ignored her. "You could have left me at the hotel for all this."

"You said you were hungry, so order some food."

"Ooooh, okay. So you like them white bitches with a black bitch's body. I see you." Lihanny smirked before rolling her eyes like she was jealous.

I smirked back at her. "Used to. I'm all for dark chocolate now," I muttered.

Her head shot in my direction, and so did Savannah's. She huffed before slamming the menu down and pushing her chair back.

"I'm going to sit in the car." She walked off.

Lihanny looked at me and burst out laughing. "Damn, you not getting any pussy tonight, boo. My bad."

“That’s not my bitch. She’s Hydiah’s mother,” I said, grabbing a piece of rib off her plate. I caught the look she gave me like she wanted to bite my damn finger off for taking it.

“Oh, yeah. I can see that now. Where she been at?” she questioned, picking up another rib and feasting on it.

“She moved somewhere with her peoples. She got herself into some shit with the wrong person, so she’s here for help,” I explained.

Lihanny shook her head. “They always come when they need something from you. But they’re nowhere to be found when you need them to be a parent to their child.”

I stared at her, wondering if she was directing that to me or herself. She looked up at me mid-bite. “Why you looking at me like that?”

“Because you’re eating like you been starving all day,” I replied.

“I haven’t. I been running around all day. Taking care of business.” She stuck her fork in her macaroni and took a bite.

“You better start feeding my baby more,” I replied just to fuck with her.

I knew the answer to the question that I didn’t even ask as soon as she looked up at me.

“What did you say?”

“I said, you better start feeding my baby more.”

She sucked her teeth and dropped her fork. “Who told you?”

I smirked. “You just did. When were you going to tell me, Lihanny?”

She sucked her teeth and rolled her eyes. “I wasn’t.”

I frowned at her response. “What you mean you wasn’t? That’s how you do?”

“I knew you were going to start sending out threats about not supplying me anymore since I’m pregnant. So I wasn’t going to tell you.”

I leaned back in the seat and crossed my arms across my chest. "So you're worried more about selling than the well-being of our child?"

She rolled her eyes at that accusation. "That's not what I said, nor is it what I meant. How am I going to provide for my child if I'm not making any money?"

"Damn. I'm offended."

"I'm not depending on you to take care of me and this baby, Hendrix. I was never taught to rely on a nigga for anything, so I'm definitely not about to start now. I don't care what you say."

"You took a test?"

Picking up her fork, she started picking through her food and nodded. "Yeah. I did, but I made an appointment with my gyn to confirm it."

"All right, how about I think about whether I'm going to let you continue to run Norfolk. Deal?"

She looked at me like she wanted to object, but instead she just shrugged her shoulders. I didn't know how to feel about her being pregnant with my child. Shit, Haylee was only 5 months. And with business and shit picking up, the last thing I needed was a fucking baby. Plus, my ass had been jumping from state to state since Haylee was born, and I knew it was going to be worse once I had this conversation with Nylah. This news was stressing a nigga out, but I wouldn't tell her ass that. I was just going to go with the flow and see how this shit played out in the end.

Chapter 24

Lihanny Wright

At Smokey Bones

Once I finished my food, I sat and waited for the waitress to bring me my check. I was low-key annoyed as hell right now, but I wasn't even about to trip because I expected nothing less from this nigga. He always thought he was in charge of somebody, but he had another think coming. I knew he was going to threaten to stop supplying me if I was pregnant with his baby. Which was why I had been making some calls, trying to come up with a backup plan just in case I needed it. When I got to Florida, I would have a meeting with a nigga named Carlos. From what I heard, he knew somebody who was pushing some major weight. And if Hendrix didn't want me selling his shit, then I was going to find another way like always. Wasn't nobody going to stop my bag especially now that I had another life to think of.

"Here you go." The waitress came back with my check.

I went to grab my little purse off the table, but Hendrix pulled out his card and passed it to her first. She walked away.

"You didn't have to pay for my food, but thank you."

"You're welcome. And yes, I did, baby mama." He smirked.

I rolled my eyes but couldn't help but smile. "Oh, my Lord. What did I get myself into?" I shook my head and he laughed.

"Get out of here. I will be the best baby daddy you'll ever have."

I scrunched my face up. "Nigga, what you trying to say? I'ma have a bunch of kids by a bunch of other niggas?"

He shrugged with a smirk on his ugly-ass face, and I picked up a fry and threw it at him. "Fuck you, nigga."

Hendrix bit his bottom lip and glared at me through those bedroom eyes. "Pregnant pussy is the best, baby. Just tell me when and where."

I burst out laughing because he looked and sounded like a big-ass creep with that weird-ass voice that he was making. My laughter stopped when I looked past him and spotted Nigel walking in with that detective, Eugene, Roy was telling me about earlier.

The waitress brought Hendrix his card back just in time, because I was standing up and gathering my stuff. Hendrix caught on to the fact that I was rushing, so he turned around to figure out what had my attention. As soon as he laid eyes on them, he looked back at me and shook his head.

"Nah, we not doing that here. I done told you there's a time and place for everything, and it's not the time or the place," he said, but I ignored him.

I was tired of him trying to make peace. These niggas tried to get me thrown under the fucking jail, and he wanted me to just brush the shit off. It was impossible and wasn't going to happen.

I walked up to their table and smiled. "Hey, Nigel, long time no see."

He looked at me with a deep scowl on his face. "Lihanny."

"How have you been?" I looked over at the detective as he looked down at his menu, pretending he didn't see us.

"Minding my business. As you should be doing," he spat before turning to his date, who wasn't paying him any mind. "Do you want to go?"

"Oh, don't let me ruin your dinner. I was just coming over to speak and to ask how Cassie was doing. I heard she's had some run-ins with the law." I looked over at Eugene. "Oh, I remember you. You're a detective, right?"

"Lihanny, why don't you just take your ass on somewhere? We're trying to have a peaceful dinner."

"Or what? You're going to try to pin another murder on me?"

My eyes darted from him to Eugene, then back to him. I thought back to what Roy told me about Eugene having some kind of relation to Nigel and Cassie. They were some nasty muthafuckas. I scrunched my face up at the thought.

"That's some nasty shit," I said.

Nigel stood up like he was about to do something. "I said, take your ass on somewhere."

Hendrix pulled me behind him as he stood toe-to-toe with Nigel. "You should take your seat."

Eugene finally placed his menu down and pulled his badge from his pocket. "All right, I'm going to have to ask you to leave before you're arrested for disturbing the peace."

I laughed, "Disturbing whose peace? Y'all?"

Hendrix gritted his teeth and grabbed me by my wrist to pull me away. "I'll be seeing you," he called over his shoulder.

We walked out the doors, and when we got outside, I immediately pulled my phone out of my pocket to call Dez. But before I could press his name, Hendrix snatched my phone out of my hand.

I looked up at him, frowning. "Give me my phone back."

His nose flared at me. "What the fuck did I just tell you, Lihanny? Huh?"

"I don't give a damn about what you told me. Those muthafuckas got me fucked up and so do you. Now give me my phone."

"You doing reckless-ass shit, and it's not just you anymore. Do what you want to yo, but I'm telling you this shit right now—if something happens to my fucking child, I'm going to snap your fucking neck." He shoved my phone into my hand before walking off to his truck.

I rolled my eyes, then headed to my Jeep as I dialed Dez's number.

"What's up, Li?"

"Get to Smokey Bones on Virginia Beach Boulevard right now," I said, then hung up.

Climbing into my Jeep, I sat there and thought about what Hendrix was saying. I sucked my teeth and laid my head back on my headrest. His ugly ass was right, but I would never admit that to his face. I didn't want to be like Patty, who placed her needs before mine. My first thought was to kill them muthafuckas as soon as they walked out those doors, but instead I was going to get Dez to follow them to find out where they lived. I needed to be smart because he was a detective, and there was going to be a lot of fucking chaos once he was put out of his misery. I learned my lesson from Malaki. Their bodies would not be found this time.

One Week Later

"Lihanny Wright."

I stood and followed the nurse who had called my name. She led me to a room where my gyn was waiting for me.

"Hey, Li," she spoke, looking up from the file she had been staring at.

I gave her a quick hug before nodding over to the file. "Is that mine?"

She looked back at it, then nodded. "Yes, ma'am."

I bit my bottom lip nervously. "Well?"

"I'm going to be a grandma," she excitedly revealed, clapping.

My heart dropped to my ass after hearing her confirm it. I was not ready to be somebody's mother. Like, my mother was a piece of shit.

"Oh, Lihanny, you're going to be fine. You aren't your mother," Daisy said as if she were reading my mind.

"I'm so damn scared, Daisy. I can't be like her." I covered my face as a few tears fell.

"Aw, Li. You won't be. You're nothing like your mother." She pulled away, gripping my shoulders. "You are nothing like her, Lihanny. And you're going to be a great mother. Now wipe your face and let me give you everything you need to get through this pregnancy."

I wiped my face and watched as she grabbed a white paper from the file and some paperwork. "These are your prenatal vitamins. Take these once a day. The other pills in there are for if you start feeling any morning sickness."

I nodded. "Okay. I have to get going. I'm going out of town, and I need to get some stuff in order."

"Take care of yourself and that baby. All right?" She pulled me in for one last hug.

"I will, Daisy. Thank you."

I left and called Alondra as soon as I was back in my Jeep. We were supposed to be doing some shopping before we headed to the airport, but I would rather shop in Miami. Virginia didn't have much in their outlets and malls. And I had a couple of outfits in my closet with the tags still on them that I could take with me until we made it to a mall.

"Where you at, bae?" she asked as soon as she picked up.

"I'm on my way to you. Is Dezzy there with you? I need to discuss some stuff before we leave."

"Yeah, he's in the shower."

"All right, boo. I'll be there in a minute," I told her.

"Okay. What did Daisy say?"

Daisy used to be our school nurse when we were in middle school. That was why we were so damn close. She was more like a mother to me, and she knew all the shit I went through with Patty. Most people would look down on that because they would think that Daisy should have reported Patty to child protective services. And she tried multiple times. But I begged her not to each time because I didn't want to lose the only parent I had left. So Daisy agreed to let her live.

"I guess I'm having a baby."

"Bitch, I fucking told your ass those tests were accurate," she shrieked.

I rolled my eyes. "Whatever. I'll be there in a few." I quickly hung up on her before she could say anything else.

It was going to take me a while to get used to the idea of being pregnant, but I couldn't lie and say I wasn't starting to love the idea of becoming a mother in nine months. It just gave me a warm feeling knowing I could show myself what being a real mother was even though mine was bullshit. Everybody knew that Patty broke me, and I always thought that there was no coming back from that. But with this baby growing inside of me, I had a second chance at building myself back up, and I was going to take advantage of it, which was why I needed to have a serious conversation with Dez.

I pulled up to Lonny's house just as she and Dez were walking out the door. He was holding her luggage as she skipped her happy ass to my Jeep. Lonny climbed in the truck while he placed her bag in the trunk.

"Hey, mama," she spoke, placing her hand on my stomach.

I pushed her hand away and sucked my teeth. "Bitch, you do the most."

"As the godmother I have that right," she said matter-of-factly, then sat back in her seat.

Dez walked around to her window. "What's good, Li? How you feeling?"

I shrugged. "I'm straight, but look, I know right now I'm not showing and shit. But when I do get big to the point where there is no hiding it, I'm going to fall back and allow you to run shit until I go into labor. I'm not trying to risk nothing happening to me or this baby."

"Yeah, me either. I wouldn't be a good uncle if I did."

I chuckled. "While I'm gone, make sure the shipment that comes in comes undetected. I told you Cassie and Nigel are fucking around with that damn detective, so I'm sure they're going to be sniffing around."

"I got you. I put people on all three of them, so we will know their every move at all times."

"Okay, good. Let me know their every move. Especially Cassie's bitch ass. She lucky I'm fucking pregnant," I huffed. I was going to keep her ass alive until I dropped this damn baby so I could give her a proper ass whooping. She wasn't getting out of this shit.

"Oh, and be ready when I get back to handle the shit with Scott. His family will be sent to Rio this weekend. He needs to be right behind them and there by next weekend because they transfer him Friday."

"All right, bet. Do you have the route they're taking?"

I nodded. "Yup, Roy sent it to me last week. I'm going to talk to Hendrix to see if I can borrow his jet. That'll make shit a lot easier for us," I said.

"I stay ready. So let me know the plan when y'all get back. Take care of my baby, Li, and, Alondra, don't make me come down there and show my ass," he said before pecking her lips a few times then pulling a wad of money out of his pocket. "Have fun, baby. Call me before y'all head to the airport."

He kissed Lonny again before tapping the car and walking away to his. I looked over at Alondra as she smiled her ass off before putting the money he gave her inside her purse.

"Bitch, you smiling hard as hell," I called her out, sitting upright and pulling off.

She laughed, "I can't help it, ho. That's bae."

"'That's bae,'" I mocked then laughed. "Y'all cute as hell though."

"Thanks. So are you and your baby daddy." She smirked.

I looked over at her and rolled my eyes. "Bitch, fuck you." I laughed.

She burst out laughing. "Yo, can you actually believe you pregnant by that nigga? Do you know how many times y'all have tried to kill each other?"

"Bitch, too fucking many for us to be about to become parents to one another's child." I shook my head.

I was sleeping with the enemy and got fucking pregnant. That shit was wild as hell to me, but it was also funny because at one point in time, I could not stand his fine ass. Still couldn't, but the shit was happening, and there was nothing that I could do about it.

"Y'all are really cute together though, Li. Despite y'all hating each other and shit. If y'all had met on other circumstances, y'all would make a bomb-ass couple."

I scrunched my face up on the outside, but on the inside, I was agreeing like crazy. We were too much alike though, and I felt like that was why we bumped heads so much.

"If you say so. We're going to go shopping when we get there because I already know that I'm not going to find anything in any of the stores here. I started to order some stuff from Fashion Nova, but I didn't want to risk it not getting here on time," I said.

"That's fine with me. I'm sick of looking at the same damn clothes and shit in Virginia anyway," she said, and I nodded, agreeing.

My ringing phone blared through my speakers in my car since I had the aux hooked up. I looked at the name on the dashboard and saw that it was Hendrix calling me. He called me early as hell this morning to wake me up for my appointment. That was at seven, and I told him it was at ten. I swore he was doing ignorant shit to get on my nerves.

"Hello?"

"Ay yo, make me fly my ass back down there, Lihanny. Didn't I tell your ass to call me when you got to the doctor's office so I could hear what the fuck they said?"

I rolled my eyes and glared at Lonny as she snickered. "I don't know who the fuck you think you're talking to. Call back and try again." I hung up, and she burst out laughing.

"Bitch, I hate this nigga."

Before she could say anything else, he was calling me back. I answered. "You ready to speak to me like you got some sense?" I asked.

He sighed like he was fighting back cursing me out, but I didn't care. I wasn't none of those other bitches he was fucking with. He wasn't going to talk to me any kind of way.

"Why can't you just listen when I tell you shit, ma?" he said in a calmer tone.

"I wasn't trying to be a hard ass. I honestly forgot because I was so damn nervous."

"What'd they say?"

"Nothing for real. I only went there to confirm it, and she gave me some vitamins. She set me an appointment for next week to do an ultrasound and stuff," I told him.

"All right, bet. I will be there. Where you going now?"

"To get some food with Lonny before we get on our flight. I need to talk to you about something, too. So when I land, can we meet up somewhere?"

"What you mean meet up? Just send me your hotel information."

I chuckled. "No can do. I don't need you interrupting my fun whenever you feel like it," I said just to fuck with him.

"Yeah, all right. Fuck with me if you want to, and you will be responsible for a hella dead niggas. Matter of fact, stay your ass in Virginia. You don't need to come out here. I'll get your cousin on my jet and bring her to you."

I sucked my teeth. "Don't nobody want to come out here. It's boring as hell."

"Then stop playing with me. I'll be at your room when you land." He quickly hung up.

"See what you did, bitch? Now we not going to have any kind of freedom." Lonny sucked her teeth.

"Girl, nobody but you is worried about Hendrix's ass. The most he will do is put Jerry on us to follow us around. He knows how much this trip means to me."

Alondra's head snapped in my direction as she looked at me with a smirk on her face. "Oh, so y'all having heart-to-hearts now? I see you."

I giggled. "Whatever. You get on my damn nerves."

Chapter 25

Lihanny Wright

In Florida

As soon as I was off that plane, I quickly rushed to the bathroom to throw up everything that I ate today. I was over this fucking trip already. I did not expect to be in the bathroom the whole ride, throwing up every damn where. This shit was for the highest fucking birds.

"Li, you okay? I got your bags."

Standing, I used my foot to flush the toilet before walking out of the stall and heading for the sink.

"Thank you." I rinsed my mouth out before washing my hands.

"Aw, bae, we might have to drive back if you going to be throwing up like that on the plane."

I turned my nose up. "Bitch, who driving sixteen damn hours? Not I." After I was good, I grabbed my bags from her.

"Yeah, you right. You might get sick in the car too. You need some water?" she asked, handing me a bottle that I didn't even realize she had until now.

"Thank you." I twisted the top, then turned it up, guzzling down half the bottle. "Let me call Bl—"

Before I could finish my sentence, she was screaming my name as she sprinted through the airport. "Lihanny!"

I dropped my bags as I ran to meet her halfway. Once we were close enough to each other, we leaped into each other's arms, causing us both to fall. We burst out laughing, then laughs turned into cries as we held on to each other for dear life.

"I missed you so fucking much," she cried.

"I missed you more, cousin. So much more."

We stayed there for a little while before I started feeling small pains. I forgot all about my ass being pregnant.

"Okay, I should probably get up," I muttered.

"Me and Hendrix gon' bank your ass if you hurt our baby," Alondra joked as she finally got to us.

"Baby?" Blair quickly stood, then pulled me along with her. "Bitch, why didn't you tell me?"

"Girl, it slipped my mind when I saw you." I took a minute to admire my cousin. Her eyes were big and doe-like and a hazel that I'd never seen on a chocolate girl. Her body was stacked with perfectly sized breasts and a butt that sat up nicely. She had on a gray spaghetti-strap one-piece with a pair of teal and gray Airmax 95s on her feet. Blair's red hair was pulled into a ponytail in the back. Her tattoos on her arms were on full display. My cousin was bomb as hell.

I walked over to Lonny and took my bags from her once again before introducing them. "Alondra, this is my cousin Blair. Blair, this is my best friend Alondra."

"You can call me Lonny for short." They met for a hug.

"Li calls me Bear." She chuckled and so did I. "So you can too."

"I was like two when I gave you that name."

"Bitch, I'm so fucking glad to see you." Blair came over and hugged me again. "And your ass is pregnant."

I rolled my eyes and smirked. "Definitely unintentional."

"Let's get out of here and get some food," Blair offered.

"We need to check into our room first."

Blair looked over at me then Lonny. "I know y'all hoes did not book a damn room. Especially not after all that shit I bought to get my guest rooms ready."

Lonny pointed at me. "It was her idea."

I sucked my teeth playfully. "Damn, bitch, you just met her ass and you turning on me already."

Alondra shrugged her shoulders before linking her arm with Blair's and sticking her tongue out.

"Remember that bitch. She lives in Florida."

Lonny quickly let go of Blair before coming to my side and kissing my cheek. I pulled away from her, laughing. "Nah, bitch. G'on back over there."

Lonny laughed. "You know I love you, girl."

Blair giggled. "Cancel that room. Let's go get some food." Blair grabbed one of my bags from me and grabbed my hand.

I smiled at her before grabbing ahold of Lonny's hand with my free one. Together, we walked out of the airport and to Blair's coral BMW truck. That shit was so fucking pretty it made my mouth water.

"Cousin, you out here doing it like thisss." I walked around the truck. She had the sunroof open, so her cream interior was on display. This shit was beautiful.

"Girl, I had to. This truck was calling my name," she said, popping the locks.

We placed our bags in the back before we all climbed in. I quickly pulled my phone out to shoot Hendrix a text because I was not trying to hear his mouth.

"Where y'all want to eat at?"

"Anywhere. I'm starving," Alondra said.

"I have a taste for some seafood."

PLUG: Come meet me at the restaurant. I know your fat ass is hungry.

Me: Yes, I am hungry, but I'm not meeting you any damn where for calling me fat.

"We can get takeout from this one place then go to my house. It's late, so I know y'all don't want to be out all night."

"We can get some food and a bottle then chill in the house for the rest of the night," Lonny suggested.

I nodded, liking the idea. "Sounds good to me."

"All right. The place is just a few minutes away."

PLUG: WYA and why haven't you made it to your room yet, Li?

Me: Because I am no longer staying there, Hendrix.

PLUG: Drop your location.

I rolled my eyes. "This nigga is getting on my nerves."

"Girl, you already knew he was going to want to know your every move. So I don't know why you acting like that."

"Is that your child's father?" Blair asked, glancing over at me.

"Sadly," I muttered.

"Is he a bad guy or something?" Blair inquired.

"Nah, he just don't take any of her shit and she ain't used to it." She chuckled from the back seat.

"It was just unexpected, but now that the shit is happening, he thinks he can control every damn thing."

"Maybe he just cares about you and your well-being. And now that you're carrying his child, it's expanded."

"That's exactly what it is. Li is used to being in charge, and he doesn't let her do that."

"I just don't like being told what to do." I shrugged.

"So he's controlling?"

"As hell," Lonny and I both said. "But not in an abusive way. In more like a protective way," she finished.

"Seems to me it's something that you're going to have to get used to, Lihanny."

"Yeah, I guess so."

***

The next morning, we got up early so we could catch breakfast at someplace Blair made a reservation at. I wasn't even hungry, but I was still going to go. After taking a very relaxed shower, I got dressed in a simple red baby tee that stopped just above my belly button, a pair of black short shorts, and my Dolce & Gabbana red sneakers with no socks. I unwrapped my hair and let the loose curls fall down my back. I placed a couple of pieces of jewelry on, put on my lip gloss, and grabbed my purse.

"Li? You ready?" Blair called out to me.

"Yeah, I'm coming."

I made sure I had my cards and ID before grabbing my phone and heading down the stairs. Blair was dressed in a white spaghetti-strap bandeau top with the matching mid-thigh skirt. Her feet were adorned by a pair of open-toe orange sandal heels that wrapped around her calf. She had her red hair in a slick bun, showing off her pretty face. Lonny was standing next to her in a baby blue strapless sundress that hugged her body to a T. Her hair was in a side ponytail, and she wore a pair of Chanel sandals on her feet. I felt out of place with what I had on.

"Um, do I need to go change?" I said, hitting the final step.

Blair looked up at me and shook her head. "No, ma'am. It's not a fancy place."

"Okay, cool. Come on."

Blair locked up her house behind us, and we got into her truck. She pulled up her music, and we jammed out the whole way to the restaurant. I had us all over my Snapchat and Instagram stories. I was enjoying myself catching up with my cousin and best friend. And I was loving the fact that they instantly clicked because I damn sure wasn't going to be able to choose if they didn't like each other.

We pulled up to the place about fifteen minutes later. The valet walked over and opened everyone's doors before accepting her keys and pulling off. Blair led the way inside the place.

"Reservations for Fulton," she spoke once we got to the counter.

"Right this way, Miss Fulton. One of your guests has already arrived," the waitress said as she led us through the crowded restaurant.

I felt out of place as hell with my sneakers on. I mean, it wasn't fancy, but everyone either had on dressy shoes or sandals, then in walks my Virginian ass with sneakers on.

"Who's the other guest?" I asked Blair as we turned a corner.

I looked on, amazed because this place was bigger than what it looked. "One of my friends. She's cool, I promise," Blair responded.

We walked past a few more tables before we were finally seated at a table where some girl was already sitting. When she noticed us, she got up and hugged Blair.

"Hey, Nylah. This is my cousin Li and her best friend Lonny. This is Nylah, my friend," Blair introduced us.

We both lightly shook her hand before muttering, "Nice to meet you," and then all of us took our seats. I mean, the girl wasn't ugly by far. But she seemed as if she was annoyed that we were here. As much as I wanted to say something about it, I kept my mouth shut because I didn't want to get Lonny started. My bitch had no kind of chill whatsoever, and we didn't come here for that.

"Could I start you all off with a drink?" the waiter asked.

"May I have a water with lemon?" I requested, then just sat while everyone else placed their drink orders.

Once she got everyone's orders, she walked away. I picked up the menu and began looking over it while I listened as Nylah talked Blair's head off about a bunch of nothing. I looked over at Lonny, and she just rolled her eyes, clearly as annoyed as I was.

"So what do you guys do?" Nylah spoke.

"We are into business management. We help sinking businesses learn to float again," I lied. "It's a sweet reward if you get the customer to buy or sell a house."

"Oh," was all Nylah said before she pulled her phone out and began scrolling through whatever was in her phone.

I scrunched my face up. "What you mean, 'oh'?"

"She doesn't mean anything by it, Li," Blair said, realizing that this conversation was about to go left.

I looked at my cousin but kept my mouth shut. There was something about this bitch that I definitely wasn't feeling. She was just giving me this off vibe. It was making me uncomfortable as fuck. And when I felt uncomfortable, I also felt threatened.

"No, I didn't mean anything by it. It's different, is all," she said.

"How is Hendrix and the girls doing?" Blair asked.

My head shot up at Hendrix's name. I knew I wasn't tripping, and I also knew that there weren't that many Hendrixes, so she was most definitely talking about my Hendrix.

Lonny's eyebrow arched as we stared into her face, awaiting her answer, because I just knew that she wasn't talking about my Hendrix. And yes, I said "my."

Entertained as hell by this, we had to cover our mouths with the menus. Before she could speak, the waitress came and took our orders.

"Girl, the girls are good. His daughter, Hydiah, is a big crybaby. She stays stomping her feet and pouting her ass off when she doesn't get her way. Then, bitch, this nigga has the nerve to have brought her white-ass mama to my house."

"Girl, what?" Blair said.

"Yes, bitch. He came back from Virginia last week with her talking about she needs to stay here until he figures some things out. Then his ass gon' tell me that he doesn't want to be in no kind of relationship with me. Talking about we not good for each other, and I cause him to lose his temper too much."

"I mean, you did tell me he had to choke you out because you pushed him when he was holding the girls," Blair replied.

"Bitch, that was a week ago, and I was drunk as hell. He sets me off every time he tells me he's going back to Virginia, because my cousin told me she be seeing him around with some bitch. He be thinking he's going to play house with my baby, but he got me fucked up," she stated.

Lonny looked over at me and burst out laughing. She didn't give a fuck, and it caused me to chuckle and shake my head. "Woo, chile," she giggled.

I looked up at Blair, who had a confused expression on her face. Then I looked at Nylah, who looked as if she was ready to go. I was feeling a little petty, so I pulled out my phone and took a quick picture of us before sending it to Hendrix.

Me: Baby mama crew!

A second later, Hendrix was FaceTiming me. I smirked over at Nylah, who was in her phone before answering. The phone connected and his face popped up.

"Yes, worrisome?"

"Where you at yo?" his voice blared through my speakers.

Out of the corner of my eye, I could see Nylah's head pop up, but I focused my attention on my phone.

"Eating breakfast with Lonny, Blair, and Blair's friend. Why?"

I looked up as the waitress was bringing our food. I wasn't in the mood to eat anything heavy, so I got a salad and some fruit. *That should hold me until later on.*

"Drop your location so I can come and get you. We need to discuss some things," he demanded.

"Hendrix, believe it or not, I have other stuff to do after this. So you can't come get me."

"Hendrix?" Nylah blurted.

I looked up at her as she stood with a pissed-off look on her face. I stayed seated and continued to dress my salad, but Lonny stood up also.

"Why the hell are you on FaceTime with my man?"

I took a forkful of my salad and stuffed it inside my mouth. "Ask your nigga why he's on FaceTime with me."

I turned the camera so that he could see his baby mama acting a fool. He just shook his head before hanging up the phone. I chuckled.

"Bitch, you think you're funny, and you ain't. Don't make me show my ass in here," Nylah said.

"Bitch, you ain't gon' do shit with your fake ass but get it whooped if you say anything else slick to her. How you was just over there damn near in tears because the nigga said he didn't want you, and now you trying to big-dog buck to a bitch he does want? You look dumb," Lonny fussed.

I looked up at her. "I don't want your nigga, boo. Your nigga wants me."

"Bitch, Hendrix doesn't even fuck with dark-skinned bitches. So try again."

I burst out laughing. "Shit, the way he be eating the fuck out of this pussy, he love his chocolate."

She went to pick up her glass of wine, but before she could do anything with it, Lonny grabbed her by her hair and started raining blows on her.

"Oh, no!" Blair quickly stood as she moved toward the fight to break it up.

When I stood, I jumped up and down, hyping Lonny up, and she continued to beat her ass. "Hell yeah, best friend! Beat that bitch's ass!"

I swear I wanted so badly to go over there and finish her off, but I wasn't even going to put myself at risk like that, so I stayed back, but not too far back.

"Alondra, please stop. They're going to call the cops," Blair pleaded, and Alondra immediately let Nylah go.

I picked up my wallet and phone, then grabbed Lonny's belongings too. I walked over to her, laughing my ass off. She looked over at me, laughing as well before fixing her ponytail. That Nylah ho was just lying there on the ground, trying to fix her hair.

"You're lucky I'm pregnant. I would have knocked your smart ass the fuck out. Dumb bitch. Blair, I'm sorry. We will be in the car."

I grabbed hold of Lonny's hand, and together we walked to the car and waited for Blair to finish up with her friend. I felt bad because we didn't come here to start shit. Shorty was kind of asking for it though with her nasty-ass attitude from the jump. I knew I needed to prepare myself though because I already knew that I was going to hear Hendrix's mouth later about this bullshit.

Chapter 26

Hendrix Brown

Thirty Minutes Later

"I appreciate you for hitting me about this," I told the caller on the phone.

"No problem. I'm not trying to fuck up future business. I'll see you later on," he said before hanging up the phone.

I sat up in the chair and started feasting on my wings as the front door burst open then slammed back a second later.

"Hendrix!" Nylah called out loud as hell.

I had just gotten Haylee back to sleep from her being up all night, and I was going to wring her fucking neck if she woke her up. Dropping my chicken wing, I looked back at her as she made her way over to me.

"Yo, I swear to God I'm going to choke the shit out of you if you wake my baby up." I frowned as I looked at her disheveled hair and the blood on her clothes. Standing, I walked in front of her to inspect the damage to her face, but she smacked my hand away and pushed me back.

"Get the fuck off of me!"

"What is all that yelling?" Savannah came down the stairs, wiping her eyes.

"Go put some fucking clothes on. And, Nylah, if you put your hands on me again, I'm fucking you up yo."

I walked back over to where my food was and sat back down. She followed me and stood over me, glaring intently. "Fuck you, Hendrix. How could you be fucking my best friend's cousin? Do you know how fucking embarrassing that is for her to FaceTime you after I talked to them about the shit we are going through?"

"The fuck you talking to them about our business for, Nylah? That's your fucking fault that you always running your mouth, not mine." I shrugged.

"Nigga, because I need people to express my feelings to since you clearly give no fucks about them whatsoever," she yelled.

"Back the fuck up, Nylah, for real."

"Then you had the nerve to get that bitch pregnant?"

"What!" Savannah yelled, walking over to us.

I huffed and shook my head because I was not in the mood for this shit. I didn't know what the hell I was thinking bringing Savannah here because now I had to hear two bitches nag. "First of all. I'm not fucking with nor am I in a relationship with either of you, so whatever the fuck I do or who I fuck doesn't concern either of y'all."

"Haylee is only seven months old, and you're barely around her. Where did you even meet this bitch?" Nylah questioned.

"None of your fucking business. Now back the fuck up out of my face, Nylah. Didn't I just break up with your ass last week? Why you still questioning a nigga like you have that fucking right?"

"She's the bitch from Virginia, isn't she? Blair said her cousin was from there. She's the reason you keep going back there. Look at my fucking face, Hendrix! She fucking did this to me, and you want to be with somebody like that?" Nylah covered her face and cried.

My head snapped in her direction at her saying that Li fucked her face up. I was about to fuck Lihanny up if she was out here fucking fighting with my baby in her stomach.

"Li did that to your face?"

"Li? Is that the girl you met up with at Smokey Bones? Your 'partner'?" Savannah did the quotation motion with her fingers.

Nylah's eyes darted to Savannah. "You met the bitch too?"

She crossed her arms across her chest. "Yeah, I met her. She doesn't exactly seem like your type, Hendrix."

Ignoring them both, I pulled my phone out and dialed Lihanny's number. This girl was going to make me knock her fucking head off. As soon as she picked up the phone, I went in on her disobedient ass.

"Yes?"

"Where the fuck you at? I'm going to fuck you up for fighting out here with my fucking baby in your stomach. I told your hardheaded ass not to be on no bullshit on this fucking trip, and the first damn thing you do is put my fucking child in danger by fighting." I was fuming, too. She was starting to piss me off with this rebellious shit.

"Are you done?" she inquired in the most nonchalant tone I'd ever heard from her.

"Lihanny, this shit isn't a fucking game yo. You could have seriously hurt my baby, man." I shook my head.

"I know that. Which is why I wasn't the one fighting."

My eyebrows dipped in confusion. "What?"

"You heard me. I didn't beat your bitch's ass. Lonny did." She burst out laughing.

I looked up at Nylah, who looked to be pissed off with steam coming from her ears. "I thought you said Li did that to your face."

She rolled her eyes and crossed her arms. "She sicced her friend on me."

"Bitch, I didn't sic shit on your punk ass. You was talking big shit, and my best friend whooped your ass, dumb ho."

The phone was on speaker, so Nylah had heard everything Li said.

"Bitch, she caught me off guard."

Li laughed. "How about you drop your location, and we will come for round two before I go handle my business?"

"Y'all not doing any more fucking fighting. Lihanny, I'll see your ass later." I hung up the phone and placed it next to me.

"Nylah, go clean yourself up yo. Haylee is asleep, so do it quietly." I went back to eating my chicken.

"Wooow. So you aren't going to say shit to her about attacking me?" she said in disbelief.

"Nylah, she didn't do the shit. So there isn't shit I can fucking say."

"That's some bullshit. You just going to let them beat her ass like that? You remember when Gloria and Victoria beat my ass after school? You took me over there and made me fight them over and over again until I punished them," Savannah said.

"That's because they jumped you, and that was in fucking high school. It was a one-on-one fucking fight. Ain't shit I can say about it." I shrugged and looked down at my watch.

I needed to be dressed and in the truck within the next thirty minutes, and they were fucking up my scheduling with their bullshit. I had an important meeting to go to about expanding my business and buying out the strip mall that was by the beach.

"Come on, girl. Let's get you cleaned up," Savannah said to Nylah.

I was stunned because they hadn't said much of shit to each other since Savannah had been here, and if they were talking, it was to throw shots at each other. The last thing I needed was my BMs to become friends. It was much more peaceful when they didn't speak.

After I finished my food, I went upstairs to the guest room I had been sleeping in and quickly stripped out of my clothes so that I could take a quick shower. I wrapped a towel around my waist and walked out the room then across the hall where the bathroom was. Once I was in, I pulled my towel off and turned the water on before stepping inside. This shit was steaming fucking hot, so I adjusted the temperature a bit before relaxing underneath the water. I grabbed my washcloth and began washing up.

I thought I was bugging when I heard the bathroom door open, but Savannah came stepping in the shower a minute later in her birthday suit. I stared at her blankly as she dropped to her knees and took me into her mouth. As badly as I wanted to stop her, I needed a fucking release. From what I remembered, her head game was stupid. I held on to the back of her head and threw mine back as she stuffed my whole dick in her mouth like the pro she was. I bit my lip to hold back from moaning out like a bitch.

"Damn, girl." I looked down at her as she slobbered on my shit then licked it up and sucked on the head.

I grabbed her head and fucked her mouth. She held on to the back of my legs to keep her balance. It wasn't long before she was swallowing my kids. Once I was done, she licked me clean, then stood with a smirk on her face. She turned and left the shower just as fast as she came. I shook my head before washing up again then turning the shower off.

After I got dressed, I headed down the stairs. Savannah and Nylah were in the living room, eating, with Haylee sitting on the floor, blabbering away. I walked past them and bent down to kiss my baby. She was making me miss Hydiah. My brother had flown down here to get her a couple of days ago.

"Where you going?" Nylah asked.

Ignoring her, I walked out of the house and climbed into the truck, where Jerry was waiting. As soon as I got situated, he pulled off and floored it to the meeting. I pulled my phone from my suit jacket and FaceTimed my brother. I expected to see him pop up on the screen, but instead it was Hydiah.

"Daddy!" She cheesed.

I chuckled at her being so close to the phone. "What's up, baby girl? You miss me?"

She backed up some and shrugged her shoulders. "Kind of. I'm having a lot of fun here with Uncle Sein and Nana and Papa."

"Damn, baby girl. You don't miss your daddy? I miss you a whole lot, Hydiah, and you just going to do me like that?"

Hydiah giggled. "Daddy, I said 'kind of.' Where's Haylee?"

"She's at the house. Daddy has to go handle some business, but as soon as I get back, I will FaceTime you so that you can see and talk to her."

"All right, Daddy. I have to go now. Me and Nana are making slime in the backyard."

"Okay, baby. I love you."

"Love you too, Daddy," she said and dropped the phone.

"Ay, girl. Don't be dropping my shit unless you're going to buy me another one," Hussein called after her, then picked his phone up.

"Ay, you curse at my baby again and I'm going to put my foot up your ass."

"If she breaks my fucking phone, you're going to buy me another one."

"I'm not buying you shit, bitch. But I didn't call for all that. You get that information I need?"

Hussein nodded. "Yeah. I'll send it to you when you hang up."

"All right. Watch after my baby, too."

"Always."

We hung up just as we pulled up to the office building in Miami. Jerry got out of the truck and opened my door.

"Don't be seen," I told him before buttoning up my jacket and walking in.

I greeted the people at the desk before getting on the elevator. Pressing the button to the basement, I put in the code to gain access. I silenced my phone, then placed my hands in my pockets.

Ding!

I walked off the elevator then down the hall. Once I made it to the double doors, I knocked twice before walking in. The expression on Lihanny's face was priceless and angry as hell. This was my second time interrupting one of her meetings while she was trying to find a supplier.

"Don't stop on my account," I said, then addressed everyone before unbuttoning my suit jacket and taking a seat in one of the empty chairs around the big table.

"Lihanny here was just expressing how quickly and quietly she handles her work," Carlos said.

Carlos was the son of the infamous Chancey Rodriguez from New York. The story of the Rodriguez family was definitely one for the books. Chancey's daughter, Harmony, was a fucking beast when she was running shit. She was the only female I respected in these streets because she handled her shit with class and grace. But she was ruthless as a muthafucka when shit got out of hand. That was until I met Li though. Her drive for this shit matched Harmony's to a T, and I could do nothing but respect that.

Harmony retired from the game a couple of years ago, but she was in the background and sometimes sat in on meetings, such as this one.

"What the hell are you doing here, Hendrix?" Li questioned, sitting up in her seat.

"I should be asking you that fucking question," I responded.

Harmony looked back and forth between us, oblivious as to what was going on. "Y'all know each other?"

"She works for me," I replied, not taking my eyes off her.

Harmony looked over at Lihanny with her lip turned up. "You on some snake shit?"

Lihanny's head whipped in her direction so fast I thought that shit was going to pop out of place. "Excuse me? I'm far from a snake, boo, so you can shut all that down and fix your face. All I'm trying to do here is make some fucking money." She turned to look at me. "But this nigga continues to stand in the way of that. How did you even know I was here?"

"I got a call from one of my allies about one of my workers trying to push another nigga's weight on my fucking territory."

Lihanny scoffed. "You get on my fucking nerves. I swear you're only doing this shit because I'm pregnant."

"You being pregnant with my fucking baby is only half of the problem."

"Wait a minute. Y'all two are together?" Harmony questioned.

"Yes."

"No."

We both spoke at the same time. Lihanny just glared at me before rolling her eyes.

"Listen, Hendrix, I don't have nothing against you, and you know I always have and always will have respect for you, but time is money. And I don't have time for the baby mama drama."

"Bitch, who asked you to come here? Who even are you?" Li mugged the fuck out of Harmony.

I stood because I knew this was not about to end well. They both were hotheaded as fuck. Harmony stood and so did Lihanny. I already knew Li wasn't about to back down from anybody, so they were going to go toe-to-toe if Carlos and I didn't gain control of this situation.

"Bitch? Little girl, I'm the bitch who will put you in a fucking grave in a heartbeat if you disrespect me again. I don't know who the fuck you think you're talking to, but you better pipe that shit down and fast before I have to put a fucking bullet in your head," Harmony spat.

"Bitch, they didn't stop making guns when they made yours. Ain't nobody scared of you or those empty-ass fucking threats you making. You better ask about me. I shoot first and never ask questions."

"That's enough." I grabbed Lihanny up and pulled her away. "My apologies, Harmony."

"Fuck her. You don't need to apologize to her ass. That bitch don't know what the fuck to say out of her mouth, but don't worry. I'll get that ass fixed real fucking quick. She got me fucked up. I don't fear no fucking body who bleeds just the same as I do."

"Bitch, you still fucking talking?" Harmony was trying to get from around Carlos, but he was holding her to make sure she didn't.

"You see my lips moving and hear words coming out, right?" Li bucked back as I pushed her along.

I grabbed her by her arm and pulled her out of the room and closed the door behind us. She snatched away as she walked to the elevator with her face balled up. She tried to leave my ass, but I stepped inside with her just as the doors were about to close.

"What the fuck is wrong with you yo? You on one today, aren't you?"

"Nigga, fuck you. Don't say shit to me, Hendrix."

"Yo, I don't give a fuck about that stank-ass attitude you got. I been patient as fuck with your ass, and I have been trying to give you the benefit of the doubt. But you really testing my fucking patience. The fuck you going behind my back trying to create enemies and shit for?"

"Because I don't have time to be worried about how I'm going to feed my fucking baby when he or she gets here. I already know you're going to cut me off."

"And you know that shit how? Huh?"

She walked in front of me and got off the elevator. "Because you didn't want me doing the shit in the first fucking place."

"That doesn't mean shit. I could have changed my mind about it, but the shit you just pulled back there proves to me that you don't need to be in this line of business."

She stopped walking and turned to me. "Why, because I wanted to have a plan B in case you did turn your back on me? I don't have time to wait until you give me the okay to keep moving your shit. Time waits for no fucking body. And before you and I both know it, this baby will be here. I don't want your money, so you providing for me is out of the fucking question."

"What the fuck is so wrong with letting me take care of you?"

"Because that's the mistake that Patty made. She relied on my daddy to take care of her, and when he died, she didn't have shit but a couple of thousand. Once she smoked that away it was me she fed to the wolves to take care of herself. She sacrificed me to satisfy her needs and wants. I fucking refuse! I refuse to depend on any nigga to give me a damn thing."

I sighed and walked closer to her and wiped her face. “Li, you’re not going to be like her.”

“You don’t know that.” She sniffed.

“Yes, I do. Look at me.” I cupped her chin in my hand and her eyes fell on mine. “You’re not going to be like her. You aren’t going to cause the same pain to our child that she did to you. You don’t have to fear that you’re not going to live up to being a good mother. I can see it when you look at Hydiah and Haylee that you got this shit in the bag already. You can’t keep doubting yourself like that. I got you, all right?”

She nodded. “I just don’t want to depend on you.”

“I know. I’ll figure the shit out. Now bring your ass on so we can discuss what you needed to talk about.” I wrapped my arm around her shoulder as we started walking again. “And why do you have this tight-ass shit on?” I frowned as I looked down at the dress she was wearing. All those sexy-ass curves were on display, and it was making my dick brick up.

“I had to be professional.” She shrugged.

“You couldn’t wear anything loose?”

“No, Hendrix. All of my clothes fit me like a glove.”

“Well, you need to buy some more damn clothes.” I leaned up against the truck and pulled her between my legs.

“Buy me some more clothes then, nigga.” She tossed her hair over her shoulder.

“I can definitely do that. Where you about to go now?” I asked.

“Me and the girls were actually about to hit up the mall and find something to wear tonight.”

My eyebrows dipped. I was not liking the sound of her trying to buy new fits and shit to go shake her ass. “Where you think you going, Li?”

“KOD.”

“Oh, all right. So what did you need to ask me?”

"Oh, yeah. I need to borrow your jet so I can get Scott out of here. They are transferring him on Monday."

"Is that the nigga who took the fall?" I asked, rubbing my hands on her plump ass.

"Yes."

"I'll take care of it. Send me the information."

"Lihanny, bring your caking ass on, girl!" Lonny's loudmouth ass yelled from the passenger's seat when they rolled up on us.

"Stop cock blocking," I joked.

Lonny rolled her eyes. "My best friend doesn't even like you for real."

"She's right." Li shrugged.

Before I could say anything else, the song "That's Just My Baby Daddy" blared through the speakers of Blair's truck. I threw my head back in laughter as they started acting up to the song. I smacked Li's ass as she twerked in front of me.

"All right now. Make me break your back out here," I whispered in her ear, then kissed her neck.

She looked back at me with a smirk on her face. "Whatever. Are you taking me shopping or nah?"

I looked her up and down and couldn't help but to run my hands all over her body. "Depends on what thanks I get."

"Why don't you ride with us and find out later?" She backed away from me, but I pulled her back and stood away from the car.

"Nah, I'm not riding in that girly ass shit. We will meet y'all there," I told her friend and cousin before pulling her to the truck. I opened the door for her and smacked her ass when she climbed in before climbing in behind her.

"Take us to the mall, Jerry," I told him before pressing the button that separated the front row and the rest of the car.

"Why doesn't he talk?" Li asked as she watched me take off my suit jacket and release a few buttons.

"I don't know. He's been like that since I met him," I replied as I turned to her.

I didn't let her say shit else as I stuck my tongue in her mouth, then sucked on her bottom lip. Pulling away, I kissed on her neck a couple of times, then moved down to her breasts where the tops were poking out. I kissed them on both sides, then released one and pulled it into my mouth. Li threw her head back and wrapped her hand around the back of my head. I licked and sucked all over her titties before pushing her back some so that her back was to the door.

"Ay, Jerry, turn the music up for me," I told him, and I pulled Lihanny's dress over her lips.

I ripped her panties off and placed them in my pocket before diving headfirst into her pussy. I had been waiting to do this since I found out her ass was pregnant. And just as I thought, her shit was wet as hell. I licked and slurped as she cried out about how good it felt.

"Oh, fuuuck, Hendrix."

I flicked my tongue around her bud before sucking on it nice and gently. Reaching up, I grabbed ahold of her breast and massaged her nipples with my hand. Lifting up, I licked my lips. "Play with that pussy for daddy."

She moved down to her clit and started rubbing on it while throwing her head back. Her moans were so fucking sexy. I went back down and stuck my tongue as far in her pussy as it would go and tongue fucked her until she cried out that shit was cumming. She bucked her hips on my face as she rode the wave. We stood just as her body stilled. I licked her clean before sitting up and wiping my face off with the wipes that I had stashed inside. I helped her pull her dress back over her hips.

"You good, baby?" I smirked and wiped her juices off of my face.

"Mhmuhm," she muttered, slowly sitting up.

"Here, taste yourself." I grabbed her face and tongue kissed the fuck out of her. She let out a soft moan and pulled my bottom lip into her mouth.

"Let's go before I say fuck this mall and bend you over right here." I opened up my door before walking over to her side of the truck and opening the door for her.

She climbed out and fixed her clothes. "You know you wrong for that." She chuckled.

"I couldn't help myself, baby."

We found Blair and Lonny, and I walked closely behind as they did their thing, buying everything in every fucking store they went into. Lihanny even found a couple of gender-neutral outfits for our baby and some cute matching outfits for the girls. I shook my head because I knew she was going to spoil the fuck out of our baby. And honestly, I couldn't fucking wait.

Chapter 27

Lihanny Wright

After we parted ways with Hendrix, we headed to get something to eat. I was so fucking hungry from all that walking we did. And right now, my stomach was screaming for some Chick-fil-A, so we went there, then headed to Blair's house. By the time we got to her house, my food was gone, and I was feasting on a fruit cup I'd gotten from there. Blair turned her car off, and I began gathering my stuff. I was going to have to take more than three trips to get these bags out from all the shit we bought from the mall.

"Lihanny, wait. Before you get out, I want to tell you that my parents are here."

I stopped and looked at her. It had been a long time since I'd seen my auntie and uncle, and I didn't realize how much I didn't want to see them until now. "Blair, I—"

"Hear me out, please."

I reluctantly got quiet so that she could say what she wanted to say.

"I know you don't want to see them, and they know that also. But my mother is hell-bent on seeing you, and she wants to explain why she left and a bunch of other shit that she didn't tell me. I don't want to pressure you into doing this because I don't want to lose you again, so if you don't want to, I'll make them leave right now, and whenever you're ready you can have that conversation with them."

I sighed and laid my head back on the seat. As much as I wanted to be upset with them about leaving me with Patty, I knew that they didn't do it to hurt me. I mean, Patty was my guardian, and at the time, she was stable and was handling her shit. They didn't know that shit was going to go left as soon as they left the city.

"I'll talk to them. I can't be upset forever," I muttered before getting out of the car along with Lonny and Blair.

Blair walked ahead of me, and Lonny came over and held my hand. We walked up the stairs, and Blair opened the door. I took a deep breath before entering the house. When my aunt and uncle came into view, they stood up. Aunt Katrice and Uncle Blake looked the same and really good for their age. Seeing my aunt made me think about my daddy because they looked just alike.

"Li—"

Before she could even say my whole name, I dropped my bags and ran into her arms. I felt like a big-ass baby as I cried my eyes out. She wrapped her arms around me tightly, and my uncle joined in on the hug a second later. I released half of my hold on her and hugged my uncle. I had missed them so much, and as much as I wanted to be angry with them for leaving me, I couldn't. I was just glad that they were here now.

"Lihanny, I am so sorry," my aunt cried.

I pulled away and wiped my face. "You don't have to apologize, Auntie Kat."

She shook her head. "No, I do. I could have fought her for custody of you and brought you with us. I just didn't want to drag you through all of that. I should have tried harder. I knew your father would have wanted us to bring you with us, but it would have been really hard getting custody taken away from your mother."

"Had you come back a few years later, it wouldn't have been that hard," I muttered and looked away.

"What do you mean?" My aunt raised her eyebrow.

I took a seat on the chair that was closest to me and prepared to tell them what I went through when they left. I had never been afraid to tell anyone what I was put through as a child because it made me who I was today. Nor did I care about being judged by anyone because it would never be addressed to my face.

Everyone else in the living room took a seat as well. Lonny sat next to me while Blair sat between her parents.

"After you guys moved, Patty started getting on drugs real heavy. She was smoking weed, popping pills, and sniffing coke here and there. It wasn't long before she started to blow through the money that was left to us. Bills started piling up, and Patty had refused to get out and get a job, so it was evident that we were going to get put out of the house we were in. I was more than willing to get a job, but because I wasn't of age, there wasn't anything that I could do. One night, Patty had called me down to talk to me about something, and one of my dad's old workers was down there with her, and she started talking to me about how our bills were due and we needed some help. As I was trying to explain to her that I wasn't old enough to get a job, I could feel him staring at me. So Patty was trying to tell me that there was another way for me to bring in money, but I was so confused and didn't understand what she meant. She was trying to put her words in a way that I understood, but dad's friend got angry and basically blurted out that he was paying her to have his way with me."

"Oh, no." Auntie Katrice's head fell into her hands as she began to cry.

My throat burned as I fought back the tears. I looked up at the ceiling as I shook my head, and my mind played back the events of that night.

"What was his name?" my uncle questioned. I could tell that he was pissed the fuck off.

"Dexter. His name was Dexter."

"Man, get the fuck out of here. Dexter is your fucking cousin." My uncle stood and paced the floor.

I shook my head, confused. "Wait, what?"

"Dexter is your father's and my first cousin on our father's side," my aunt said as she wiped her face.

"Oh, my God," I heard Lonny said.

"Did it stop there?" Blair asked.

"I wished it did. She pimped me out until I was eighteen, and the only reason it stopped is because I met my ex-boyfriend Malaki. He moved me out of there."

"I'm going to fucking kill both of them," my uncle raved as he pulled his phone out.

"It's going to be hard killing Patty because she's already dead. She died a few months back from cancer," I revealed.

"Good for her," my aunt muttered, then looked up at me with a side-eye when she realized that she didn't whisper it. "I'm sorry."

"No, don't be. I'm at peace now that she is gone," I said honestly. "But can I ask you why you left?"

My aunt sat up straight, and my uncle stopped pacing the floor. "Patty had something to do with Karter being killed."

"That's crazy. She was devastated when she found out he was shot."

"Yeah, because that bitch is a good fucking actor. The only nigga Karter ever trusted was there that night it happened. Karter told him not to come, but he showed up anyway to look out for him. He saw the whole thing go down, but before he could react, it was too late. He said he saw Patty there with two other dudes. He doesn't know if she was the one who shot him or if one of the other niggas there did, but he was positive it was her."

I sat up. "Who was the man who saw it go down?"

"Big B," my aunt said, shocking the hell out of me.

Everybody always thought that they were enemies, and to hear that my father trusted Big B was really crazy news.

"I thought they hated each other," I said.

"Yeah, in the beginning they did. It was bad, too. There were so many times when they tried to kill each other. But one night your father saved Big B from being killed by some other niggas from out of town. After that, they called a truce that nobody knew about, and they got really close. That's why everyone thinks Big B killed him, because last they heard they were beefing," my uncle revealed.

"Oh, wow," was all I could say.

"Lihanny, I am so sorry. Had we taken you—"

"Auntie Kat, don't do that to yourself. I don't blame either of you for what happened to me. The only person who is to blame is dead and gone. I feel no hate toward you or Uncle Blake, and I never will."

My uncle walked over to me and pulled me to my feet then into a hug. "I'm going to rip that muthafucka's dick off when I find him," he whispered in my ear before kissing the top of my head.

I nodded, then hugged him back. "Thank you."

We sat and talked some more before Blair damn near kicked them out so that we could get dressed to go out. It was like a weight had been lifted off of my shoulders after talking to them. I couldn't believe that the nigga who took part in taking my innocence from me was my fucking cousin. Or the fact that Patty was responsible for my dad's death. I swear if her ass weren't already dead, I would have killed her. And as soon as I got back to Virginia, I was getting her casket dug up and her body burned. She didn't deserve to be laid next to my father.

"Oh, Lihanny, there's something else I forgot," my aunt said.

She went into her back pocket and pulled out a piece of paper that had an account number on it along with a PIN. *SunTrust Bank*. Taking it from her, I gave her a confused look.

"Your father didn't hustle all his life to leave only a couple of thousand when he died," was all she said before giving me one last hug then going to get in the car where my uncle was waiting for her.

I walked back into the house and headed to the bedroom so that I could get dressed. As I was putting on my makeup, I looked up the number to the bank and dialed them. After placing the account number then PIN in, I waited.

"Your account balance is $24,650,800. To repeat your balance, dial one . . ."

My fucking mouth fell to the floor and so did my phone. I looked up at the ceiling and all I could do was cry. My daddy was up in heaven and still making shit happen for me.

Monday Morning at 5:30 a.m.

"Do you see them yet?" I asked Dez.

"Nah, not yet. You good back there?"

Today was the day that Scott was being transported to Greensville to serve out his sentence. We had the jet at the private airstrip waiting, and now we were just waiting for the bus to come past. The plan was to get Scott out, then blow the shit up. We had the spikes on the ground so that when they drove past us the tires would blow and they would have to stop. Hendrix hit up a friend of his from the bomb squad and got some high explosives. We got them placed underneath the bus last night. We had exactly one minute to get Scott out of there before the shit blew up once they stopped completely.

My ass had been throwing up all morning, and I was over it. I had the hugest headache, and I couldn't wait until I could go get back in my bed.

"Yeah, I'm good."

"Oooh, here they come," Lonny said, causing me to sit up.

I looked to my left to see the bus behind a police car. I pulled out my gun and cocked it back.

"Showtime," I said to myself.

The police car zoomed past us, and as soon as it hit the spikes, it started spiraling out of control. The bus was next since it was going just as fast, and the police car stopped before it could hit the spikes. We knew that we were going to have to get out and handle this shit right now before they got out of their car. Dez gave the signal to the truck that was behind us, which had our backup. I was only to get out of the car if she went left. So I watched on as Dez hopped out along with the other niggas, and they started laying the officers out before they could shoot first. Half of the team took out the officers while the other half stormed the bus. The engine was off, so I knew that they didn't have long before they had to get out of there. I was on pins and needles, and I looked back and forth between my watch and the bus.

"Get out of there, baby," Lonny whispered to herself as she looked on.

We heard a scream before they came storming off the bus. Dez was holding on to a pissed-off Scott along with another nigga we had to take to perfect our plan. They got in the truck and backed up just as the bus blew up.

Boom!

My eyes began ringing at the sound as Dez pulled away. Once we were clear of the scene, I looked over at Scott.

"Nice to see you again, old friend."

"What the fuck? That nigga cut off my fucking finger," Scott fussed as he held his bleeding pointy finger.

"We had to, or they were going to come looking for you."

When it got out that the bus was blown up, they were going to look for evidence to see who made it out of the fire. We left Scott's finger at the scene so that they would find his DNA.

"Who the hell are you people?" our extra pawn questioned from the back seat.

I rolled my eyes and pulled out the folder I had on him. "Ulysses Zanderfield. Mass rapist. Sentenced to life in prison without parole," I read aloud before looking back at him. "You like fucking little girls, do you?" I scoffed before cocking my gun back.

He shook his head frantically. "What? No. That's not tru—"

Before he could lie like all of those sick muthafuckas did, I blew his brains out. Scott covered his ears. "Yo, Li. What the fuck?"

I shrugged my shoulders. "You should have thanked him for helping us out."

"What you take this nigga for if you were just going to kill him?" he asked.

"Because, Scott, if every prisoner is accounted for, they were going to start asking a series of questions. But if at least one of them escaped, then they would have reason to believe that he was behind the whole thing, and they would go looking for him. But he's dead and will be burned to a crisp, so the case will go cold."

"You're a fucking genius, you know that?" Scott chuckled.

I smiled. "I'd like to think so also."

"I'm still pissed off about my fucking finger, but I'd rather lose that than my life. So I appreciate you."

I nodded. "Not as much as I appreciate you. When you get to Rio, tell your girl I said thank you also for trusting in me to bring you back to her. And if there's anything y'all need, call me."

He nodded and got comfortable in the seat. It took us about thirty minutes to arrive at the airstrip where Hendrix's jet was waiting for us. We all climbed out of the truck. Dez pulled out some keys to uncuff Scott's arms and legs. I walked around the car and pulled him in for a hug.

"Thank you, Scott."

"Thank you too. You be careful out here. Stay on your toes at all times."

I nodded. "Always."

Scott dapped Dez up and hugged Lonny before making his way to the jet. Before he got on, he waved at us once more. We climbed back into the truck after the jet took off.

"Please take me home to my bed." I laid my head back on the seat and relaxed.

My week was already starting off as a good one. I just hoped it stayed that way.

Chapter 28

Hendrix Brown

A Few Hours Later

The sound of my phone going off woke me out of my sleep. I rolled over and saw that it was my brother calling me.

"Yo?"

"Ay yo, this nigga just popped up at Mom's crib looking for Savannah."

I sat up and threw my legs over the bed. "The fuck? How that nigga know where she stay at?"

"Her bigmouthed-ass parents must have told him."

"Stay there. I'm on my way." I hung up the phone and made my way to the bathroom so that I could brush my teeth and wash my face.

While I got myself together, I texted Jerry to come pick me up and take me to my mom's. I had flown down here last night to pick Hydiah up and take her back to Florida, but it was late as fuck so I crashed at a hotel. I put Hussein in charge of finding out the information on Savannah's husband before that nigga could come looking for her. My plan was to cancel his ass before he became a problem, but here he was already on some bullshit by going to my mom's crib. I was about to dead all that shit though.

By the time I was dressed and ready, Jerry was downstairs waiting for me. I quickly hopped in the back, and he sped out of the spot he was in and headed to my mom's crib. I dialed up my homeboy, Russo, who got the information on this Francis nigga.

"What's good?"

"I need that tracker right now," I told him.

"Say no more." He hung up the phone, and a second later, an app appeared on my phone.

I clicked on it and saw where that nigga Francis was. I had Russo put a tracking device on his phone, so no matter where he went, I could find him with no problem. Instead of going to my mother's house, I passed Jerry my phone so that he could go to that location instead. I was going to get rid of his ass before he became an even bigger problem for me.

We pulled up to the Ramada on Military Highway. It couldn't tell me exactly what room he was in, so I called Russo back up.

"Yo?"

"I need you to get into the Ramada Inn Suites on Military Highway and tell me what his room number is," I said.

"Gotcha, give me one second."

I grabbed my gun from under the seat and placed it on my body.

"He's in room 218," Russo said.

"Good looking out." I hung up the phone as Jerry drove to that side of the hotel. "Send him the money for me. I'll be right back."

I hopped out and took the stairs to the second floor. After walking down the hallway, I finally stood in front of his door. I looked around to make sure nobody was around before pulling out my gun and twisting the silencer on.

Knock. Knock.

"Who is it?"

I placed my hand over the peephole so that he couldn't see me.

"Who is it?" he repeated before opening the door.

I smacked him with the butt of my gun before he could say anything else. "Aw, shit." He fell back into the room, and I walked in and closed the door behind me, then locked it.

"Who the fuck are you?" he questioned as he looked up at me while holding his nose.

"Don't worry about who the fuck I am. I heard you like to beat on women."

"What? I would never," he said.

Pew!

"Aaah, fuck! Please, I swear," he cried as he held his foot. "I've never hit a female in my life."

"The fuck are you doing here?" I inquired.

"I just came to get my wife back. She gave birth to our daughter, then disappeared a few weeks later. My baby girl needs her breast milk, and her parents thought I might find her here."

I chuckled and shook my head after realizing that Savannah had played the fuck out of me. "You should have stayed your ass where you were."

I lifted my gun and sent two shots to his head. Turning around, I wiped my prints off the door and the peephole before heading back to the truck.

"Take me to my mom's house," I told Jerry, twisting the silencer off the gun and putting the safety back on.

After placing it where I found it, I pulled my phone out to text Lihanny.

Me: What you doing, baby mama?

Baby Girl: Trying to go back to sleep.

Me: How did the shit go?

Baby Girl: Just as planned. Now please, leave me to bed.

I chuckled but didn't text her back. Her moody ass needed all the sleep that she could get. As the days went by, her ass was getting meaner and meaner, but I liked that shit because I could tame her mean ass.

We pulled up to my parents' house, and I got out of the truck. I used my key to get in, and the smell of food immediately smacked me in the face. I headed straight to the kitchen, and my mouth watered at all the food my mother had laid out.

"It smells so good in here, Ma," I spoke, making my presence known.

She turned around and looked at me. "We had a visitor today," she said, ignoring the compliment I gave her with her rude ass.

"Already handled it. I need to leave Hydiah here while I go put my foot in Savannah's ass for lying to me, too."

My mother's face frowned up. "What do you mean?"

"That nigga didn't beat her ass. I could see it all over his face when I accused him of doing so. He said he was only here because Savannah left him with a newborn high and dry. The baby needs some breast milk, so he came to find her."

My mama shook her head. "What the hell is wrong with that girl? Having babies, then dipping out on them the second she gets a chance. Something can't be right in her head."

"Don't even worry about it. I'm going to figure it out as soon as I eat."

My mama took that as a sign to make me a plate. Not long after, my pops, Hussein, and Hydiah came to join us. And we all sat and ate breakfast together. I low-key looked around the table and thought about when it was time for me to do shit like this with my own family.

I was always raised with the idea that a family was supposed to eat together at a table, and I was going to pass that down to my kids and wife once I got to that point. As I thought about it, I found myself wondering if Lihanny was going to be that wife I spoke of. My phone vibrated in my pocket, and I looked at it to see that it was a message from Lihanny.

Baby Girl: Your baby mamas are following me.

Nylah Ingram

In Virginia, Fifteen Minutes Earlier

"There she goes right there," Savannah pointed out.

My head went in the direction that she was pointing in, and sure enough, that Li bitch was coming out of an apartment complex. I rolled my eyes at that bitch. I couldn't stand her ass, which was why I was sitting in the car waiting to follow her. My life with Hendrix was going great before this bitch came along ruining shit for me. I was supposed to be the last woman to bear Hendrix's kids, then here comes this ratchet ho trapping my man. I didn't even understand what Hendrix saw in her anyway. She didn't have any kind of class, and she was black as hell. Hendrix didn't even like girls his color, so for him to have been fucking her was shocking to me.

Late last night after Hendrix left, I dropped Haylee off at my mom's house, and Savannah and I hopped on a plane to come here. I didn't know exactly what our plan was, but we were definitely going to snatch this bitch up, then kill her, from what I understood. It was Savannah's idea to do so. We had a conversation after Li's friend snuck me at the restaurant. We came to the agreement that we would get rid of this bitch, then share Hendrix with each other.

"Hurry, follow her," Savannah said.

I quickly placed the car in drive and followed her, careful not to get noticed. I wasn't trying to risk her seeing us, so we both had on hats and hoods over our heads.

"I hope she is going somewhere secluded," I said. I wasn't trying to risk someone seeing us take her ass. Then we would go to jail, and she would have Hendrix to herself. That was the last thing that I needed to happen.

"She's turning. She's turning," Savannah yelled.

"Bitch, I fucking see her. You don't have to yell." I rolled my eyes and turned right.

She drove up a little more before making another right, then another. We drove for a few more minutes before we pulled up to the back of a tobacco store.

"What do we do now?" I said.

Savannah pulled out the guns she took from Hendrix's stash and passed me one. "We go get her ass," she said before hopping out of the car.

I quickly placed the car in park before getting out as well. Looking around, I made sure that there was no one in sight before I followed Savannah to the car. We got to driver's side, and Savannah held the gun up to the window.

"Bitch, get out of the car."

Li looked back and forth between me and Savannah before smirking. I aimed my gun at her. "Do you think this is a fucking joke?"

Smirking still, she nodded before laughing. Savannah used the end of the gun and busted out the window. The shit caught me off guard, so I jumped back a little, then looked around.

"Bitch, are you crazy? Somebody could have heard that," I fussed.

Savannah ignored me and opened up her door. Li was no longer smirking. Instead, she looked pissed the fuck off. Like, I could have sworn her eyes were all black, and I was starting to rethink this whole fucking plan.

"Get your ass in the car." Savannah pointed the gun at the back of her head.

"Y'all bitches better hope you fucking kill me." She gritted her teeth.

"Shut the fuck up and get your ass in the car." Savanah smacked her upside the head with the gun, and she immediately fell to the ground.

I gasped. "Bitch, now look what the fuck you did."

"Is she dead?" Savannah asked with wide eyes.

"I don't fucking know. Check her pulse."

"Bitch, you check her pulse."

I sucked my teeth and rolled my eyes. "You were just big and bad a second ago." I bent down and felt around for a pulse. "She's alive. Let's get her in this damn car before somebody sees us."

We placed the guns down and picked her up from both ends, then walked to the car. Savannah dropped her legs to open the door before picking her back up and placing her inside. She quickly grabbed the guns and jumped in.

"Where to?" she questioned.

"I don't fucking know my way around here." This entire plan had gone to shit, and I wished that I stayed my ass in Miami.

"Just drive around for a minute. I'm sure there's an empty building around here somewhere."

I shook my head and placed the car in reverse. "Remind me to never do a fucking crime with you again."

I turned around to back up and could have shitted my fucking pants seeing a big black SUV pulling in behind us. I immediately began to panic. "Bitch, it's Hendrix."

Savannah looked back, then ducked, like that was going to fucking help. "How the fuck did he find out?"

"I don't fucking know, but I'm telling him it was your idea."

The two front doors and the back door opened as he, Jerry, and Hussein got out and then stormed to the car. I tried to lock the doors, but before I could, they were being snatched open.

Hendrix pulled me out of the car. "What the fuck are y'all doing here?"

"Man, look." Hussein grabbed his attention, and his eyes fell to the back seat where Li was out cold.

He quickly snatched the door open and picked her up. "Ay yo, take her to the fucking hospital." He passed her off to Jerry.

Hendrix turned to me and glared back and forth between me and Savannah. "If something happens to either her or my fucking baby, I'm putting a fucking bullet in both of y'all. What the fuck were y'all thinking? Huh?" he yelled in my face.

"What you yelling at me for? It was all her idea," I cried.

"Bitch, shut up. You're the one who said you wanted revenge," Savannah said.

"Where the fuck is my daughter at, Nylah?"

"I dropped her off at my mom's house," I whispered.

"Get y'all stupid asses in the fucking car." He grabbed me by my arm and pushed me to the back seat, and Hussein did the same with Savannah. "Take Li's car to mom's house, then go to the hospital to sit with her until I make it up there," he told his brother before climbing into the driver's seat.

He was fucking fuming. I could feel the heat radiating off his body. I was definitely regretting doing this shit now. "Hen—"

"Don't say fucking shit to me, Nylah. I swear to God I'm fighting the fuck out of myself to not shoot both of y'all dumb asses. What the fuck is wrong with you bitches these days?"

"Who you calling a bitch?" Savannah bucked.

"You most definitely don't need to say shit to me right now, because I had a fucking conversation with Francis, you lying-ass bitch. Tread fucking lightly, Savannah."

That shut her ass up really quick. She sat back and didn't say anything else the entire ride to wherever we were going. I played with my fingers in nervousness the whole ride. I just knew this nigga was about to take us in the middle of nowhere and shoot us in the face. I closed my eyes and prayed that God got me back to my baby girl. When I opened my eyes, we were at a small-ass house. The shit almost looked like a shack.

"Get out," he said before turning the car off and hopping out.

Savannah and I slowly got out of the car and followed him into the shack. I was scared as fuck at this point. I just knew I was about to die.

"Hendrix, don't kill me please. I promise I won't do no shit like that again. I was just angry that you wanna be with her and that you got her pregnant. But I'll back off now, I swear. Just please don't kill me," I pleaded, refusing to step into my death.

He just looked at me. "Get in the fucking house. I'm not going to ask you again. Don't fuck with me."

Sobbing, I walked into the house and jumped when he slammed the door behind us. I thought he was about to shoot us right there, but I realized that he wasn't even in here with us.

"What the hell?" Savannah said, walking over to the small-ass window. "He's leaving."

"Oh, my God. What is he going to do to us?"

Savannah sucked her teeth. "Please shut the hell up with all that crying."

"Bitch, fuck you. If it weren't for you, I would be back in Miami with my baby," I fussed.

"Girl, ain't nobody put a fucking gun to your head and forced you to come out here."

I ignored her and walked down the small-ass hallway, where I found a room. It held a twin-sized bed and a little-ass box TV. I walked in and closed the door before climbing into the bed. All I could do was sit here and get ready to accept my fate.

Chapter 29

Lihanny Wright

A Few Hours Later

"Mhmm," I groaned as I grabbed hold of my head. My eyes slowly opened as I looked around the room I was in. Seeing that I was in a hospital bed made me think about why I was in here in the first fucking place, and I immediately got pissed off.

"Stop moving so much, ma." Hendrix came over to me and sat next to the bed in the chair.

"I'm going to kill both of those bitches. They could have fucking harmed my damn baby."

"I'm taking care of it. You need to relax. You have a big-ass concussion and some swelling in your brain. I told your hardheaded ass to get checked out for the pain you were feeling after the crash. Now the shit has gotten worse since one of them hit you in your head."

I rolled my eyes. "You need to get your bitches in check," I said as my eyes went to my stomach. "Is the baby—"

"The baby is fine. Heartbeat strong as fuck." He cheesed. "It's most definitely going to be a boy."

"I hope so too. I most definitely do not want a girl. When can I get out of here?"

"You're going to be in here until the swelling goes down, ma. They need to monitor you overnight. If you leave, you can die in your sleep."

I huffed and laid my head back. "I hate hospitals."

"Well, get comfortable because you'll be in here for a while." He stood. "Are you hungry?"

I nodded. "Starving. I was heading to Feather 'n' Fin when I saw their dumb asses following me. Both of those bitches are dumb."

Hendrix shook his head. "I can't believe they did this shit."

"Where are they?"

"In the hole. They're going to stay their asses in there with no food or water until I feel like they've learned their lesson."

"Let me beat their asses. Or shoot them at least," I said.

"Nah. You don't need to do shit but sit here and worry about yourself and my baby. I got the other shit covered." He bent down and kissed my lips softly. "Jerry went to go get you some food."

"Tell my bae I said thank you," I joked.

"Stop fucking with me before I bring the baby mama crew back in here to finish you off." He laughed.

But I didn't find shit funny. "That's funny to you?"

He covered his mouth with his hands before shaking his head. "Nah. It's not funny."

"Get out of my damn room, Hendrix. You're lucky I didn't leave your daughters without mothers, because I could have easily killed both of those bitches, and you know it."

I was doing him a favor by texting him and turning my location on for him to find me. It took everything in me not to pull my Desert Eagle out and put a hot one right between their eyes. Ol' stupid-ass hoes. I couldn't wait to drop this fucking baby.

"I was just playing, baby. Don't act like that." He smiled.

I rolled my eyes. "I'm not your baby."

"You are my baby. Now stop acting like that. But check it. I wanna holla at you about this moving weight shit. The only way I'm going to agree to let you handle shit is if you do it after you have our baby. When he or she turns six months old, you can run shit again. But I don't want you near this shit while you're pregnant."

"I don't want it," I said.

His eyebrows dipped. "What?"

"I said I don't want it. After I tie up a few loose ends, I have plans to open up a smoothie shop."

"When did you decide this?" he asked, walking over to the bed.

"When I was in Florida and found out my father left me a shitload of money. I was only pushing weight until I made enough to live comfortably. I can do that now, so I don't need to be in the streets. But that doesn't mean that I want you to bring in some out-of-towner to handle shit. Nobody knows the ins and outs of this shit better than Dez. He deserves to be in charge."

"I already spoke with him. He was who I was going to put in charge while you were on maternity leave."

I nodded. "He handles his shit with an iron fist for sure. So it's in good hands."

"I'm proud of you. You know that?" he said as he stared at me intently.

I smiled and nodded. "I'm proud of myself. I thought I was going to be doing this shit forever."

"Shit, me too. But in all honesty, I'm kind of glad I didn't kill you all those times."

I burst out laughing. "Oh, whatever, nigga. You couldn't kill me even if you tried. Lihanny is invincible."

"Invincible my ass. You just got Punk'd by two suburban bitches."

I punched him in his arm and burst out laughing. The shit was only funny because those bitches were from the suburbs, which was why they both looked so damn scared holding those fucking guns. Scary-ass hoes.

Chapter 30

Hendrix Brown

Nine Months Later

"Lihanny, I know your ass did not just fucking pee on me again. I told you about doing that shit," I fussed as I climbed out of the bed.

"Hendrix, shut the hell up. Ain't nobody pee on you. My damn water just broke," she yelled, moving the cover off of her body.

"Oh, shit." I rushed over to her and realized that she wasn't even in pain.

"Grab the bags while I put some clothes on," she said.

She was naked because her ass stayed peeing on herself in the middle of the night. She was a month over her due date, and it was hard for her to get her ass up to make it on time. After she slipped her clothes on and I was ready with the bags, I walked her down the stairs.

"Go get in the car, baby, while I get the girls," I told her, placing the bags by the front door.

"Hurry. I think he's coming now," she cried as she held the bottom of her stomach.

It was crazy that she went from being calm as hell to in pain within minutes, but I quickly went up the stairs and rushed into the girls' room. It took no time for me to put their jackets on and throw them over my shoulders. When I got downstairs, Li was in the car, taking quick breaths with tears running down her face. I knew my baby was in a lot of pain.

"Hendrix, hurry up!" she yelled.

I placed a seat belt over them before running and hopping into the driver's seat, then speeding out of the driveway. I placed my hand on her stomach. "Hold on, baby. We almost there."

Three hours later, we welcomed Hendrik Karter Brown into the world. I was crying harder than Lihanny's ass as I cut the umbilical cord then grabbed my son from the doctors. "Damn, he looks just like you, Li." I wiped my face and bounced him a little.

"Let me see," she muttered softly from being exhausted.

I bent down some so that she could see his face. She broke out in a big-ass smile, and tears started to come from her eyes. "Awww, I love him so much." She kissed his head.

I bent down and kissed her a few times before handing him over to the doctors so that they could clean him up and get his measurements. As soon as he was out of my arms, my baby boy started crying like crazy.

"What the fuck are y'all doing to my baby?" Lihanny tried to sit up in her bed.

"Relax, ma. He just wants me to hold him. Let them do their job. I'm going to go get the girls." I bent down and kissed her lips before leaving the room. I walked down the hall to the visitors' room, where our entire family was waiting. They all stood when they saw me, and I couldn't even hide the smile on my face.

"It's a boy."

They all came over and embraced me and gave out congrats. I picked up Haylee and grabbed hold of Hydiah's hand. Every single one of us headed to the back to see Li and Hendrik. Nobody said shit to us either. We were deep as fuck, squeezing into that delivery room. Lihanny was holding him and feeding him a bottle. Hydiah climbed onto the bed, and I placed Haylee on the other side of her so that they could see him.

"Meet your brother Hendrik," Lihanny said as she bent him down some so that they could see him.

"Aww, he is so cute," Hydiah said, grabbing his little hand, and he held on to hers.

"Cute!" Haylee shrieked, causing us to all laugh.

I was complete like a muthafucka. I had two beautiful daughters and a handsome-ass son. The last thing I needed was to make Lihanny my wife. And that was to come in due time.

Lihanny Wright

A Few Days Later

I hope y'all didn't think that I forgot about that snake bitch Cassie. I told y'all that as soon as I dropped my baby, I was going to come for her ass, and that was what the fuck I meant. The same night they released me from the hospital, I was sitting outside her house, waiting for the perfect time to make my move.

"You ready, bitch?" Lonny said from the passenger's seat.

I looked over at her and nodded. "Damn right."

We climbed out of the car, and I tossed my hood over my head. Jogging to the door, Lonny bent down and popped the lock. Quietly, we closed the door and walked up the stairs. We looked in every room until we found these nasty muthafuckas in the bed together with Nigel in the middle. He and Eugene were spooning while Cassie was turned in the other direction. Lonny slammed the door shut and flicked the light on, scaring them out of their sleep. Eugene jumped up and reached for his gun. I pointed mine at him.

"Aht aht aht. Don't even think about it. Lonny, grab it," I said, never taking my eyes off of him.

Once she grabbed the gun and had one pointed at Eugene and the other pointed at Nigel, I walked over to the side of the bed where Cassie was looking like she'd seen a ghost. I dropped my hood and smirked down at her.

"I bet you thought I forgot about your opening your mouth, didn't you?" I grabbed her by her head and dragged her out of the bed.

"Li, please."

I hit her in the head with the butt of my gun. "Shut the fuck up, bitch. Now you're going to watch as we shoot these gay muthafuckas."

"You dumb bit—" Before Nigel could finish his sentence, Lonny blew his brains out, causing Cassie to scream.

"Bitch, shut the hell up," Lonny said before turning the gun on Eugene and putting him out of his misery.

"Oh God!" Cassie cried out.

"The fuck are you crying for, ho? You weren't doing all this when you were fucking snitching on me, were you?" I kneed her in the back of her head before letting her hair go.

I held my hand out, and Lonny placed Eugene's gun in my hand. "Get the fuck up, Cassie," I spat.

She sniffled and cried as she slowly stood. I grabbed her and stuffed Eugene's gun in her mouth. She cried hard as hell as I placed her hand on the gun then her finger on the trigger.

"Rot in hell, bitch," Lonny said.

Pow!

I snuck into my and Hendrix's bedroom a few hours later. He was on the bed knocked out with Hendrik lying on his chest. I shook my head and walked off to put Hendrik in his bassinet next to the bed. Once he was comfortable, I stripped out of my clothes and climbed under the covers. Hendrix pulled me to his body and buried his face in my neck.

"You all right?"

"I am now."

The End